RACHEL
TO THE
RESCUE

BOOKS BY ELINOR LIPMAN

Into Love and Out Again

Then She Found Me

The Way Men Act

Isabel's Bed

The Inn at Lake Devine

The Ladies' Man

The Dearly Departed

The Pursuit of Alice Thrift

My Latest Grievance

The Family Man

*Tweet Land of Liberty:
Irreverent Rhymes from the Political Circus*

The View from Penthouse B

I Can't Complain: (All Too) Personal Essays

On Turpentine Lane

Good Riddance

RACHEL TO THE RESCUE

ELINOR LIPMAN

Mariner Books
Houghton Mifflin Harcourt
Boston   New York

First U.S. edition 2021

Copyright © 2020 by Elinor Lipman

hmhbooks.com

Published in Great Britain in 2020 by Lightning Books,
an imprint of Eye Books

Library of Congress Cataloging-in-Publication Data
Names: Lipman, Elinor, author.
Title: Rachel to the rescue / Elinor Lipman.
Description: First U.S. edition. | Boston ; New York :
Houghton Mifflin Harcourt, 2021.
Identifiers: LCCN 2021007269 (print) | LCCN 2021007270 (ebook) |
ISBN 9780358653257 (trade paperback) | ISBN 9780358653233 (ebook)
Classification: LCC PS3562.I577 R33 2021 (print) |
LCC PS3562.I577 (ebook) | DDC 813/.54 —dc23
LC record available at https://lccn.loc.gov/2021007269
LC ebook record available at https://lccn.loc.gov/2021007270

Printed in the United States of America

1 2021
4500826648

For Jonathan

The president's unofficial 'filing system' involves tearing up documents into pieces, even when they're supposed to be preserved . . . It was a painstaking process that was the result of a clash between legal requirements to preserve White House records and President Donald Trump's odd and enduring habit of ripping up papers when he's done with them . . .

— *Politico*, June 2018

1

THE BAD NEWS FIRST

Unless I amend it, my resume confirms that I truly did work for the forty-fifth president of the United States, if you can call my daily torture-task a job. Even when I hide behind my formal title (Assistant, White House Office of Records Management aka WHORM) I eventually confess that I spent my days taping back together every piece of paper that passed through the hands of Donald J. Trump.

How would a person end up in the administration's most unnecessary office? Unemployed, I had searched every online job site, including USA.Jobs.com, where I typed in Washington, D.C., and for fun, under locations, "White House". I rationalized it this way to my one-sided friends and family: 1600 Pennsylvania Avenue is the People's House. It doesn't belong to any one man or woman or administration, so calm down.

I hadn't worked on any campaign nor did I have family connections, but someone must've liked my professional qualifications, which I could claim as the personal assistant/typist/proof-reader/errand-runner for a wealthy New Yorker who intended to self-publish a memoir after his parents were no longer alive to read and disown him. But he died, a fatal heart attack at the breakfast table, before he'd dictated anything beyond his freshman year at, of course, Yale. My White House security clearance sailed through, probably due to my bare-bones employment record, and bachelor's degree from a college in a red state.

A distracted woman interviewed me for the entry-level job in slapdash fashion. She said my duties would involve a lot of reading; in fact nothing *but*. Well into the first term of the 45th president, I found myself in a cubicle, one of a dozen men and women of various ages reading incoming mail. There was the positive, the negative, the donors in search of favors; the dangerous, the hate letters and the love letters, the requests for pardons, for clemency, for commuted sentences, for loans, for business advice, for autographed photos; the macaroni paintings, the coffee mugs, the velour renditions of the president; the edibles. The wedding invitations addressed to President and Mrs. Trump were sent to the East Wing. Under the law, letters we would've tossed had to be kept — even those griping about service at Trump hotels and building supers in Trump residential buildings.

I didn't complain about the brittle, discolored, sometimes crumbling paper that had been irradiated before delivery. I look back and wonder, did I stand out in some way in that entry-level correspondence job? Was my lateral move a reward or a punishment? Was I especially hard-working or just expendable? Whichever — someone must have noticed that I was a nimble restorer of paper in need of mending.

So, after only thirteen weeks in the Office of Correspondence, I moved to the Old Executive Office Building, upholding the Presidential Records Act. Unstated job description: tape tape

tape. Did I get the easy ones, the rare memo that had been merely ripped down the middle? No. I got the confetti. Thankless task? How about an unnecessary one? How about the nagging reality that the leader of the free world was unteachable?

I knew from my days in Correspondence that the President didn't actually read what the world wrote to him. So, it was no small irony that my very own email reached him, or someone with the power to hire and fire. I didn't mean to send it; should not have composed it above a department-wide email about refrigerator courtesy. Just for fun, or so I believed, I described my daily grind in terms unflattering to the shredder-in-chief, addressed to my alleged best buddy in the office, which I mistakenly thought — with the judgment one can have late at night after too many Cape Codders — he'd find amusing. I also wrote that I might as well be slaving away in Tehran because every day I identified with the Iranian student militia in "Argo", who reassembled shredded documents. Probably not a smart reference, nor was my post-script that said, "It would be nice to have a president who had a learning curve." And then my tanked-up finger hit "reply all".

It was the epistolary equivalent of death by cop. I didn't get past Security the day after I sent it. Though I do appreciate that my somewhat treasonous e-letter now resides in the National Archives, not one thing about my three long months on Team Scotch Tape is helping me make friends in 2020.

Luckily my health insurance was good till the end of the month. After being figuratively kicked to the curb, I wandered in something of a daze across 17th Street. Well, halfway across, at which point I was knocked unconscious by a big black car driven by what the newspapers would one day diplomatically refer to as "a personal friend of the president's".

2

VISITING HOURS

A POLICEWOMAN had figured out from the "mom & dad" listing on my phone, how to reach my next-of-kin. Almost a full day later, when I regained consciousness, they were at my bedside, trying to look chipper.

"You were hit by a car, sweetheart," my mother said with a sob.

I asked if I was dying.

"No, no, not at all. Just some broken bones."

"Do you know who we are?" my father asked.

"Bill and Hillary Clinton," I said, managing to move one corner of my mouth into a half-smile, my inner actress floating up from the bottom of my mental swamp.

"She's okay!" he crowed.

I tried to sit up, but got no farther than the first inch due to the pain in my midsection. I yowled.

"Just broken ribs, thank God," said my mother.

I moaned, "Whaddya mean 'thank God'?"

"It could be so much worse!"

"And there's a concussion — either when you were hit or when you bounced off the car," my father said.

"Who hit me? Did they stop?"

"On 17th Street, with the world watching? They had to," my mother said.

A male doctor or intern or resident or nurse with a shaved head was carefully, slowly buzzing my mattress up to a slight elevation. "Good morning! Nice to see you back in action."

"Am I? Did you have to restart my heart or anything? With paddles? Was I technically dead?"

"What a question," said my mother.

"No and no," said the man, who turned out to be a nurse, and of the height and strength I would soon find out could lift a person from bed to wherever she needed to be next.

I asked where I was.

"Washington, D.C., hon," said my mom.

"I know that. I meant what hospital."

"G.W. Best in the biz," said the nurse, pointing to the embroidered letters on his scrub.

"How'd you get here so fast?" I asked my parents. "Was it fast?"

"The accident was yesterday," my mother said. "We got on the first Acela—"

"Faster than flying," said my father. "Believe me, we checked."

"Thank you for coming," I said, my voice suddenly choked.

"Are you in pain?" my mother asked.

"Are you kidding? How about 'agony'?"

"Your head or your middle?"

"Everywhere."

"It was one of those big VWs," said my mother.

"A Touareg," said my dad.

"How did you find all this out?"

"We know what the police know."

"Was I run over or just hit?"

"Hit. Bumped. Thrown up onto the car," my mother said. "Then slid off when the driver slammed on her brakes."

I asked if it had been my fault. Neither answered immediately. Finally, my father said, "You weren't crossing at a pedestrian walkway."

I don't remember if I asked my next question out of hope or dread or too much handling of White House press releases. "Did this make the newspapers?"

"In a police report," said my dad. "Location, driver, victim of course. There were lots of witnesses."

"And, hon," said my dad, "we now know that you were fired."

For the first time, I staged fogginess. "I *was*?"

"You were seen being escorted out of the building, and the security guards knew you, so with a phone call or two up to your department, they learned you'd been . . . separated."

I said, "Now I remember. I would've told you if I hadn't been nearly killed."

"She wasn't almost killed, was she?" my mother asked the nurse.

"Not even close," he said.

My dad asked me if I'd been promised a severance package, or two weeks' notice? Or letters of reference?

I closed my eyes, prompting the nurse to say, "Maybe she needs a snooze."

My mother said, "Aren't you supposed to keep waking patients up every few hours if they had a concussion so they don't slip into a coma?"

"We're on it," said the nurse.

I asked if I'd been cut and bleeding and needed stitches.

"Miraculously no," said my mother.

"Give it to me straight," I said.

"One black eye," my mother said. "But not so bad. It's already turning yellow. A little foundation will cover it."

I asked if she had a mirror in her purse. She said too quickly, no, she didn't.

"You know what the good news is?" my father said. "No damage to your spine! Everyone breaks a rib or two. I once broke a rib sneezing!"

I asked the nurse if it was okay to sleep, or was my mother right?

"Since you're awake and carrying on a conversation and there's no bleed, and your pupils aren't dilated, you can sleep."

"She *was* bleeding, though," my mother said.

"Not that kind." He touched his head. "Inside."

"Now that we know she's out of the woods, I could use a sandwich and a cup of coffee," said my dad.

I asked what time it was and how long I'd been here.

"Almost noon," said my mother. "The accident was early yesterday, during rush hour."

That sounded right — sacked as I arrived for work.

"Call us if you need us," my mother said. "I think your phone is with your backpack, somewhere."

I said, "Go have lunch. I won't need to call you."

"She's very alert," my father said. "Sounds like the old Rachel."

"Thank you for coming all this way," I said.

"We're not going anywhere — just to the cafeteria. Did you think we're sending you home to that fourth-floor walk-up with a room-mate who's never home?"

"Third floor," I said.

Mom kissed me on the cheek, gingerly. Dad gave my closest,

un-tubed hand a squeeze. "You're doing great," he said. "Can we bring you anything from the cafeteria?"

I said no thanks. And try to relax. I didn't die.

"Don't even say that!" my mother wailed.

They finally left, walking backwards, waving, but no relief visible in their strained smiles.

The nurse said, "Nice folks," then asked about the pain. I said, "On a scale of one to ten? Nine and a half."

"Ouch. Sorry."

"Whatever you're giving me for the pain, it's not working."

"We can give you some extra-strength Tylenol."

"That's it? How about morphine?"

What about that question made him smile? "Morphine isn't for broken ribs, darlin'."

"Opioids?"

"No and no. The pain tells us a lot. You don't want to mask it."

"Yes I do. Then what's in the I.V.?"

"Nutrition."

"You're nice, too," I said.

"I try."

He left with a reminder that he was only a call-button away, here, practically in my hand. I lay there, wondering if it was okay to press my ribs diagnostically or if that would send a splintered one into an organ. Did the police still have my phone? My backpack? I was repeatedly moving my legs and wiggling my toes. Everything down there worked. I could feel socks on my feet and the blanket on my shins. How long does a concussion last, and does it fix itself?

Five minutes later? Fifteen? The nurse was back, leaning halfway into my room. "There's someone here to see you."

"Who?"

"A woman."

8

"A doctor?"

"No. She has a big bunch of flowers."

How bad could that be? Was it visiting hours? I said okay.

This visitor must have been at his elbow, because she walked right in, fur-coated, brief-cased, leather boots to her knees, carrying a giant arrangement of flowers.

I didn't know this person. "Are you sure you're in the right room?" I asked.

Her answer was, "I'm an attorney."

"Seriously?" I said, meaning, *Don't tell me I'm being visited by a literal ambulance chaser?*

"First of all, how are you?" she asked.

"Terrible. My entire ribcage is killing me. And I have a concussion."

"I won't be long. Thank you for agreeing to see me."

Had I?

"I represent the driver whose car you ran in front of, and I hope you know that they weren't at fault."

My now-favorite nurse had stuck his head back in and asked, "Everything good here?"

"Could you get us a vase?" this visitor asked.

"She's a lawyer," I told him. "She represents the driver who ran over me." If I'd been able to roll over to one side and turn my back on her as an act of dismissal, I would have. Instead, I closed my eyes and simulated wooziness.

"Rachel?" I heard her say — not in the whisper you'd use when addressing a patient who was drifting off to sleep, but a rebuke. "I have a few questions I'd like you to answer."

I murmured, "I'd better not. My parents aren't going to be thrilled that you barged in here."

"Are your parents attorneys?"

Huh? No, they weren't attorneys, but both were excellent

diplomats. As owners of a paint and wallpaper store, they'd negotiated with customers who wanted their money back after the room had already been decorated or their kid's scribbles hadn't come off with Mister Clean's Magic Eraser. I said, "No they aren't *attorneys*" — adding a sarcastic twist to that word as if it were too pretentious for ordinary speech.

"I think they'd be interested in why I'm here, as you will be, too," she said.

Now that she mentioned it, I was a little curious. I waited, staring with what I hoped was a cool lack of tell-tale interest.

She took off her gigantic coat and tossed it across the foot of my bed. Before I could say, "hey!" or "ouch!" she turned girlfriendy. "Rachel, I apologize for coming on too strong. Do you think you could grant me a few more minutes? I'll leave the second you ask me to."

I said, "Just know that I'm being monitored. The nurse's station is watching what's going on. That nurse, that big guy, told me that he once caught a patient getting smothered with a pillow—"

"Don't be ridiculous. I'm a member of the bar."

"Then please back away. I'll hear what you have to say, from over there." After she'd sat down on the squeaky plastic armchair, I added, "I hope you're not expecting me to comment or sign any papers or whatever you came for."

"You're sounding very cogent to me, which comports with what I was told, that you weren't seriously injured."

That did it! My whole body was sorer than it had ever been, and my head had never felt this heavy and off-kilter. "I'm *very* injured. I'm in intensive care!" Was I? No one had said that, but hadn't I been knocked unconscious? "I'm a ten on the pain scale. And you don't know me when I'm uninjured so you can't judge how cogent I am."

She took out her phone and started scrolling. After too long without a question or comment, I asked, "So who *was* the driver?"

"A client of mine."

"No kidding. Famous?"

"Of course not," she said, still scrolling diligently.

I asked her if I could borrow her phone.

"I'm sorry. It's strictly for work."

"I think it's work when the victim wants to call her next of kin."

She let out an exasperated sigh. "Number?"

Oh dear. Their mobile numbers were in the Cloud, not what remained of my memory.

Another nurse, this time a woman with a shaved head and very long earrings entered the room, briskly. Had a monitor summoned her? "What's wrong?" I asked.

"Nothing. Just gonna get your vitals and look in your eyes."

"Don't they ever leave you alone here?" the lawyer asked.

"Please wait outside," I said.

As soon as she'd left, I told the nurse, "I don't even know her. She's a lawyer. She represents the person who ran me down."

"Ran you down? On purpose?"

Well that was a new thought. Had someone on the inside, in the White House, in the press office, in the family quarters, wanted to shut me up? Was Scotch-taping everything that the president touched so embarrassing that I had a price on my head?

"I worked for the Trump Administration. I was fired for sending an insulting email."

"Please don't confess to anything I'll have to testify to in court. That happens, you know."

"I didn't threaten him. I don't even remember the exact

wording, but it was along the lines of *what an idiot you are.* I'd had a little too much to drink when I wrote it—"

"I don't want to know that! I don't want to testify that you got hit by a car because you weren't in full control of your faculties."

I said, "No, no, the drinking was unrelated to the accident, just to the stupid email I wrote."

She had no comment except, "Temp is normal. Let me look at your pupils." When I opened my eyes wider, the light hurt.

"Good?" I asked after some back-and-forthing with her pen-light.

"Good enough."

"I hurt everywhere."

"We know." With that, she produced a small, white paper cup containing the alleged pain reliever, and poured me a glass of water. I took the pill and drank the entire glass. "Good," she said. "Hydrating's good. Call us if you need to pee. It'll be good to get you up."

After making a notation in my chart, unfortunately out of my reach, she asked if she should send my guest back in.

Permission wasn't necessary. The lawyer was peeking in from the open door.

"Okay," I said. "Let's get this over with."

"I'll get right to the point. My client would prefer *not* to settle through her insurance. I have a check that would cover—"

Then this visit *was* about money. Shouldn't I check with a lawyer, an insurance agent, my parents, the police? I was shaking my poor heavy head: *no, sorry.*

Even a concussed layman knows that you turn down the first offer. And just from living in the real world, I surmised that when a lawyer comes calling and offers a check before anyone asks, the payee probably has a good case.

I said, "It must be against some legal ethics to negotiate with someone in the intensive care unit. I mean, isn't that a real no-no — like *here, change your will. Sign this. Leave everything to me.*"

"That makes no sense, and does not apply—"

Should I ask how much the alleged check was for? Did I look as if I were wavering? Possibly, because she tried, "Let me remind you, as you turn down a check at this juncture, that you were fired."

"So?"

"Lost income? Earning potential? Hard for a jury to calculate how employable you'd ever be."

Jee-sus — a jury! I said, "Please leave. You can keep your check. It's probably for some laughable amount anyway, since you consider me unemployable."

Was it just a bargaining strategy when she said, "So this is your final decision: *I'll take my chances. If I'm never able to walk again, I might be able to get disability.*"

I said, now up on my elbows, the pain almost taking my breath away, "I can walk! Do you see a bedpan? No, because I can get up and pee on my own! And that was a really nasty thing to say, by the way. If you had such an innocent client, you'd be doing this through the proper channels, not sneaking into my room."

"Don't be foolish," she said, gathering her coat and briefcase.

"And I am *not* okay. I hurt everywhere. And my vision is blurry. I hope I'm not brain-damaged."

How was that? I didn't want to sound too well or too sharp. If there was a settlement ahead, it was best that I appear like a defendant pleading not guilty on the basis of insanity — a lot diminished and a little dangerous.

3

AM I VIRAL?

WHEN I WOKE from my potentially life-threatening nap, my mother was at my side, brandishing my backpack and announcing, "Not lost! Not stolen! Not run over!"

"Wallet?" I grunted. "Phone?"

She itemized aloud: wallet, phone, charger, the plug part that goes into the outlet; keys, headphones, lip gloss, tampons, sunglasses, gum, a Snickers bar. Did I want to use the phone? Anyone I needed to call?

Was that a note of social optimism I'd heard — perhaps a reference to a previously unannounced boyfriend who'd be sick with worry somewhere?

"Just charge it," I said.

My father, so clearly wanting to do *anything*, said that he'd spotted the outlet! With some ceremony, he affixed the phone to the cable, the cable to the adapter, the adapter into the outlet. He asked if he should jack the head of the bed up a bit — he'd be careful; he'd seen the way the nurse had done it. I said yes, okay, but slowly. Stop if I scream.

Had I really been out cold and phoneless only one day, I wondered, because as soon as the phone came to life, there was a slew of voicemail, email, and text messages.

Before I could open or answer anything, a call came in with a D.C. area code and no I.D. "Aren't you going to answer it?" my mother asked.

"No."

She took the phone from me. "Rachel Klein's line. This is her mother speaking."

What was that look I was getting? Intrigue? Excitement? Her whole face was signaling: *Wait'll I tell you*. She was saying yes, yes, no, yes, no, I don't know, and finally "No comment." And finally, "You're welcome . . . Beverly Klein, the usual spelling . . . her mother."

"Who was that?"

"A reporter!"

"A reporter for what?"

"I didn't catch it. A man. Very polite."

"Did he say how he got my number?"

"I didn't ask—"

I tried without success to prop myself up on one elbow. "A reporter calls out of the blue and you just answer the questions without asking why the hell he's calling and how he got my number?"

"I wasn't thinking clearly! I'm sorry! My only child was hit by a car. You know what it's like when the police call and the first thing you hear is, 'There's been an accident'? You lose your mind!"

"Worst call of our lives," added my dad. "A nightmare! And

when you try to reach the doctor's, it's only 'press one' for this and 'two' for that. I've never been so frustrated! And when you finally reach a real person, she can only say next to nothing because 'anyone can claim to be a patient's parent!'"

"I'm sorry. I wasn't thinking of that end of things." I took the phone back, put it down on the side table, changed my mind, and rested it on my chest. Would all these text messages, emails and voicemails explain why a reporter wanted to speak to me?

Boom! Someone had captured my accident on a phone and posted it on Facebook. One of my cousins wrote, *I tried to call Aunt Bev & yr dad, but they weren't at the store and their voicemails were full!!!! OMG R U OK? LMK!*

My first instinct was *open Facebook*. But look under what or whom? I didn't know which paparazzi wannabe had posted it, or how they knew it was me.

"What?" my mother was asking. "Did you find something?"

I told her that concentrating was hard and reading harder — not a lie: I had halos shimmering on the periphery everywhere I looked. Easier: hitting the number of the nameless reporter who'd just called.

A man answered with a distracted "Associated Press. Loftus."

"This is Rachel Klein. Someone from this number just called me."

"Oh wow. I didn't know if you'd be able to talk."

I asked if he knew about the accident from Facebook, and if that was true, how did he know it was me in the video?

"You don't know?"

Would that be information gleaned from a police website that over-shared? "An accident report?" I asked.

"No. The press briefing."

The press briefing? Had there been news so major, so life-changing — the president resigned or died or been assassinated?

— so that the press was going down the list of every single employee for comment until someone answered his or her phone? "What happened?" I whispered.

"You don't know? I assumed you did."

"Give me a sec." I checked text messages first: more OMGs and R U Oks????, plus "press briefing", "press conference", "press secretary", "White House".

I hit the speaker icon and said to my hovering parents, "Listen to this, in case I'm hallucinating." He summarized, clearly from notes, that before some underling press secretary took questions on matters of state, politics, and presidential hot water, an even more junior staff member read from a slip of paper, offering Rachel Naomi Klein — spelled it — recently of the Office of Presidential Records and before that The Office of Correspondence, get-well wishes from The President and First Lady. Further: thankfully, Ms. Klein had sustained injuries of a non-life-threatening nature soon after leaving the Eisenhower Executive Office Building.

My parents were smiling for the first time since I'd opened my eyes. Good Democrats both, yet my father put his arm around my mother's shoulders and gave her a squeeze. Was their daughter more important than either of them realized? More beloved by the office that canned her?

"Did anyone say, 'who's Rachel Klein?'" I asked the reporter.

"He didn't have to. He stated what your last two jobs were."

"Then what?"

"Well, you know the White House press corps . . ."

"No she doesn't!" my mother yelled.

"Well someone asked what 'recently' meant. 'Could he be more specific: did that mean resigned? Fired? Retired?'"

"Oh, crap," I said.

"Which one was it?" the reporter pressed.

"What did the spokesperson say?"

"He'd find out and get back to us."

"Why would it matter? I was a nobody. I mean, in the great scheme of things, I only worked there like a minute."

"Well, let's just say everything is suspect."

"*Me*? I'm suspect?"

"Not you. Maybe what happened to you."

I said, "I'm very tired. Did my mother tell you I had a concussion?"

"I knew that. Sorry. Can I call you back later?"

"Please don't."

"One more question: Do you know who was driving the car that hit you?"

"Do *you*?"

"I'm working on it. I mean, I have the license plate number—"

My father asked, loud enough for it to carry through the phone, "Do you think Rachel might've been hit on purpose?"

"No one said that. 'How do you spell 'Rachel'?"

I said, "Doesn't the Associated Press have bigger things to cover? There are people dying in refugee camps on every continent, including ours!"

"Would I be wrong to assume that you were fired for cause?"

My father was shaking his head, frowning and gesticulating like a man worried about a daughter who might never get another job. *Not a word!*

But how would a "no comment" sound? I asked, "By 'cause' do you mean I did something that the White House didn't like — a fire-able offense?"

"It's a simple question: can you tell me why you were fired?"

I blame what followed on exhaustion, on my phone blowing up with email dings and ring tones, on the sharp pains in my ribs, on my dry mouth, my concussed brain. I told him, "Okay; I wrote a critical email, a joke really, and hit 'send' by accident."

I told him it wasn't that bad — merely a rant about my stupid job, and maybe, probably, some venting about Donald Trump's learning curve. That's all. Yes, it had gone to my whole department, an inadvertent "reply all". And yes, I suppose it *was* the kind of thing you pound out late at night in a fit of pique, but by the light of day don't send.

4

SOMETHING'S GOING ON

THE PAST TWENTY-FOUR hours had improved my mother's mood, color, and appearance. Was it only the application of lipstick and the jaunty scarf tied in the manner of a talented accessorizer? It shouldn't have been a surprise. When not frantic over her only child's brush with death, she'd always been charming. She could close a deal with the fussiest, most impatient customer, who claimed to have found nothing in dozens of wallpaper books and was now considering stencils.

Newly cheerful, she distributed the abundance of post-press conference flower arrangements and inappropriately celebratory balloons to patients who might be less heralded than the now-famous me. Yes, she knew I was in pain, but how about thank-you notes?

"Could *you*? I'll sign them. You'll say 'Rachel is still recuperating but didn't want any more time to go by before thanking you.'"

"You spend enough time reading your emails. Maybe you could manage *writing* one or two an hour?"

"To people I don't even know?"

"Oh really?" she said, waving a large, monogrammed card. "You don't know Ivanka and Jared?"

I asked if that was a joke — Ivanka and *Jared*? Had she shown me what they'd sent before it was re-gifted?

"Nothing special. Tulips."

"For once I might be giving this White House some credit," said my dad.

"For the flowers? Or the shout-out?"

"Both. I say that as an employer: even if the person who's hit by a car is leaving under . . . not the best of circumstances, you rise to the occasion. Do you remember that guy who worked for us who was an actor? Brett, Brent, one of those names? He falsified his resume, claimed he'd worked at Farrow & Ball? Always late, knew nothing. But if he'd been hit by a car on his way out the door, your mother and I would've waved the white flag and done the right thing."

"He was very good-looking," my mother said. "And a little too popular with the decorators."

Someone else, an L.P.N., an R.N., a secretary, knocked. Another flower arrangement — birds of paradise and hollyhocks. Huge.

My mother helped herself to the card, took it out of the envelope, lifted her eyebrows.

"From . . .?"

" 'Your friends in Correspondence. We miss you. Get well soon!' "

"Didn't they let you go?" my dad asked.

"Correspondence was the first job, before my transfer to Scotch-taping."

"And this is no bunch of daisies," said my mother.

"Something's going on," I said.

My next visitor was a white-coated resident, who entered after an insincere rap on the door. She had a long black braid down her back and a lilt-y accent. My mother asked when I'd be discharged.

Stethoscope earpieces in place, she didn't answer. "Deep breath," she was saying to me. "Another. Another."

"Ow!" I said with each intake.

"I know," said the doctor. "Even one cracked rib can make every move very painful."

I had three, the X-ray had shown. "Is it a hairline crack or are they smashed? Because I worry that they're all splintered and could puncture something. Plus, they hurt like hell."

Without even a disclaimer such as *unlikely but . . .,* she said, "Rib pain can cause poor inspiratory effort, insufficient lung expansion and subsequent pneumonia."

"But she can go home with any of that, right?" asked my mother.

"The attending will be in later. He's the one who has to sign off on a discharge."

"Put in a good word for her," said my mom. "And *us*! She'll be getting excellent care at home."

Home. We hadn't discussed my destination upon discharge. I waited till the doctor left before saying, "I'll be going back to my apartment."

"With no one to look after you?"

That parental inference was my fault. I'd painted an unflattering, inattentive portrait of my room-mate, Elizabeth — not the warmest person, not prone to caretaking or even having a single meal together. "You're coming back to New York, and that's that," my mother said.

"This time we'll fly," said my dad. "Or rent a car if you'd prefer."

I said, "I think I should stay in D.C. until I figure out what's going on. And by the way, who's paying my hospital bill?"

"Your insurance, we assume. Otherwise we'd be hearing about it."

But a private room like this one with two reclining armchairs and a view? Maybe this was the time to tell them that an attorney representing the mystery driver had paid me a visit. No, I'd wait till the counteroffer came, not wanting to hear that I'd been crazy to turn down money at this juncture in my jobless life.

I told them they should go back to New York, which was like telling them to put me up for adoption. I tried, "What about work? Aren't you bored, sitting around here, eating cafeteria food and watching me sleep?"

No and no.

"At least take a break. Go to the National Gallery, the Smithsonian, The Vietnam Memorial."

More protests; only their in-patient daughter held their interest. They were in no hurry, with the reliable staff back at the store, with the suitcase they remembered to pack before running for the Acela, with their prescriptions refillable at the chain drugstore that D.C. shared with New York, and that perfectly adequate Airbnb a short cab ride away in a safe neighborhood.

Since the arrival of flowers from my East Wing non-grudge-holding co-workers, I was working up some resentment over not hearing from one single member of Team Tape — until I remembered that along with my marching orders went the end of my dot.gov address. They'd have to know my personal email, which no one had ever needed.

I wrote to my former boss, *You probably heard I was hit by a car after being escorted out of the building like a criminal. In case you were wondering, I'm alive. The White House sent flowers. I should be discharged in another day or two, despite my serious injuries. Have you hired a replacement yet?*

Didn't get-well wishes pronounced at a national press conference give me standing? Not that I wanted to return to Scotch-taping the president's confetti, but might I now, in an unsung, nearly secret office, be something of a trophy?

The first question I asked any reporter calling me was "How'd you get my number?" It didn't take much sleuthing on either of our parts: My mother had bragged on Facebook about the press-conference shout-out, at the same time she was reassuring her friends that I would survive without permanent damage. All any reporter or blogger or Tweeter had to do was glance left on her page, to "Works at Klein Wallpaper & Paint, New York, New York," easily Googled, and where actual, over-obliging humans answered the phone. You're trying to reach their daughter, Rachel? Sure! Such an easy request for people-pleasing employees Murray and Mary-Jo, since my cell number topped my parents' hand-written list of whom to call in an emergency.

Until we squelched that free-for-all, the calls poured in. And why was every reporter, to a person, asking me if I'd ever seen the driver in the White House?

"How would I know if I'd seen her? I was knocked out."

"What about afterwards?"

"Afterwards? When I was lying in the middle of the street, unconscious?"

"Miss Klein," they'd say psychiatrically, "We understand this is a sensitive subject."

I said, "I'm going to recover from this. It's not like I have a fatal illness."

"Who's paying for your hospital stay?" was another favorite question.

"I am! My insurance is . . . I have a COBRA."

I'd shut my phone off, only to find a glut of messages when I turned it back on.

"I think I've turned into gossip," I told my parents. "Which makes no sense."

"You were hit on your way out the door. You could've been killed. The White House in its own way was celebrating that you survived."

I was an unemployed nobody, suddenly famous in a limited Washington, D.C., cable-news way. The calls kept coming, as if getting hit by a car outside the Eisenhower Executive Office Building couldn't be an innocent accident. Maybe upon my discharge, after my parents had fetched my pin-striped navy-blue suit from my apartment, after the hematomas had faded, I'd call a press conference of my own.

5

THE BUZZ

MY PARENTS WON the recuperation-location battle. We were heading north in a rental car, chosen for its roomy backseat. Their closing argument: in D.C. I'd have only a nonchalant, near-stranger of a roommate; whereas they'd take turns staying home from work so I wouldn't have to lift, bend, cook, eat or sneeze without assistance.

As they were painting a rosy picture of our reunited nuclear family, I'd remind them that my visit was temporary, that Ruth Bader Ginsburg hadn't missed a single day of work after breaking three of her ribs. And surely I'd find another job in D.C., maybe even in one of my old departments.

When that prospect wasn't seconded, I added, "I know I was fired, but then I got those televised get-well wishes and flowers from Ivanka and Jared . . . Maybe my old boss is thinking, 'She sent one toxic email by mistake. She was a really good worker. Everyone deserves a second chance.'"

My mother said, "You'd want to go back to that job you hated?

Do you think that taping scraps of paper back together is a good use of your talents?"

"You're not thinking I'll come to work at the store, are you?" I asked the silent front seat.

Too quickly they protested: No, of course not! Do you think we sent you to college for a career in paint and wallpaper?

I said, "*You* both went to college."

They reminded me that the store had been in the family since 1953, and they'd brought it into the twenty-first century. Wallpaper reproductions of Warhol and Lichtenstein! A cappuccino machine!

"It was a good family business," said my dad. "And don't forget: I *majored* in business."

"How many people can say that their jobs feel like their life's work?" my mother asked.

I couldn't. Had they forgotten the three summers I'd worked at Klein Wallpaper & Paint? I was okay at the cash register, but terrible at offering artistic opinions. I had even less patience with the customers who couldn't decide on which shade of white to paint their walls. Chantilly Lace? Cotton Balls? Crème Brûlée? Mascarpone? Mayonnaise? I might advise a dithering customer, "You paint the walls, the ceiling, the moldings; let it dry, put back the furniture, hang up the art and the curtains, and you know what happens? You never give it another thought."

Which was not the attitude that gave Klein Wallpaper & Paint five stars on Yahoo. I reminded my parents of that — how I wouldn't contribute anything to the business except cranky reviews.

"Were you like that at your last job?" my mother asked.

She meant impatient and unhelpful. I said, "I hated it, but I did the work. I didn't complain more than anyone else did."

My mother twisted herself around as much as her seatbelt

allowed. "What you did, and what you might mention to these nosy reporters calling, was speak truth to power."

I had? Could that be the takeaway from my rude and fatal e-etiquette?

"You need to start thinking of yourself as a whistle-blower. You announced to your fellow citizens: 'Your tax dollars are paying me for doing a stupid, unnecessary job.' How many people in this administration have done that? Nobody."

I said, "But I *was* a nobody."

"If all the nobodies in that administration got fired for telling off the president, you'd all get a name!"

"What kind of name?"

"As a group, like a team. Like the Secaucus Seven, or the Gang of Eight or the Three Amigos."

"Highly unlikely. You're giving me way too much credit. I didn't resign in protest—"

"But you have the goods — he could *not* help ripping up everything he read, no matter how many times he was told that every paper that crossed his desk had to be saved for posterity!"

I said, "Could we drop this subject? It's exhausting. I'm going to close my eyes."

She dropped it only until we were in the ladies' bathroom at the Clara Barton service area on 95 North. "I have an idea," she announced from the next stall.

I waited until we were side by side at the sinks before saying, "Okay, what?"

"I think you know that Murray's son Doug is in marketing?"

I said no I didn't, and wasn't he the goofy one who'd done deliveries for KWP?

"No, that was Mark, his younger brother."

"And Doug came to mind why?"

"Because if he's in marketing, he knows his way around the

media. It's like advertising, only instead of placing print ads like our guy does, he helps clients get themselves attention."

"No, thanks. I have all the attention I can handle."

Still, back in the car, she ran this unformed idea past my father, who said, "Dougie *did* work for us one summer, driving the van. When he was at Harvard."

"Not Harvard! I'd remember Harvard!" my mother scolded.

"B.U.?" he tried.

Back under the blanket they'd bought just for this commute, I said, "One of Murray's sons went to Wesleyan. I don't know which one, but he used to brag about it. Early decision."

"That was definitely Doug," said my mother. "He majored in whatever it is that gets you a job in public relations. And his dad thinks he's a shark!"

I said, "It doesn't matter. I'm not going to hire him."

"'Hire' might not be the right word, if you know what I mean."

"If you mean he wouldn't charge me, dream on."

"But it's us," said my father. "As good as family."

"And I don't think *you* realize what you've been through," my mother said. "Your phone was ringing off the hook, and you were taking those calls, one on top of the other—"

"And not sounding always . . . compos mentis," said my dad.

I asked if a neurologist had used that phrase, or was it their home-grown diagnosis?

"Your father shouldn't have said that. He meant that when a call woke you up, you could sound dopey. You were a little *fuhmished*, that's all."

"I'm better. And I'm managing."

"Only because your phone's turned off! And when it's on, you can't just keep saying 'No comment.' Sometimes an explanation is the right way to go," my mother added.

"These calls aren't going to go on forever."

"I think you need back-up, and I think he'd be willing to help," my mother said.

"The shark? You talked to him already?"

My father said, "I don't think the word Murray used was 'shark.' I think it was 'sharp.' This one was the *sharp* son."

I said, "I'm drifting off back here. Wake me when we're home, if I haven't slipped into a coma."

When I turned my phone back on, I learned that a White House correspondent for BuzzFeed had unearthed the name of the driver who'd hit me: Veronica Hyde-White. Why was this news? Only because some official who spoke on the condition of anonymity said that Rachel Klein had been fired for criticizing the President. Pretty dull stuff, I thought. No one other than Beverly Klein considered me a whistle-blower or a brave big-mouth willing to speak truth to power.

I supposed I could talk to this Doug. I Googled him from the back seat. He had an actual company, an office in Soho, and a list of clients whose identities he protected. I liked that — his website made it sound as if the people who needed marketing help also needed discretion.

If my parents were right in characterizing Dougie as family, grown-up now, grateful for the decades of his father's employment and the resulting roof over his head, food on the table, clothes and tuition, perhaps he would spare me a few hours of non-billable time.

6

WHY ME?

I wasn't returning to my childhood home, the stuccoed Tudor in White Plains, New York, where I'd been raised, in the turret-like room with midnight-blue shooting-star wallpaper, but to my parents' sleek new luxury apartment, so close to the U.N. that it was named The Emissary. Can you call an apartment with only one bedroom "luxurious"? The developer certainly had, given their view of the East River, an indoor dog park they didn't need, a gym, a dry cleaner on the premises, a concierge, a service called the "Invisible Butler", whereby someone would water your plants or feed your exotic tropical fish when you're away. They explained: true, two bedrooms would have been ideal, but it was either that, or these marvelous amenities. I'd get the fold-out couch, which was new, ergonomic, patented. It had its own alcove and full bath, didn't it? And the terrace and the accompanying sunsets—well, not the *actual* sunset but the one reflected off the Pepsi sign in Long Island City. And need they point out how much better an elevatored building and one-floor living was for my recovery than three flights up in D.C.?

To be fair, they had reason to believe their nest was empty. My ghost-writing job had come with room and board, provided by the would-be memoirist. How did I know that jobs don't go on forever the way my parents' had? Given the pace of my boss's dictation and my tolerance for his meandering digressions, I thought I'd be employed for at least a few years. What none of us were factoring in was me finding him face-down, without a pulse, on the breakfast-room floor eight months into our collaboration.

After the autopsy proved he'd had a heart attack, and I was cleared of any suspicions, I searched online for jobs, all in east-coast cities with subway systems. "Washington, D.C.," my parents had reassured themselves. "You'll visit. *We'll* visit. Holidays! You'll jump on the train, three hours and twenty-two minutes away! We don't know why our friends are feeling sorry for us."

Post-hospitalization, this was my first visit to what was now the family home, featuring the latest in wall fabrics and saturated colors; a showroom of sorts. I found it depressing in ways I didn't want to articulate — where did I belong in these 4.5 rooms? Instead I asked about the tangibles: Where was my stuff? What happened to the drawers full of off-season clothes, the sweatshirts bearing the names of old boyfriends' schools? What about Monopoly and Clue and Life and Trivial Pursuit that had been reliably on a particular shelf in our famously dry basement? The dartboard, the ping-pong table, the cross-country skis, the snow tires, the boxes of Nana's meat, milk and Passover dishes?

What Goodwill and Housingworks wanted, they got, I was told.

"I would've kept a lot of my stuff if you'd asked."

"We did ask," my father said. "We sent pictures and asked what you wanted to keep."

That sounded vaguely familiar. "What did I say?"

"You wanted almost everything, but we negotiated."

"And where's the stuff I decided to keep?"

"In storage! Right here in Manhattan. You can visit it any time you want."

I knew what the problem was — my former nonchalance, attributable to having rather easily found room, board and a stipend, not realizing how soon that would pass away with the man who hired me. Hadn't they figured a visiting daughter with a chronic short job-incumbency into the landscape? Apparently not.

Lying around the apartment, watching TV, trying to lower myself into, and up from, the recliner was more painful than being on my feet. I was encouraged to drop by the store; no, not to work; no lifting, no straining; just to get up and dressed and reintegrated into society. *Everyone's asking for you — Murray, Mary-Jo, the neighboring merchants*, they both reported. I said sure. At least I could ring up sales, assuring customers their wallpaper, border and paint choices were brilliant. Half days, okay?

As for the phone calls that kept coming into Klein Wallpaper & Paint for me, I had a prepared speech: "I don't know why you're calling me. I was hit by a car, period. Well, not *period-period* because I was running out of the EEOB, after some unpleasantness at work, which I am not going to elaborate on. Yes, my name got mentioned at a White House press briefing, but just a get-well wish, and by an assistant's assistant. I have to get back to work now. Goodbye."

That proved ineffectual. No one said, "You're right. What was I thinking? Sorry to bother you." A new rule was codified:

if anyone calls for me, say I'm not there, and would have no comment anyway. So why, on my second day back at work, was I hearing my mother yelling in her publicly mellifluous voice, "Phone call on line two for Rachel!"

Before I could project more than a puzzled look at this deviation, she whispered, "It's not a reporter. It's a nervous woman who says she'd lose her job if anyone found out she's calling you." With her hand over the receiver she added, "I asked what was so sensitive, and she said she had information about the driver of the vehicle that almost killed you. Is that true, that you were almost killed? She couldn't know more than what the doctors told us—"

I reached for the phone to cut off her agitating.

"Rachel will be with you in a minute. She's with a customer," jabbing the air toward the office. I obeyed, unhappily, and found my father at the partners' desk, eating the same salami sandwich that was his daily lunch.

"Want to sit? You okay?" he asked, half-rising from his chair.

"This'll be quick," I told him, then most professionally into the phone, "This is Rachel Klein. Who's calling?"

"I can't say. I have some highly sensitive information you might find useful." Her voice was sit-com nasal, making me wonder if she was trying to disguise it.

"About?"

"About the driver of the vehicle that almost took your life: Do you know her identity?"

I said I did — police report, lawyer's visit, BuzzFeed. "And you know her how?" I asked.

"I can't say." Then, with no lead-up, no warning, no "are you sitting down?" she said, "She's having sexual relations with the president."

"Trump?"

"Of course Trump!"

First impression: crackpot/liar/crank call. Yet who in my position, after months of taping presidential scraps back together, getting the heave-ho, nursing grudges, wouldn't feel scandal-hopeful? My apparently stunned expression made my father ask, "What? What did she say?"

I motioned — *not now. Shhhh.*

"Are you still there?" asked the woman, "because I just told you something that most people would consider game-changing."

"I heard you. I'm trying to figure out why—"

"Why what? You think it's implausible that a woman would have sex voluntarily with Donald Trump?"

"No! Trying to make sense of why you're telling me instead of — name the place — the *Post*? CNN?"

"You were their victim! Where do you think Veronica was headed when her car ran you down?"

"To see the president?"

"Yes! Where she goes, still goes, every Tuesday and Thursday."

Had my accident happened on a Tuesday or a Thursday? What day had I woken up in the hospital?

"Did you hear what I said? Veronica was rushing to the White House when she hit you."

"I heard you. I just don't know why I should believe you and what I'm supposed to do with this alleged fact."

There was a pause, then, triumphantly, "Veronica is a doctor of optometry."

"So?"

She harrumphed at my apparent cluelessness, then explained, "She's hiding behind 'doctor.' She thinks it's the perfect cover. If asked what business she has at the White House, she can say that the president is a patient, and the reason her visits are a state secret, not on a log, is — she'll pretend she hates admitting it — his ego."

"Seeing an optometrist has to be a state secret?"

"Have you ever seen the man in glasses? Even to view an eclipse! Of course not! It's a phobia! He thinks reading glasses make him look old and studious in a way his base wouldn't like. And have you ever had a glimpse of the words on the tele-prompter? They're gigantic. He reads at a fifth-grade level. Veronica gives him exercises. It started that way; legit examinations."

I said, "And then they fell in love?"

"'Fell in love!' Are you twelve years old?"

"Do you think insulting me is going to help you make your case?" prompting my father to pantomime *hang up, hang up!*

"I'm not looking to help myself. It's for the country."

"For the country how?"

"Seriously? He announced he was running for re-election his first day in office! I'm taking an educated guess, based on your name and location, as to which side you're on."

"You want this to get out and you think I'm the one to leak it? Why not call some anonymous tip line yourself? Or call a reporter from a phone booth?"

After a pause she said, "I tried that. First thing they ask is for a number where they can call you back."

Having been reminded of that wise journalistic practice, I said, "I'd need that, too. And your name. And *your* source."

"I can't."

"Then don't ask for my help. You've made me very uncomfortable, and that's on top of the physical pain from the accident, and the severe . . ." — what was a potent-enough word? — ". . . *disorientation* I'm already dealing with." Then, only a guess, I said, "If you know so much, you must be Dr. Hyde-Whatever's friend or sister or daughter or employee. Or witnessed this first-hand in the White House."

"I told you, I can't say."

I said, "Well, you've mistaken me for someone who: A. cares; and B. has some kind of standing—"

"You do have standing! You're her victim; *their* victim! The woman who nearly killed you was speeding to the White House to fuck the president!"

I winced, then asked in psychiatric, accusatory fashion: "It sounds to me like a hate-leak. Do you know this Veronica?"

She whispered, "I can't go public. I can't be the source of this. I'd lose everything."

Now I was torn. I wanted to hear who she was and what was at stake, but why tie up the store phone knowing my value as a snitch was debatable. I said, "No one is going to run a story based on one dubious source quoting another dubious source."

"But I told you — it's a game-changer! I have evidence. I know her!"

I said, "Now we're getting somewhere. How do you know her?"

After a pause and embedded in a wail: "Simon and I are in love!"

"Simon is . . .?"

"Simon Hyde-White, her husband!"

I could only say in slow-witted fashion, "So she's married?"

"To a wonderful man!"

I needed time to digest these declarations. I asked if I could call her back.

"No. No calls. Your caller ID could pop up, and Simon or Veronica might be standing right there."

"She knows about you and her husband?"

"No!"

"But sometimes you're all together in the same room? Be-

37

cause you three work together? Or live together?"

I heard what might be her choking back a sob or faking one. "You have to swear to God you'll never tell a soul that I called you."

Before I could swear or not swear, she continued, "I never intended to share this much, but here goes . . ." She lowered her voice to barely audible. "I'm their real-estate agent."

How did that explain one iota of this? I said, "But . . . well, I don't get—"

"I sold them one apartment — a duplex, two bedrooms up, parquet floors, gym, parking space included. I showed them thirty or forty listings over the course of a year. Maybe fifty. Nights, weekends. We became very close! And I've got an exclusive on it as a resale."

I said, "If it's true, I'm one of how many people who know that the president of the United States is dating his optometrist?"

"But you're one of the only people I could think of who has nothing to lose. You don't have a job. He can't get you fired; he can't ruin your life. He's not going to make up a name for you on Twitter."

I'd heard enough. I said I didn't see what was stopping her from being her own whistle-blower. With only an abrupt "Sorry," I hung up before I had to hear the same refrain: she can't, she couldn't, she'd lose everything.

My mother, apparently waiting for line 2 to go dark, joined my father and me within seconds. Leaving out the sexual part of the story, I told them that the caller was claiming that the driver of the luxury vehicle that almost killed me had been on her way to the White House for her regular appointment with the president when I — don't quote me — ran in front of her.

"Is she a member of congress or the cabinet?" my mother asked.

"She's the president's optometrist," I said. "Very hush-hush."

"Why?"

"Because he doesn't want his base to see him in glasses and think he's an elitist."

"What does she want from you?" my mother asked.

"She thinks he's keeping a big secret from the country, and she'd like me to leak it."

"Myopia?" my mother said. "That's it? That's the headline?"

"I know," I said. "Hardly worth leaking."

"Maybe we need to call a lawyer," said my father.

"Or the *Daily News*," said my mother. " 'Trump to eyeglasses: drop dead!' "

"I'm doing nothing. I doubt she'll call back, since I gave her no encouragement whatsoever."

"How come we didn't know the driver was a doctor?" my mother asked. "Did you Google her?"

I hadn't. We gathered around my father's computer screen. He typed. We found Veronica Hyde-White, indeed an optometrist . . . British, alma maters, medical licenses, affiliated hospitals, insurance information, University of Manchester BSc., Manchester Royal Eye Hospital.

"Hit 'images,' " I instructed. Several photos appeared, each telling the same tale. Even wearing a white lab coat in an optometric milieu; even as a brunette bride a dozen years before, and most definitely as a more recent blonde with a smaller nose, we noted long hair and legs, and a wide, toothy smile.

My mother nudged me. "Do you see it?" she asked.

I certainly did. What she was referring to was Dr. Veronica Hyde-White's studied resemblance — though slightly over-the-hill and less fashionable — to forbidden first daughter Ivanka Trump.

7

WHOSE MOVE NOW?

I WASN'T YET BRANDING myself a boomeranging adult child. My parents had begged me to stay with them, to recover at the Emissary, hadn't they? The pain radiating from my ribcage was waning, but could still surprise me, and the concussion triggered less-than-normal sight, balance, motivation, and what felt like a head that had doubled in size.

At the two-week juncture, while I was feeling no less unmoored and uncheerful, my mother suggested gin and tonic on the terrace. Once seated, we commented on the especially bright pink of the sky, the last gasp of the patio tomatoes, and agreed, yes, the surcharge for the river view was worth every extra $10,000.

We were gathered, I soon learned, for life coaching. My father had diagrammed my career on a piece of graph paper, listing my writing and editing skills, the political experience gained in the capitalized Executive Branch of The United States Government, the diplomacy involved, and of course, my experience and life-long dedication to retail.

Next, on his laptop, a curriculum vitae — mine, as evidenced by my name centered on the first line and a head shot that was two hairstyles ago.

"You know what it sounds like?" I asked after skimming. They looked hopeful, anticipating employment optimism. "Like it was written by a doting parent, with zero objectivity."

"Why? Where?"

"First, it's in the third-person, which is creepy. You don't say things like 'where she ably carried out,' then in the next line 'performed brilliantly despite' . . . And then when you use 'competently' it sounds like one of those medals for participation. Don't you see enough resumes to know what's convincing and what's bullshit?"

"It's only a draft," said my mother. "You're the editor. It was just the idea of getting something down on paper."

"It's not like I was going to sit home for the rest of my life. Of course I'll be getting another job, and my own place, and a bedroom with a bed. I'll go back to D.C. and I'll get hired by someone who thinks that my last job was ridiculous, so that getting fired was completely understandable."

"A badge of honor!" said my father.

"Whistle-blowing," my mother reminded me.

"Don't think we're worried about you! I know you'll get a job and make new friends," he added.

"Male and female," said my mother.

"Look how well you did with your last move," my father continued. "You found a job, an apartment, a room-mate, and passed that background check, one-two-three."

"You know who finds an apartment and a room-mate and some kind of job? Just about every kid graduating from college."

Then, expressly to guilt-trip them, "How soon do you want me out?"

With that I was expecting a rush to protest such uncharacteristic inhospitality. Instead, a pause, followed by a nod between them — *You tell her . . . No you.*

"I get it," I said. "You had your own space, and privacy, and you used to slip out to dinner straight from work, and knew that if you brought home leftover Chinese for lunch the next day, you could count on it being in the fridge in the morning."

"Do you think we begrudge you our leftovers?" my mother asked. "Because all this conversation is about is getting the ball rolling."

My dad said, "For example, judging by the hour you get to the store, you could put the mornings to better use."

"I'm not sleeping in. I'm catching up. It's homework. I have to read the newspaper and watch cable news."

"*Have* to?" my mother repeated.

"After all of this stuff I'm suddenly involved in? I mean, I wake up in the hospital and next thing I know, they're talking about me at a White House press conference! And then my phone starts ringing. Mom's the one who named me an influencer."

"I did?"

"You said I was a whistle-blower."

"That's not a job," said my dad.

I didn't tell them that I'd sent an email, cold, to Doug at his self-described boutique agency that promoted people and their causes. I'd studied his website, which promised "buzz-building" and "thought leadership". Under "Current Roster" were group photos of what seemed to be bands — none I'd heard of. I wrote to the info@ address, explaining who I was vis-à-vis Klein Wallpaper & Paint, long-time employer of Doug's dad.

Doug himself wrote back, but in the manner of the busiest person who ever sat at a keyboard, "Rachel, sure. Make appt. to see me."

Disappointing, unfriendly, even arrogant, such a reply didn't move me to make any such appointment. To his credit, he tried again at the end of the day. "How's Friday, 9 a.m.?" I knew the way the world worked. He was squeezing me in before his first real appointment of the day. I wrote back and said, "I'll be there. Thanks."

So now, at sunset on the terrace, I used that outreach as evidence of my forward motion and initiative. It was received with relief and toasts: to Murray, to Dougie, to family, to health! *L'chaim!*

I heard back from the driver's attorney, but a different one from the hospital visitor, a Mr. Gilbert Winslow. When I asked him what happened to the first lawyer, he said, "Nothing. We work as a team."

I said, "I didn't appreciate that visit. I'd just come to. She barged in with a honking bouquet of flowers, and demanded a vase from the nearest nurse."

His answer to that made me think that Attorney Number One was present and had slipped him a crib sheet. "Those flowers, I understand, were beautiful...from imported bulbs," he told me.

I waited several, long, dignified seconds, then asked what he was calling about.

"Do you have a few minutes?"

I did. I was in my pajamas, eating oatmeal in my parents' breakfast nook. I told him I needed to get a pen and paper so I could report our conversation to my (nonexistent) lawyer.

"Would you like me to call you back?"

All I had to do was reach over to the refrigerator and detach the magnetized notepad labeled *Let's Go Shopping!* "No, I'm ready."

His voice became more remote. I asked if he was on speakerphone and who else was there.

"Attorney DiMartino, whom you've met."

Oh, her, as suspected. I said, "I don't remember much of that conversation in the hospital. I was in a lot of pain. I mean, on a scale of one to ten, like eleven."

That prompted him to ask politely how I was feeling now.

"A little better," I said. "But it's a slow road."

"I'll get right to the point. You asked why we were calling. Do you remember that Attorney DiMartino, on behalf of our client, offered you, in a good-will gesture—"

"The check I turned down?"

"It was . . . yes, a check."

"You just called it a good-will gesture. What she told *me* was that the driver didn't want to go through her insurance company, that she wanted to settle privately. I have to say, that seemed fishy."

"Without your even knowing the amount of the check, you found the gesture fishy?"

Should I dip my toe into the scandalous waters this early? I did. "I've learned more since that visit and I think your client has a good reason to buy my silence."

Attorney DiMartino said, "That is absurd. Not to mention libelous."

"Do you know anything about Dr. Hyde-White's private life?" I asked.

"She's an ophthalmologist," said Attorney Winslow.

"No, she's not. She's an optometrist," I said.

In case they were wondering how I knew that, I volunteered the semi-truthful answer: "I used to work at the White House, don't forget — where she was a frequent visitor."

It was exactly at this juncture that I began to wonder if my head injury had caused a drastic change in my personality. Was I now someone to be reckoned with? Had these lawyers met their match in a way I might not be able to follow through on? I was jobless, without prospects, so why keep saying no to untold amounts of money? I asked, hoping to sound blasé, "As for a settlement, what are you offering now?"

Attorney Winslow said, as if even *he* was embarrassed, "Then, as now: ten thousand dollars."

"Ten thousand dollars after what I've been through?"

"Let us point out," he said, "that there was no long-term disability, no damage to a vehicle, no loss of property. And we understand that your COBRA plan covered your hospitalization."

Another note must have passed between them, because he added after a rustle of paper, "And no loss of income due to your job status at the time of the accident."

Their offer made complete sense in terms of compensation for running into the street without looking, but I confess that I was hoping for five times that amount. Is this where I should make my counteroffer? Finally I said, "I guess you don't understand what this ordeal has done to my life, not to mention my health. Besides, aren't we dealing with a billionaire?"

"A billionaire? Who's a billionaire?" Attorney DiMartino sputtered.

Attorney Winslow said, "Our client is Dr. Hyde-White. She's making a good-faith effort because she is a compassionate woman and a medical professional. And may I add, she is a blameless driver with a spotless record who is sympathetic to your jobless state. How many drivers not at fault would make such a gesture?"

I said, "She was speeding. And she's British, which can be lethal on a two-way American street. Plus, I know why she was going to the White House."

"Why?" said Winslow. "Let's hear it. Let's hear whatever it is that you think you know."

I settled on what I thought was an assertion several degrees short of libel. "I happen to know that Veronica is not just the president's optometrist."

I expected . . . what? A denial? A threat? Instead, only silence. I said, "Did anyone hear me?"

"Whether Dr. Hyde-White is or isn't the president's optometrist, we cannot confirm," said Attorney Winslow.

I said, "I know. Big state secret — that he needs glasses."

"We wouldn't know. She's ethically bound by doctor-patient confidentiality. And we happen to know she signed a non-disclosure agreement, because we reviewed it."

"I bet she did. Which must be standard if you're having sex with the president of the United States."

I heard a satisfying gasp from Attorney DiMartino.

"Check it out," I said. "I heard it on very good authority."

"We've heard quite enough, young lady," said Attorney Winslow. "We don't find your supposition credible."

Attorney DiMartino's voice came through, louder than before. "You're forgetting who you're dealing with," then set forth, as if announcing six separate medal winners, the surnames constituting the *Mayflower*-heavy firm I was tackling, solo.

Finally, the weight of that landed. They were Alden, Winslow, Fuller, Billington & Schwartz. I was a nobody in pajamas, alleging a presidential affair, based on nothing more than the phone-booth testimony of an unknown crank.

Whose move now? I didn't want to sound as over my head as I actually felt. And wouldn't $10,000 cover a first and last month's rent, plus a security deposit?

"Could you make it twenty thousand?" I asked. "I'm sleeping on my parents' couch."

"Not our problem," snapped Attorney DiMartino.

"Nor our decision. We'll speak to our client, and get back to you," said Attorney Winslow.

Attorney DiMartino wasn't finished, "Who told you—" she yelled. But her better-mannered partner killed that line of inquiry with a firm and frosty, "Good day, Miss Klein."

8

I MEET DOUGIE

WHAT AN ATTENTIVE and gracious host, greeting me at the elevator with, "Rachel! I've been reading about you!" Murray's older son had taken a turn for the fashionable since the last time I'd seen him, approximately five Passovers ago. On this day his khakis were turned up, exposing his ankles; sockless, black loafers, a pink shirt, a skinny tie. Were madras jackets back in style? They must be.

I asked where he'd been reading about me.

"I do my homework. Associated Press, BuzzFeed, HuffPo for starters. You used to tape stuff, right? That was your whole job? Remind me: voluntary or involuntary separation?"

"If you mean did I quit in protest or was I fired, I was fired."

"So you didn't quit in protest?"

"I might've, eventually . . ."

He couldn't have looked any less impressed. Had I thought

that a denim skirt and a lilac twin-set borrowed from my mother would hit the right note when presenting myself to an image-maker? I couldn't disguise the yellowish-green vestige of the hematoma on my forehead, but bangs would've helped. Stupid of me to have turned down the haircut my mother had offered. "Too expensive; you've already done so much," I'd told her, hoping that landed as punishment for suggesting I abandon their couch.

Doug waved an ID badge at some invisible device and opened the glass door that declared this the offices of WAY! Inside, everything was gleaming white and chrome. "Meet Rachel Klein," he said to the young man whose t-shirt bore the name of a band I recognized from the website. Doug's office was at the end of the hall — water view, with framed tabloid front pages crowding one wall. I asked if these were clients. "Not yet," he said.

He sat down behind the glass console that seemed to be his desk. I took the guest chair, upholstered in an abstract jungle print, the first splash of color I'd seen so far. "What has Rachel Klein been up to since I last saw her?" he asked.

"Besides the stuff you've been reading about?"

"Correct. I meant what do we have to work with?"

"Not much right now. I'm recuperating, plus helping out at the store."

Apparently, a reference to his father's workplace was all it took for him to ask, "Everyone knows that my Dad and Mary-Jo are a couple, right?"

I told him we did know, but we honored their wish—

"To keep it secret from Mark and me?"

I told him I only knew because Murray had confided in my dad, in an employer/employee/EEOC kind of way. When he squinted at that, I said, "Equal Employment Opportunity Commission? You know — so the relationship was out in the open and not unwanted sexual attention."

"As in, 'I'm shtupping Mary-Jo. Okay with you, Kenny-boy?'"

What to say to that? I further explained that Murray had asked my father to join him for a serious sit-down lunch at a nearby Italian restaurant; that his dad had seemed so nervous that *my* dad thought Murray was going to tell him he had an incurable disease. But then, whew — nothing bigger than that he had feelings for Mary-Jo, and *Danken Gott* she returned those feelings.

"You'd think he'd say at least that much to his own kids, wouldn't you?"

I said, "He was doing the right thing. Telling my parents was the equivalent of going to Human Resources—"

"He told *both* your parents?"

"I think that was understood." What I didn't tell Doug was that when the news of the workplace romance broke, my mother took credit, *wanted* credit for the match, which she'd been promoting in ways she swore were subtle. I'd witnessed some of those subtleties: meaningful looks and coy shrugs that translated to *Why not him? Why not her? What are you waiting for?*

I asked how he knew about the romance if it was such a big secret.

"From my mother, who heard it as a brag. You must know the divorce wasn't his idea. He was shell-shocked for years."

It was hard to picture Murray bragging about anything. I said, "I'd think you and Mark would be happy for him."

"Totally. I mean . . . *Dad*? Only an asshole son would say, 'Why don't you see what's out there? Why not try Tinder? Maybe you can find a single, thirty-nine-year old who's dying to tear your clothes off.'" With that he leaned back as far as his spring-loaded chair took him, and smiled as if he'd just said something agreeable.

So that's why I was there: his daddy issues. I said, "He must have his reasons. Maybe he thinks—"

". . . That I'd curl up in a ball, like when they dropped the bomb about the divorce, that we're still nursing some fantasy about our parents getting back together, like it hasn't been a hundred years since they split? I was a kid! What kid likes that news? Maybe the one whose father's a monster — not the guy who puts on an apron and makes dinner every night and does the dishes!"

"Is it Mary-Jo? Do you have something against her?"

"It's not about her! It's about honesty!"

All I had to offer was one of my mother's theories: "Mary-Jo was the baby of about eight or nine kids, at least one of them a priest. Her mom would never approve of her daughter dating a divorced Jew, let alone sleeping with him. It was a secret for such a long time, that maybe it's hard to be out."

"And he couldn't confide in me and Mark?"

I wanted to say, *Enough already! Ask him! Email him! Tell him you know; that everybody knows and you're fine with it!*

He glanced at his watch. Had he squandered whatever potential time I'd been allotted? I asked if he had another appointment.

"No. We're good. Sorry . . . back to you." And apparently back to a list of generic questions he posed to any potential client. "Where does Rachel Klein want to be in five years?" he asked, his face reset to benign curiosity.

"Where? As in what city?"

"No. Life-wise. Jobwise. Status-wise. Where do you see yourself?"

I should've prepped. What would make me sound as if I had success potential? "I see myself running my own firm—"

"In five years? That's aggressive."

Was aggressive good or bad? Just when I thought he was going to declare me an unsuitable candidate for anything but Klein Wallpaper & Paint, he said, "First, we get you on TV."

"As what?"

"As *what*? As the person who had the *cojones* to say 'I don't care if I'm tossed out on my ass. I don't care if I have to go live in my parents' basement — I refuse to work for Donald J. Trump!"

I corrected two things: My parents no longer lived in White Plains, so no basement; and I hadn't quit in protest. I'd been fired. And as far as TV . . . he could do that?

"It's totally what I do, so I need the goods."

I'd brought notes, took them out of my purse, unfolded the two pages, but didn't relinquish them when he motioned for them. I began with, "Okay. You know I was hit by a car—"

"Ouch! Uber or taxi or random driver?"

"A big VW, driven by a woman named Veronica Hyde-White."

"Spell it."

"First I have to get this out of the way . . . your fees . . ."

"Forget it! You're not getting any bill. It would be" — air quotes — "pro bono. It's a great phrase. Latin. Mark taught me. Did you know he went to law school?"

I told him I did; my parents had gone to his graduation.

"My dad went alone. I mean, of course my mom went, and her boyfriend. But not Mary-Jo. What was up with that?"

With every exchange, I was feeling less and less inclined to accept the gift of Dougie's buzz-building. I began my backpedal with, "It's tempting, but I'm not sure I'm ready for TV. I'm still recuperating from the accident."

"Which put you in a coma, right?"

"Knocked me unconscious—"

"I like 'coma.' Can you get me a copy of your medical records?"

I said no. I only had a concussion and a few broken ribs.

"We're dropping the 'only.' You suffered a head injury that put you in a coma. Some people don't wake up from that and the plug gets pulled. You bounced off a car going how many miles an hour?"

"Someone told me she was speeding—"

"Who told you?"

"An anonymous call came into the store—"

"Why anonymous? What did they want?"

"It was a woman. She had some personal information about the driver she thought I could use."

"Good stuff?"

"I don't know if what she told me is even true. And I don't want to be sued for libel if it went public."

"Public? I'm not your public. This" — he traced the perimeter of the office with a sweep of his hand — "is your safe space. Nothing goes farther than here." He winked. "Unless I want it to."

"The caller . . ." I stopped, inhaled and exhaled for effect. "Okay — she claims that the driver is the president's optometrist."

Dougie's whole bearing went from eager to deflated. "Optometrist? That's the big reveal?"

I whispered, "She claimed that Dr. Hyde-White was late for her appointment with the president, and was speeding to the White House when she hit me."

"That's it?"

"You can see why it's all very hush-hush. It's like a state secret—"

"What is?'

"That he needs glasses."

Without picking up a phone, he barked into an invisible intercom, "Jace, get me my brother!" Seconds later I heard, "Marko! You'll never guess who's in my office . . . Nope. Ha! No . . . It's Rachel Klein! Want me to put her on speaker?"

I said, "Please don't."

"She vetoed that! But listen, she thinks we need to confront Dad. Everyone knows! I'm thinking a dinner as an intervention. We say, 'Out with it, for crissakes! We both know you and M.J. have been hooking up for months, maybe years, and what the fuck's the big secret? . . .' I know. I know." Then, an aside to me: "He's reminding me he wanted to confront him from the get-go, that I was the one stalling."

I just sat there. Could I leave? How rude would it be to reject the unwelcome services of WAY!'s founder and CEO?

"Bye, dude! Love ya!... You'd better — like the minute the bar exam is over."

I put my notes back in my purse. "I guess he didn't ask what I was doing here, or why I needed the services of WAY!," I said.

"Do you like the name? I crowd-sourced it on Twitter, and that was the favorite. I sent the first t-shirt to the guy who added the exclamation point. Everyone thinks the name captures our mission."

I said, "I'm not sure that I have a mission. But it was really nice seeing you after all these years. And so touched that you weren't going to bill me."

"Are you sure? I love a challenge and I love 'whistle-blower.' And don't take this the wrong way: but at WAY! we love a makeover."

I went back to the store, straight to Murray's side at the paint agitator. I waited for the racket to end then said, "I just came from a meeting with Dougie. All he talked about was how you never told him and Mark, explicitly, that you and Mary-Jo are a couple. They're going to ambush you at a dinner. If I were you, I'd take the initiative."

"In what way?"

"You invite *them* to dinner and show up with Mary-Jo."

"Holding hands," my eavesdropping mother called from the paint chip strips. "Right, Mary-Jo?"

"I'm not listening," she said.

"We're all behind you," my mother told Murray, "so do it already."

"Good thing there's no customers here," said my dad.

Murray, glancing Mary-Jo's way, said he'd think about such a get-together. It was hard to find a night when both boys were free.

I said, "No excuses. Ambush *them*. Invite them to brunch, like this Sunday."

"Won't it look like you came back from WAY! and tattled?" he asked.

"So what? I think your secret romance was the only reason he made the appointment in the first place."

Had Murray and I ever had a conversation that bordered on the personal? No. Yet his next question seemed to go deeper. "Did Dougie bring you into his private bathroom?" he asked.

Despite my emphatic no, he continued. "I chose the wallpaper. Well, Mary-Jo and I did. We used York's Tropics Banana Leaf, the green-on-green one with pink accents. Across the ceiling too. Everyone who goes in there comes out smiling."

I said, "I wasn't there long enough to use the bathroom."

"It's loud," said Mary-Jo. "I wouldn't want to live with it, but we thought it fit WAY!"

"Dougie's attitude was if you don't like it, you're not a good fit with the company," said Murray.

"Really? Was he serious?" I asked.

Murray said, "That was Dougie being Dougie."

My parents had gone back to their various tasks. Murray asked if I'd scheduled a follow-up.

"He spent a lot of time with me. But after we talked, I realized that WAY! and I weren't a good fit."

Murray looked disappointed. But Mary-Jo's glance said, *I know. Believe me, I know.*

9

I RETURN

I PRINTED OUT MY Dad-fashioned resume, now seeing the wisdom of how he'd massaged my proof-reading/errand-running for the deceased memoirist into "ghostwriter". From there, he'd catapulted me into the White House offices of correspondence and presidential records "management". Well, I did manage my own desk, didn't I? And "ghost-writing" was only a minor overstatement, having strengthened and enlivened the bland passages my late boss believed to be anecdotes. I'd have to explain to potential employers that I couldn't supply a letter of reference due to his sudden death, nor one for the immediate-past White House job, due to reasons I'd provide in person.

After a dinner I'd prepared (rigatoni, red sauce, salad) and had labeled "a family meeting", I announced I was ready to put myself out there.

"In what way?" my dad asked.

"Job hunting!"

Both parents looked disappointed, as if hoping for less "hunting", and more "starting Monday".

"Anything so far?" my mother asked.

I said I hadn't got around to the actual search, but was planning to post my resume on Craigslist and ZipRecruiter.

My dad said I was thinking small. "Have you contacted employment agencies? Or your alumni placement office? People like to hire Duke grads," he said.

My mother asked if I'd be moving back to D.C., where, after all, they'd been covering my rent.

"Knowing you wouldn't want to be sleeping on your parents' couch forever," my dad added.

"If a job turns up in D.C., sure," I said.

"There must be a 'position wanted' section in the *Washington Post*," my dad said.

There was. We learned this after the dishes were cleared to make room for my laptop. I found "upload your resume" on the *Post*'s job site, and its companion, "Search for your next candidate".

We collaborated on a new paragraph beginning with "My dream job would be . . ." which mish-mashed my handling of confidential documents, proofreading, editing, client facing, and congeniality. We had to digitally subscribe to the *Post* on the spot in order to upload these claims, a small price to pay for what would surely and brightly lie ahead.

Responses came right away, none relating to my stated dream job. There was salesperson, district sales, sales rep, sales development, sales consultant — undoubtedly due to an algorithmic take-away from my Klein Wallpaper & Paint retail experience.

More of that; more of nothing I wanted to answer or pursue. Around midnight, after receipt of "life model" and "adult actress for MFA project", I added a sentence to my dream-job paragraph that I thought expressed who I was, hire me or hate me: "For three months, I worked for the Trump administration, but left as a matter of conscience."

At 10:05 the next morning, an email arrived, with a phone number and the message, *Please call ASAP.* I did, and a woman answered with only an unfriendly, "This is Sandra." When I identified myself as the ghost-writing job seeker, she asked if I could come for a screening interview.

"Screening?"

"Not with the actual employer, whose name I can't reveal, but with me."

"Can't reveal because . . .?"

"He's famous."

"May I ask what he's famous for?"

"Books," she said.

"What kind?"

"Best-sellers."

"Novels?"

"No!"

"Can you be specific?"

"I cannot."

"A hint?"

She paused before whispering, "He's famous for getting under the skin of presidents."

Woodward? Bernstein? But would they need to peruse resumes online?

She asked where I was located.

"New York City at the moment. Where are you?"

"D.C. obviously. Can you make it later today?"

I asked if this was an emergency of some sort because I'd have to make arrangements—

"Tomorrow then?"

I said doable, yes, but couldn't a screener happen over the phone?

"Absolutely not. It has to be in person."

I said okay, tomorrow. Please email me the time and location, preferably in the afternoon, preferably at a public place.

"Four p.m. I'll email you the address."

"A restaurant or coffee shop is fine."

"His home is his office," she said.

I didn't say, "He could be a murderer. I could be walking into a sex-trade trap." I said, "I'm sure you'll understand why I can't come to a stranger's house."

"Hold please."

When she returned, her answer was a guarded, "Kirby Champion, okay? Famous enough? You can tell someone that's who you'll be meeting . . . if you make the cut."

I said, okay, yes, send address and Metro stop. And of course I knew the name. *Vaguely, but would do my homework.*

I was sure my practical parents would advise against my running down for just one bite. They'd want me to have a few things lined up so if this job didn't pan out, I'd have scheduled fallback appointments.

"How about running down to Bloomie's this afternoon?" my mother asked, "unless of course you have a suitable interview outfit we may not have seen."

I said I had what I needed. I'd worked in the White House, remember? I owned a suit. It was navy blue. Besides, this was a preliminary interview with an underling, possibly a gatekeeper, judging by her—

"Please, Raitch — no attitude," my dad said.

I reminded him that I'd been hired on the spot by poor, late Mr. Lancelot Wheeler, based on a single, very cordial interview and a typing test. Have a little faith.

Was this optimism on my mother's face? "If you make it to the next round with this author . . . someone like him might be interested in what you found out about the optometrist. I mean, it can't be mere coincidence that he wants to meet you."

"Bev, please remember it's not about Rachel," my dad said. "Besides, that sorry chapter of her life — her miserable job and her accident and whatever that anonymous caller said the driver is up to at the White House — I thought we agreed it's time she puts all of that in a box and leaves it here, out of sight and out of mind."

My mother was at the sink, brushing crumbs off the breakfast place-mats she'd collected, but looked up. Her eyebrows were raised and readable. *That's strictly your father's opinion*, they were saying.

10

PASSING MUSTER

WHEN I CALLED MY room-mate from New York, she said she'd
assumed I'd be moving back, since rent plus utilities had been
covered during the hiatus. Wasn't I lucky to have parents who
hadn't cut me off as hers had done; hadn't turned their backs on
me, afraid of what their pious friends were whispering — oh,
one thing: there would be three of us now. I'd be cool with her
girlfriend in residence?

This was news, orientation-wise. "*Girlfriend* girlfriend?" I
asked.

"Yes, girlfriend, partner. Yasemin."

"New relationship?" I asked.

"No. Just the live-in part."

I told her I'd be arriving the next day for a job interview,
dropping my stuff off before the 4 p.m. appointment.

"You won't believe how clean it is now. And organized!

Things like flour and sugar and lentils in big glass jars. Even the cereal gets put into plastic containers."

"This is Yasemin's doing?"

"For sure. And get this: she cooks. And she knows how to get groceries delivered so they're here, like five minutes before we get home. We eat in most nights."

She failed to add "...and you'll join us." But still, for Elizabeth, it was close to a welcome mat.

Within minutes of arriving at the tall brick townhouse on O Street in Georgetown, I understood why my contact, Sandra (tweed-suited, gray pageboy, velvet headband), had insisted on an in-person interview. Her unapologetic, appraising gaze traveled from my black pumps upwards to my suit, blouse, face, hair, and back down again. In another situation where rudeness wouldn't have come at a price, I might have said, "Why don't you take a picture?" but here, like an eager applicant, I said, "Hope I'm passing muster."

"So far, yes. Please understand I have to do this, because Mr. Champion, as a male employer, cannot. And it's not about looks. It's about presentation. Being presentable. Some candidates come for interviews dressed for the gym."

"I always dress professionally," I said. *Surely if I get this job, I'll shop.*

"Please be seated," she said.

Now, face to face, I was the focus of a new kind of diagnostic stare. To establish myself as unspooked and unfazed, I broke the stand-off with, "You probably want to know about my time at the White House."

"I'll get to that. First," — pointing to my resume — "wallpaper and paint? What's that about?"

"Just summer jobs, and part-time for a few weeks when I was home recuperating from my accident." When that didn't seem to clarify anything, I added, "*Klein* Wallpaper & Paint. My parents own it . . . It was founded by my paternal great-grandfather in 1925."

Still frowning, she asked, "This accident you referenced . . . Did you have to go on disability?"

It wasn't a lie to say, "I did not. I never took a single sick day."

"I've had candidates ask, first thing, how many sick days do I get. How much vacation time? What about parental leave?"

Noted: *don't ask*. She was staring again, so I offered, "Here's an interesting fact about my job in the Office of Presidential Correspondence: every piece of mail had to be irradiated."

She said "Of course it would be," then asked if I ever had direct contact with the president.

"For better or for worse, no."

"I don't mean did you have lunch with him. I meant did he ever walk through the department and exchange some pleasantries. Or yell at someone?"

"In my second job, White House Office of Records Management, I did have direct contact with him." It was a version of the truth; wasn't every single thing I taped back together ripped by his own two hands?

"This part about getting fired . . . were you planning to elaborate on that with K.C.?"

I said I would if he brought it up, but—

"No, I meant, work it into the conversation. And if you're holding a grudge against the president, still better."

Was this a trap? Was she sabotaging my interview because one of her relatives was applying for the job? "That seems a risky thing to do in a job interview," I said.

64

"Not with K.C. He can't advertise 'assistant needed who hates Donald Trump', but getting fired by forty-five's administration is a good start. I have a question I ask everyone: 'Could you handle working with someone whose goal is to humiliate the president on every page?'"

I said yes, I could. And I think I'd be very good at it. Could you tell me more about what the job entails?

"You'd be transcribing phone calls."

"Whose?"

"His! This isn't going to win you a Pulitzer. This is, for lack of a better term, an extra pair of ears. He needs all conversations with his subjects recorded."

"Is that legal?"

"It's for accuracy, for posterity, for someday the Kirby Champion library. It's not to blackmail them."

"That's good," I said.

"You seem smart. And you graduated from Duke. He'll like that. His middle daughter's applying there."

"If she wanted to ask me anything about the school . . . I mean, if I'm working for her dad."

She picked up a catalogue and was flipping through it. Office supplies, I guessed; its glossy cover featured a copy machine and two attractive employees, one pressing a button, the other frozen mid-collating.

Was I being dismissed or tested? I asked if my interview was over.

"I'm waiting to hear whether K.C. is free to meet you now. I've already texted him." She asked if I'd read any of his books.

"I downloaded the one about the Bushes—"

"Not the best example, because he liked them, which got in the way. You know he's a muckraker, right?"

"I'd love to work for a muckraker."

She emitted a hmmphh that I interpreted as *of course you'd say that.*

Was it premature to thank her? Before I could, she added, "Tell him you don't shut your phone off at night. In fact, tell him you barely sleep."

"He'd expect me to be available around the clock?"

"When you publish a book a year, you get ideas twenty-four/seven."

"And he has to share them on the spot? They can't wait till morning?"

"You'll figure it out," she said.

In the narrow closet of an elevator, we went straight to the third floor — bypassing 2, which housed the living quarters, I was told, her tone suggesting I must never, ever, press that button. The space was one long enormous room, street view to back garden, with golf-themed wallpaper, palace-sized Persian rugs, and bookshelves holding multiples of Kirby Champion's hardcover books. At one end of the room was a massive antique desk, its surface strewn with file folders, newspapers, mail and, presumably, manuscripts. Behind it, under the bay windows, was a table holding what looked like the latest delivery from the office-supply catalog: packages of pens, Post-its, spiral-bound notebooks, plus photographs of tall female children. I waited in the upholstered chair facing the desk, and practiced arranging my features into an expression I hoped was both intelligent and accommodating. "He'll be with you soon," Sandra said. "Don't touch anything."

Maybe ten minutes had passed when a male voice boomed, "So you're the one I'm supposed to like!"

It had to be Kirby Champion, though his round, florid face bore little resemblance to the younger, more chiseled one I'd found online. He was wearing a suit in an orange and blue plaid, made louder by his size — six feet four or five, for sure. He shook my hand, then perched himself on a corner of the desk. "Give me all the reasons why I shouldn't hire you."

"Shouldn't hire me? Or *should*?"

"Should *not*. I like to know where the landmines are."

How truthful should I be? Wouldn't the smart answer be something benign and lovable? I started with, "I used to work for a writer, Lancelot Wheeler—"

"Hold on! Wait! Did you say 'Lancelot'?"

"I did."

"Surely an affectation, though I love it!"

"He swore it was his real name. His parents were huge *Camelot* fans."

"And he didn't hate it? Didn't go by Lance, or use his middle name? Like 'L. Bartholomew Whatever?'"

I liked that he'd plucked Bartholomew out of thin air, and I told him that.

"Where were we? You were about to list your bad habits."

I decided to view this as improv, where the audience had thrown out the phrase, "crackpot job interview." I began again. "So Mr. Wheeler had a heart attack and I was questioned by the police, even though I was the one who called nine-one-one."

"You didn't kill him, did you, with one of those drugs that simulates a heart attack?" He laughed heartily.

"I definitely did not kill him. And why would I? I mean, without him I was out of work, and I was extremely fond of him."

"Fond? How fond?"

"Not like that. He was gay. Plus, about fifty years older than I was."

"Wait! Then his parents couldn't have seen *Camelot*! Not the musical! Not if he was eighty!"

I said, "I'm only quoting Mr. Wheeler. I didn't do the math."

"And if you had known the year *Camelot* opened, would you have challenged him?"

Was the notion of challenging a boss related to the toxic email that proved fatal to my White House career? Was he crediting me with speaking truth to power? I said, "I'd like to think so."

"And I trust he hadn't just redone his will without any witnesses present and left you his fortune because you had a gun to his head?" More hearty laughter.

I forced a companionable laugh at the same time I was wondering whether every conversation I'd have with this man would be a parlor game.

"What else? I'm still not convinced that you have bad habits."

I said I was getting to that. "The job came with room and board. I had meals with him. I saw how he ate — all the wrong things — steak every other night. Ice cream, whipped cream, mayo on French fries. Twice as much butter as his toast needed. I could've said something. Or at least learned CPR."

He pretended to lick the point of an imaginary pencil, then intoned, "Doesn't know CPR. Buy defibrillator for the office. What else? C'mon. You were fired, right? By Trump."

"Not directly by Trump." I was going to elaborate about my reply-all drunken email minus the drunken part, so I backtracked, figuring a Trump grudge was a better job qualification. So I said, "Actually, I was fired because I told the truth in an email."

"Directed toward Donald Trump, right? Who eats steak every night! And ice cream! You've given me hope!"

"I wrote that email late at night. To a co-worker, or so I thought. It wasn't meant for his eyes." Was this my opportunity? Having pronounced the word "eyes," should I tell him about the adulterous doctor of optometry?

Don't be stupid, I told myself. He could steal it. I'd be like the Winklevoss twins whose idea got turned into Facebook. Maybe I could just whet his appetite. I said, "Since leaving the White House, random people call me—"

"With job offers?"

That was a good notion. I said, "Some. But mostly because I was run down about a minute after security escorted me out of the EEOB."

"Run down? On purpose?"

"I don't think so . . ."

"Hit and run?"

"No, she stopped."

"She? Name?"

I hesitated, but it was public record. "Dr. Veronica Hyde-White, hyphenated."

"What kind of doctor?"

"Optometrist."

"Are these calls about her? *From* her?"

"Not her directly."

"Don't be coy."

I leaned back in my chair and crossed my arms. "If you were me, would you tell all before you were hired?"

He grinned, exhibiting exceptionally white teeth. "I hire for attitude! So far, so good. How's this: you write it all down; write about these calls you're getting. The who what when why how. Redact whatever you consider money in the bank."

"Now? You mean as my writing sample?"

He was shaking a box of pens onto the desk, but my question stopped him. "Writing sample?" he repeated.

"So you can judge my spelling and punctuation, and, well, writing — to help you make your decision."

"Which decision?"

"The job! Your opening. The reason I'm here."

And just like that, this big, jovial muckraker, said, "I don't give a rat's ass about your spelling. The job's bloody well yours if you want it."

11

WHEN CAN YOU START?

AFTER A HANDSHAKE and a backslapping "welcome aboard," I asked Mr. Champion for something in writing.

"Salary and benefits? That kind of thing?"

I said, "I wouldn't want to find out this was an unpaid internship."

Once again, he laughed appreciatively. Was I about to work for my best audience, ever? I said, "This is a real job, right?"

"Of course! I'm sending you downstairs. My sister deals with the nuts and bolts."

Did he mean . . . was he the brother of . . . *Sandra*? "Would that be Sandra?" I asked.

"She'll be civil, now that you're on the team. And thrilled that she's done with the finding and the screening." He pushed his reading glasses back up his nose, and tapped my handwritten, vague account of life since the accident. "This," he said.

"Needs more?"

"It begs a hundred questions."

"Like . . ."

"Like there's something pretty big that happened when you worked for Trump, and someone's either trying to get it out of you or trying to shut you up."

Should I admit he was totally off base? I said, "Not exactly. But you're good. I do know more. I was too stunned to ask the latest caller anything except 'How do you know what you're alleging, and why tell *me*?'" I glanced behind him at the framed photos of daughters at various ages, arms tucked around each other's waists, numbers pinned to their race-wear and skiwear. But no wife.

If he saw me studying them, he didn't acknowledge it. He said, "This big secret you're holding onto — does anyone else know? I mean, anyone who'd use it?"

"Do you mean write about it? No."

He grinned. "In that case, I thank you for this future scoop."

Scoop? I told him I'd brought up the alleged interesting tidbit when I was negotiating with the lawyers about a settlement—

"You were negotiating *yourself*? Without a lawyer?"

I confessed, yes, unfortunately — couldn't afford one.

"Who's their client? The driver? Her insurance agency? Whoever fired you at the White House?"

"The driver. I was asking for more than they were offering—"

"Which was what?"

"Ten K."

"And you said, 'I have some intel that would embarrass your client'?"

"Pretty much."

"And their move?"

"They said they didn't find me credible. I haven't heard from them since."

"How much do you want?"

"Well, more than their ten K—"

"No! I didn't mean for compensation. Here."

Did he want me to name my own salary? I asked if he could give me a range.

"How's ten per cent above your last job? Sandra can work out the numbers."

"Fifteen per cent?"

"Twelve-and-a-half per cent above whatever Donald Trump was paying you. I'll text Sandra."

When I told him I was thrilled and grateful to be part of the Champion team, he said he was pleased, too, having interviewed a half-dozen candidates before me. And not one of them had more than garden-variety hatred for the president — none personal, just political.

"Well . . . good for me!"

"One sec." He'd picked up his phone. "Sandra — we're hiring Miss . . .?"

"Klein," I supplied. "Rachel."

"And have her sign the T.I.P."

"Tip?" I repeated when he'd put down his phone.

"Transfer of intellectual property. Essentially, what news breaks here, stays here."

That sounded reasonable. I went downstairs and signed it.

My mother squealed, "I'm ordering all of his books the minute I get off the phone! Congratulations! Kenny! Pick up! Rachel got the job with that author!"

My dad was on the office extension within seconds. "Sweetheart! What's the actual job? And when do you start?"

"Tomorrow. And I'm not totally sure what the actual job is — his human resources person-slash-sister said I'd be recording his interviews."

Apparently they were too relieved to mention that I might possess talents beyond pushing a button on a recording device. Anticipating that, I told them that I'd beat out a half-dozen other candidates.

"I'm not the least surprised!" my dad gushed.

"Did you have to finesse the part about getting fired?" my mother asked.

"Just the opposite. I think it was my grudge-holding that put me over the top."

"Salary?" my mother asked. "Not that we care."

"Twelve-and-a-half per cent higher than my last job."

"Health and dental?"

"One thing at a time, Bev," said my dad.

"Both," I said.

"I know you're going to find the job fascinating," said my father. "I took a look at his past works: these interviews are going to be with senators and campaign managers and chiefs of staff—"

"And ex-wives and girlfriends," added my mother.

"Starting tomorrow!" said my dad. "Your mother and I thought you'd have to go back for another interview, and maybe a third. You must've aced it."

I said I had to get off, was in an Uber, almost at Nordstrom Rack, hoping to find outfits that announced "journalist at work."

"Then nothing Bohemian, please," said my mother.

"Can we help?" my dad asked.

I said, "I think you're forgetting that I never spent a nickel while under your roof. But thanks."

"Is he a nice man?" my mother asked. "I was worried that he might be very . . . brash, considering the books he writes."

I spoke an utter truth: "I'm still recovering from how nice he is."

After a successful shopping trip that spilled over into nearby Macy's, rendering two skirts, two sweaters, one shirt in two different colors, tights, and a pair of red suede shoes I couldn't resist, I went back to the apartment, unpacked my suitcase, laid out the new purchases for subsequent admiring, and went out again to buy a bottle of something.

"How ya doin'?" the wine-shop clerk asked. And though I knew it was his standard, meaningless auto-greeting, I said, "Great! I just got a new job!"

"Congrats. I remember you," he said. "Vodka, right?"

"My Cape Codder phase. That's over."

He pointed to the Prosecco I'd brought to the register. "Good choice. Good price. Having friends over to celebrate?"

Had this clerk just asked me a personal question? I said, "Only my room mate. Well, two room-mates. The second one is new. I haven't even met her."

I signed the credit-card reader with my index finger. He bagged the bottle. With nothing left to transact, I volunteered, "The other two room-mates are girlfriends . . ." And in case that needed elucidation, I added, "A same-sex couple. Though I happen to be straight."

He smiled and murmured, "What a coincidence."

"I'm Rachel Klein."

"Rachel Klein, just like your credit card says. Good to know."

"My new job? Do you know Kirby Champion, the author? That's who hired me."

"I don't. But congratulations."

"Thank you." When I didn't pick up the bag, he asked if there was anything else. I said, "Just that I've worked in retail, and

I think you're exceptionally good at client facing." His name badge said "Alex", which I pronounced with some oomph, as if committing it to memory.

He pointed toward the back of the store where an older man appeared to be lecturing about something in the Loire Valley section. "That's my dad, client-facing in action. We're a team."

I made a mental note: next time, tell Alex that I too had parental employers, in retail. The Loire Valley customer was heading toward us, juggling three bottles. I said, "I should run. First day of work tomorrow."

"Knock 'em dead," said Alex.

It had to be Yasemin in the kitchen, hard at work with a cleaver on a lump of raw meat, her long dark hair loosely pinned up with what looked like a bamboo kebab skewer.

I introduced myself — hardly necessary, because her first question was, "How did it go?"

I held up the bottle: "I got the job!"

She rinsed her hands, crossed the room and gave me a damp, congratulatory hug. I said, "I feel like my luck is changing. My ribs didn't even hurt when you hugged me."

"Sit," she said. "Entertain me while I cook. Do you eat lamb?"

Did that mean I'd be joining them? I said, "Yes. I eat everything." I put the Prosecco in the fridge, cleared mail off the table, and, to show I wasn't taking reentry for granted, set a mere two places.

"Hey! Three plates and three salad bowls. Can you do vinaigrette?"

I said I could follow a recipe for vinaigrette. I'd look online.

When I returned with my phone, she asked about the job. I began with the name "Kirby Champion," which produced a "You're fucking kidding me?"

"Is that bad?"

"I work for D.O.J. He calls a *lot*, always hoping to hit on a leaker."

I said, "That could be me harassing federal employees from now on."

"Lessons at the knee of a master harasser. Should be fun."

I asked her if Elizabeth had filled her in on my checkered federal career.

Yasemin said no, just that I was recovering in New York from a car accident. But she'd Googled me. "You're kind of famous," she said.

"My fifteen minutes..."

"Your new boss must've Googled you, too, and said, 'Hmmm. She told off the president. Just what I need!' Can we open the bubbly now?"

I retrieved the Prosecco from the refrigerator, uncorked it and poured us each a glass in etched flutes I'd never seen before. Yasemin raised hers. "May your fifteen minutes turn into fifteen years, or fifty, and your name added to the jacket of every snarky book!"

From a kitchen stool, I sipped my drink and watched her sear chunks of lamb. Had I fallen down a rabbit hole into Opposites Day? How else to explain all of this — unaccustomed domestic cordiality? A friendly exchange with a heretofore low-key wine clerk? And the best topsy-turvy development of all: a famous muckraker had hired me precisely because I'd been fired.

12

I CAN DO THAT

SANDRA HAD FASHIONED a cubicle for me with a four-screen cherry-blossom room divider. She promised a telephone with intercom capability so that her brother could buzz me rather than bellow. Anything else I needed?

Lots. I was sitting at an olive-green Army-surplus desk, on a folding chair, staring at a computer monitor circa 2010. I asked if I could get a comfortable chair — something ergonomic, adjustable, and tilty?

"Maybe. We'll revisit that when you've made it through the trial period."

I said, forcing a smile, "Then I have two goals to shoot for."

There was no official orientation, just a summons in the form of a loud "Klein! C'mere!" I jogged across the long, golf-papered great room to find my new boss on the phone, holding up a note that said, **ANON!!** He returned to scrawling words on a yellow legal pad, pages flying, his receiver hunched between ear and shoulder. Ear pods, I thought. I'll tell him about those.

Whatever answers he was getting seemed to be making him happy. "You saw that?" he'd ask. "You *heard* that?" with sharp "whens?" and "wheres?" thrown in, sounding impeccably journalistic to me.

After hanging up, he grinned. "That's what I call a helluva source."

I asked how one knows that an anonymous caller is legit. Couldn't anyone call and say "I have some dirt"?

"Excellent question. Because I know everyone who works at 1600 Pennsylvania Avenue!"

"You know them personally?"

"I know the roster. And you know who wants to talk? The haters. By the way, they all hate him."

I asked what was it about this latest phone call that made him or her a great source.

"The insults. POTUS this and POTUS that — like a pet name gone bad." He flipped pages, forward then back. "Here it is! 'Brought her dog to work. Trump's kid played with him. Loved him. POTUS made new rule: no mutts at WH.'"

Was that big news? I asked if he could give me another compelling quote. Same page, halfway down: "How's this? If POTUS spills D.C., has fit. Yells for aides."

"Spills? Meaning leaks?"

He looked at his own scrawl, squinted, then said, "No, not leaks. D.C. is Diet Coke. He drinks at least a dozen a day."

It was too soon and too judgmental to ask if this was the caliber of tips his sources were supplying. "What else?" I asked.

"This one won't surprise you: He keeps a can of hairspray in every bathroom, plus one in his desk drawer. And you know what desk that is, don't you? The Resolute Desk!"

"Did you ask how she knows what's in every bathroom?"

"I didn't have to ask! She's on the housekeeping staff — that, by the way, is totally off the record. She knows first-hand that the hairspray in the Obamas' bathroom belonged to the First Lady and only the First Lady."

I hoped I was looking more engaged than disappointed. To change the subject and to demonstrate a grasp of his bibliography I asked, "Will this book be a sequel to *Insufferable*?"

"Trump-wise, by definition, yes. But it's tricky. I might have to do one version where he's out — removed, defeated, or dead — and another where he's reelected. Maybe just a matter of verb tenses."

I asked how far along he was.

"If you mean pages written — *nada*. I'm still in the research phase. Luckily, these things kind of write themselves." He smiled. "No one ever accused me of being a stylist. But what would you rather read? A prize-winner or a page-turner?"

I thought it best to answer "page-turner, for sure."

"You'll help with the writing," he announced. "Hey, don't look so alarmed. You'll be transcribing the interviews. All you'd have to add are the he-saids and the she-saids and pepper the quotes with 'allegedly.'"

Don't get nervous, I told myself. *I can do that*. Thinking of what Yasemin had told me about his reputation at DOJ, I asked if, after *Insufferable*, potential sources still took his calls.

"You mean am I shunned because I'm a pariah?"

A solicitous employee might have disputed that, except that he looked so pleased with his own word choice. I said, "Pariah, in the best sense of the word."

"Here's what you'll find out; here's why they take my calls: They're frustrated. They want to talk. They know everyone squeals, so they figure out a way to get to me. I'm safer than the *Washington Post* or *The New York Times* or the Associated Press because those leaks end up in the morning paper, or online, in five minutes. With me, their insults won't show up for six, eight, nine months. In a book — and the president doesn't read books!"

I chuckled along with him, then asked if the work in progress had a title. It did: "The Blight." He asked what I thought of it. "Be honest. It's only a place-holder."

I said, "My only qualm would be if it was mistaken for a book about an actual blight."

"You mean crops? Not a chance; not this blight. Trump's photo will be plastered on the cover. Plus a subtitle — not a hundred per cent yet — something like "The diseased presidency of Donald J. Trump.""

"In that case 'Blight' could work," I felt obliged to say.

"My publisher doesn't like it, so if you wake up in the middle of the night with some brilliant title, write it down. Do you keep a notepad by your bed?"

I said, "From now on I will."

"I used to have a little gadget that I could talk into. Good for memos, but bad if your wife is a light sleeper."

I didn't respond to that; didn't want to speak of personal matters on my first day, so I asked, "What would you like me to do now?"

"No more interviews today. Maybe just some good old-fashioned editing." He opened his top right-hand desk drawer, took out a folder and handed it to me. It was my redacted synopsis of the undisclosed affair. "I want you to flesh this out. I'm looking for nuance, but loud. Take as much time as you need. Do you have your notes with you?"

Notes? I said, "I think I've already reconstructed the conversation in these pages."

"I need more. Wasn't that our unspoken deal? I hire you and I get the goods? This is well-written, but no heat, no juice, no news. There has to be more. I mean, *is* there more?"

"There's more. A lot more." I took the file and said okay; I'd try to supply more juice.

"Good, good. Shovel on the dirt. I didn't hire you to be a fact-checker."

I went back to my cubicle and turned on the computer. Password? That required a trip to the first floor to ask Sandra, who gave it up with a second reminder of my trial period. Back at the keyboard, I closed my eyes and concentrated. I could do nuance. I remembered how the real-estate girlfriend had bounced from nervous to annoyed to impatient to weepy, in between non sequiturs. *She's an optometrist! She's sleeping with the president! I love her husband!*

My recall was pretty good for someone who'd been recovering from a concussion. I refashioned the conversation as dialogue, introduced new adverbs ("angrily", "belligerently", "passionately"). When I reread the draft, it was long enough for an entire chapter. Might I be writing history? I dug in, embellishing with atmosphere: the glug-glug-thwomp of the paint-mixing machine, the mingled office smells of the Mister Coffee and my father's salami sandwich; falafel sputtering from the Hallal truck on Lexington Avenue. The affair between Veronica and the president might not be proved in these pages; it might not hobble a presidency, but suddenly I had a way with words.

13

HOW, WHEN, WHERE
AND WITH WHOM?

DID I HAVE TO KEEP my work confidential? I asked at dinner
— again a Yasemin triumph (eggplant casserole and my first
fattoush salad) — if our kitchen table could be a cone of silence
on the nights I needed to debrief and confide.

"We're all ears, and our lips are sealed," said Yasemin.

"As long as you didn't sign an N.D.A.," said Elizabeth.

"Which wouldn't apply to conversations around a kitchen
table," said Yasemin.

"Can't be too careful," said Elizabeth.

"First, is a T.I.P. the same as an NDA?"

"Are you spelling 'tip'?" asked Yasemin.

"No. I'm not sure about the T, but the I.P. stands for intellectual
property."

They exchanged a look that suggested legal disapproval.

I said, "Neither Mr. Champion nor his sister mentioned an NDA. Apparently, I earned his trust on the basis of . . . nothing I can name."

"You worked in the White House and that's his beat. He was lucky to get you" — a startlingly supportive sentence from the room-mate whose path I'd hardly ever crossed, pre-Yasemin.

I said, "I sat in on a phone interview Mr. Champion had with a source. Then he shared the high points with me," hoping that would satisfy any curiosity I may have mistakenly stoked. I chewed my next bite of salad, eyes closed as if transported, then asked, "What makes the dressing tangy?"

"Buttermilk," said Yasemin.

"That's it?" Elizabeth asked. "He interviews people and then gives you the highlights? That's the whole shooting match?"

Yasemin said, "You're forgetting who I am to Rachel — a relative stranger who works for the Department of Justice. I could be a Trump appointee who'd go running to one of my higher-ups."

"Isn't my girlfriend the most reasonable person you ever met?" asked Elizabeth.

"And the best cook!" I said.

Was Elizabeth looking less than thrilled? Maybe my compliment sounded as if I were taking nightly dinners for granted. I quickly added, "Not that you need a third wheel at your table. I'm planning to get out, to do stuff. It's time I resuscitate my social life."

"We don't need dinner à deux seven nights a week," said Yasemin. "Besides, I always make too much, and Lizzie is too cool to bring a lunchbox to work."

"How, when, where and with whom are you going to kick-start your social life?" Elizabeth asked.

"She'll go online," said Yasemin. "Unless she already has a beau."

I said, no, no beau. And not keen on going online. I thought I'd stick with real life.

"Real life is fine if you worked out in the world," Yasemin said.

"Instead of a job with no co-workers; not even an office building where you could strike up a conversation in the elevator," said Elizabeth.

"Mingling in an office never ends well," I said.

Yasemin gestured: *more. Elaborate on that topic.*

I said, "It's hardly worth mentioning, but when I worked in WHORM, I thought there was something going on between me and another Scotch-taper. Nothing overt. Nothing spoken, just a few coffee breaks."

"But?" asked Yasemin.

"Doesn't matter. He's the one I emailed too late at night with the smack talk about Trump that got me fired."

"He blew the whistle on you?" asked Yasemin.

"No. I hit 'reply all,' so it wasn't his fault."

"Has he been in touch to say he's sorry you were fired?" asked Yasemin.

"Or visited you in the hospital after you were run over?" asked Elizabeth.

"Or sent flowers or a card, for crissakes?" asked Yasemin.

I said no, none of the above.

"He's an asshole, clearly," said Elizabeth. "He's off the list. Goodbye, asshole."

"Back to the drawing board," said Yasemin. "Okay; have you spotted anyone you'd want to ask out — which you'd do, right? This being the twenty-first century and presumably okay even for a straight woman" — causing Elizabeth to fake a loud cough.

"Very insecure, my girlfriend, just because I once or twice in the past dated a man," Yasemin explained.

Did I have to address that? I didn't. I said, "It's too early to make my move. We've only met once, and he was behind a counter."

Yasemin said she and Elizabeth would be excellent romantic consultants. They weren't silly, competitive girls like the ones I must've dealt with in high school who'd made me . . . frankly, gun shy. Who was it? Where did I meet him . . . a *him*, right?

I said, "He works at the wine store."

"Which wine store?"

"On Sherman, like four, five blocks."

"Has to be Varsity," said Elizabeth.

"Let's go," said Yasemin.

"We're still eating," I said. "Please pass the eggplant."

"What time does it close?" Yasemin asked.

Elizabeth was already tapping her phone. "Nine o'clock week-nights. Plenty of time. We'll call it 'I'm out of vermouth,' which is true. And you'll have time to sex yourself up."

Yasemin said, "Elizabeth has a limited vocabulary in these matters. She means 'change into something more fetching and put on lipstick.'"

Elizabeth said, "It's almost eight. You two go. Yasemin's definitely the better wingman. I'll do the dishes."

I said, "It doesn't mean he'll be there tonight."

"Then you'll leave him a note, woman!" said Yasemin.

Elizabeth asked, "What's his name?"

"Alex."

Her phone was now at her ear. Within seconds she was saying, "Just checking that you're open . . . And to whom am I speaking? . . . Thanks, see you soon."

Whatever answer she'd heard was making the formerly dry, cold Elizabeth smile.

I changed into jeans and my new navy-blue velour turtleneck, which made Yasemin say, "A turtleneck. Really? Don't you have anything more come-hither?"

I returned to my closet. There was a pale pink silk blouse, tags still hanging from the armpit, that I'd bought for a staff holiday party, never attended due to getting sacked. I put it on to avoid another veto, added my bat mitzvah pearls, and when I returned to the front hall asked, "Do I look like I'm trying too hard?"

Yasemin said, "Don't take this the wrong way, but not in the least."

Sure enough, it was Alex behind the counter, ringing up a tuxedoed customer's half-dozen bottles of wine, necessitating a trip to a back room for a take-home carton. Once he'd returned, packed the bottles, and opened the front door for the departing customer, Yasemin and I stepped up to the counter.

Alex pointed at me. "Prosecco, right? Celebrating the new job?"

"She's Rachel," Yasemin announced.

I said, "Yup, today was my first day."

"How'd it go?"

Yasemin said, "I'm going to browse, okay? Back in . . ." — she surveyed the rear of the store — ". . . the Kosher wine section."

Alex said, "Best selection in the city, we think." Then back to me. "Day one? So far so good?"

"A little overwhelming, but pretty good."

"Remind me where you're working."

I said, "It's more 'for whom?' than 'where?' — for Kirby Champion, the political journalist."

"Is that what you do — journalism?"

"I seem to, all of a sudden. I'm his only assistant. When I worked at the White House—"

"The *Trump* White House?"

"Just for a few months. I answered an ad, and next thing I knew I was sorting presidential mail."

His smile faded to one of mere professional politeness.

I said, "I saw that."

"Saw what?"

I replicated his near-frown. "Trust me. No Republican can be *the* research associate for Kirby Champion, enemy of the people."

His smile returned. He put his right hand over his heart, covering the words "& Spirits" on the bib of his apron. "We serve everyone, regardless of race, creed, religion, age, who they love or who they vote for."

"Go, Varsity," I said.

He asked what brought me here tonight. Kosher wine, too? He could recommend a really decent white and a red.

"Just Vermouth, for my room-mate."

"Dry or sweet?"

"She didn't say..."

He pointed to the far reaches of the store, where Yasemin was pretending to be occupied. "You could ask her."

"Not that one. The other one who's home doing the dishes."

"Okay, does she drink martinis?"

I said I didn't know, we didn't use to socialize, but that sounded right. I'd seen big green olives in the fridge.

"Dry vermouth, then. The sweet one would be for Negronis — which are very in now. Or Manhattans."

The vermouths were on a shelf directly behind the counter. When his back was turned, I murmured, "Any brand is fine. It was just an excuse to come by."

He turned around. "I didn't catch that."

I edited myself to, "I thought we had a nice conversation the other night."

That's when I knew I'd made a mistake, had misjudged and misunderstood, because his answer was the dreaded brush-off, "I'm flattered..."

With hope abandoned I said, "You're probably nice to everyone. Not to mention married."

He turned back to the shelves, chose two bottles, put them on the counter. Facing me again he said, "I'm not. Are you?"

I shook my head.

He held up a bottle in each hand. "You can return whichever one the absent room-mate doesn't want."

I said, "That's very accommodating. Thank you. Definitely ring up both."

He slid a store flyer across the counter and handed me a pen. "I'll need your phone number. Protocol. In case I have to chase down the unwanted bottle."

I wrote my number along with my name and email address. I asked if he worked *every* night, or had I just hit it right.

"Monday through Friday. My dad gives me weekends off."

Did "weekends off" carry any meaning beyond paternal altruism? I refrained from saying I didn't work weekends, either — too pushy even by the standards of my socially aggressive advisers. I was saved from a conversational at-bat because Alex stepped up: folding the flyer in half, then quarters, then once more, he slipped the resulting square into his shirt pocket.

"Safe and sound," I said, "unless you forget to take it out before you throw the shirt into the washing machine."

"I won't forget." And after a pause, "Rachel."

Yasemin was chatting with a middle-aged man in a yarmulke. "We're all set," I called to her.

She yelled back, "I made a new friend. His rabbi is a lesbian! He wants to have us over for a Shabbat dinner. I told him you're Jewish!"

Alex was bagging my two bottles and grinning.

I said, "Isn't this a great country we live in?"

14

I'M NEW AT THIS

I PUT THE FINAL POLISH on my Hyde-White summary, then emailed it to Mr. Champion. It came back immediately with margin comments that were all queries. *Who called you? What do you know about her? Name? Number? Anything?* I wrote back, *If this can be totally off the record, she's the real-estate agent for the driver of the car that caused my accident.*

I heard a bellow, "Klein! Come here! You're going to school on this one!"

He didn't mean literally. He pointed to the chair. "You know who ran you over, right? Remind me. The name. She's an eye doc? In the District?"

"Veronica Hyde-White, hyphenated."

"Watch me," he said.

He found her office number in thirty seconds and called it. When someone picked up, he mouthed *front desk*. Then brightly, "Perhaps you can help me, though this isn't a medical matter. I'm not a patient — at least, not yet." He winked. "Great! I was at the doctor's open house — lovely place, perfect for me, but I've misplaced the real-estate agent's card. Could you supply her name? — if the listing is still on the market, of course."

He asked her to spell it, and was that Mandy with an A? "Thank you so much," he told her. "Of course I'll need the firm she works for. You wouldn't happen to have her number handy?"

More happy-conspiratorial nods to me. He thanked the receptionist, hung up, handed me the note and said "Mandy Cullinane. You'll call her now."

I would? To ask what? "How did you know there was an open house?" I asked him.

"I didn't. She'd assume there was if I said I went to it. And a little charm goes a long way."

I needed a half-minute to collect my thoughts, and signaled that by holding up one finger, walking a few yards away, coming back. I did a fast rewind of the last day and a half. Here I was, employed, hired by a successful author who'd put his faith in me as a first-rate grudge-holder. Did it count that Mandy asked me to swear I wouldn't tell a soul? Had she even waited for my answer? I began with, "This is unconfirmed. She could be lying. It could've been a crank call . . ."

"But . . .?"

"She asked me to leak something." I sat down again. "It's probably unnecessary for me to start with 'This is off the record.'"

"Correct, but a good impulse. Go on."

"Okay, Mandy called me at the store. I took it in the back office—"

"Irrelevant. Get to the good stuff."

Without further build-up I blurted out, "Veronica the optometrist was on her way to the White House to have sex with the president when she hit me."

This was rewarded with a most gratifying, exaggerated double-take, plus a fist-pound on his desk. "Lord have mercy. Do we believe her?"

"I didn't at first. She wouldn't tell me who she was, or how she knew this until I said, 'Why should I help you?'"

"Help how?"

"Leak it. Go public so she didn't have to." I paused, getting a feel for my own narrative potential. "Because she and the optometrist's husband are madly in love."

"Holy shit!"

"I know! I was hearing one bombshell after another!"

"Why the hell *you*? Did she say?"

"Yes! She assumed I'd want to get back at the driver who hit me, and the president who fired me. Oh, and I was the best candidate because I had no job, no name, so nothing to lose. I wasn't going to become Nasty Rachel Klein or Shifty Rachel Klein or Nervous—"

"I get it. And what's her goal if this goes public? Did she say?"

"No. Only that it would be my patriotic duty."

"Bull. Shit. She's hoping the affair would be one Pussygate too far for FLOTUS who'd divorce POTUS, freeing him up for the eye doctor—"

"Freeing up Simon Hyde-White, who could then run into the arms of—" I looked at the Post-it — "Mandy Cullinane of Cornwall Parker."

"We need another source. Witnesses? Are there emails? Phone calls? Did the husband record conversations? Maybe invoices?"

"Invoices?"

"Do we even know that Veronica treated the president, let alone — I'm being careful here — had relations with him? Tell her you need proof that the optometry went below the belt."

Hadn't Mandy told me she had evidence? I'd like to think that the new me, under the tutelage of Kirby Champion, would've asked what "evidence" meant. At my desk, I wrote a script. I'd call and I'd say, "Rachel Klein here." Then shrink-like, I'd wait for her to speak. If she'd ask how I found her, I'd say "You're a real-estate agent. I know at least one of your listings. It's not as if you work undercover."

Nervous and reluctant, I dialed the office number. A man answered. Yes, he could give me Mandy Cullinane's cell. She'll be happy to hear from you. Was I looking to rent or to buy?

I got off quickly, exceedingly ill-equipped to assume a fake identity as a potential house-hunter.

I used my own phone to call Mandy. She answered in chipper fashion. I said, "This is Rachel Klein. Are you alone?"

"I'm driving! I could've had a client in the car. What do you want?"

"That thing you told me — Veronica and the president, you and Simon? Both situations. Are they still . . . operational?"

She didn't answer right away. The music that had been playing in the car went silent. "Yes and yes."

"I need proof. It can't be just you telling me this. I need something concrete, and I'll need at least one other source."

"Like you're a fucking reporter all of a sudden? Let the press do their job. You'd just be offering a tip." And then she was gone.

As I sat there, contemplating my failure to get proof, evidence or satisfaction, my phone rang. The caller I.D. said, jangling the rest of my nerves, S. Hyde-White. I answered with only a "Yes?"

He was British, too. Without anything resembling an introduction he barked, "Simon Hyde-White here. I need an affidavit."

In case there'd been a mistake, I stated my name, then, "An affidavit from me?"

"Yes, from you! To say that Veronica was driving the car that hit you."

"The police have that on the accident report—"

"The accident report's missing! It's like it never happened. So I bloody well *do* need you to confirm that she hit you as she was speeding to the White House for an assignation with the president!"

Just like that.

I said, "I don't know she was speeding to the White House, let alone to see the president."

"I'm telling you now! What man would make up a humiliating set of circumstances like that?"

I pointed out that different men have different motives, that people frequently exceed the speed limit, and few to none of them are hurrying to hook up with the president.

"Then why are there a half a dozen calls to the White House, ten, twenty, thirty seconds apart, like they'd been dialed frantically? For sure she was calling him to say, 'Had an accident! *Caused* an accident. Might've killed someone. With all those cops, I had to stop. Don't know how long I'll be delayed.' *You're* the missing accident report."

"But I'd be lying if I swore in an affidavit that I knew where she was going or why!"

"I'm telling you right now: She was shagging the president! You're hearing that straight from the injured party. Me! You need a source? Now you have one."

I scribbled: **rules of hearsay diff in UK?**

"I still don't see why you need an affidavit."

"I'm establishing a timeline. All you have to swear to is that you were hit by such and such a vehicle driven by Dr. Veronica Hyde-White on such and such a day at a speed of fifty miles per hour in a thirty-mile-an-hour zone. You have the license-plate number, right?"

"I don't know any of that! I was knocked unconscious. I'd be perjuring myself!"

"On a piece of paper?"

"I'd be signing it! Same as if I took an oath in a courtroom. What do you even need it for?"

"I'll make it simple for you: in the event I go public with this—"

"With what? My *accident*? It's already public enough that it got a shout-out at a White House press conference."

"Not the accident — the affair! Veronica Hyde-White and Donald J. Trump. My marriage was for nought. It's over; done with; dog's dinner."

His marriage was for nought? An odd phrase. Had something been promised that wasn't delivered? "Are you a U.S. citizen?" I asked.

"Irrelevant!"

Was it? I asked how he'd found out about Veronica's affair.

"She admits it! And she's a scientist. She has physical evidence if it comes to that."

"Comes to what?"

"His denial. If he calls Veronica a liar. If he says, 'Her? Have you seen her? She's forty-seven years old! I wouldn't shag her!'"

"Didn't she have to sign a non-disclosure agreement?"

"Sod that!"

Could you sod a confidentiality agreement? I asked which part would he leak — the affair or the myopia?

Instead of answering he returned to ranting. "His wife put up with the porn star and the Playboy bunny. But shagging in the White House, under her own roof — she'd walk."

I'd started taking notes and chastising myself for not writing down every syllable from the beginning of the conversation.

"Are you there?" he asked.

I was digesting as I was scribbling. Obviously, Mandy had speed-dialed him the second she and I had hung up. Did the adulterous Dr. Hyde-White routinely confide in her cuckolded husband? Were they allies or enemies? Spouses or soon-to-be ex-spouses? I said, "This is all so foreign to me. My parents have been married for over thirty years. It sounds like you're rooting for your wife's affair."

"You don't need to understand anyone else's marriage! You just need to be so affronted by the president of the United States having an affair in the White House that you run with this very well-sourced intelligence to either *The New York Times*, the *Washington Post*, the *Wall Street Journal*, *The Guardian*, the *Daily Mail* . . . I don't care!"

"Then what? The news breaks. Trump denies it."

"I told you! Veronica has proof! She has invoices, plus there are duplicates of every prescription with his name on it. And she's a scientist! She's stored his DNA in the freezer. And trust me: she'll be holding up those knickers!"

"Where?"

"At a press conference, with a lawyer present, who, by the way, specializes in exactly these kinds of man-hating cases."

I said, "I don't see how any of that helps. Isn't her ultimate goal to be the fourth Mrs. Trump?"

"Precisely."

"But why is it *your* goal, too? Why are you pushing her into the arms of the next guy?"

"God, woman! Haven't you ever heard of an amicable divorce?"

"Not like this! Not an aggressively amicable one. Holding a press conference and holding up her knickers seems . . . pretty counterintuitive. How does that get her marching down the aisle?"

"We only go there if the whole thing goes pear-shaped, if he denies the affair. Believe me, Veronica isn't the kind of woman who'd slip silently into the night, or even to the sidelines. And believe me, no more extending his line of credit. You know how many invoices he's ignored?"

"All of them?"

"Every goddamn one. But she was willing to comp him so her business card could say 'by appointment to the President,' the way the queen issues a royal warrant to tradespeople, who can brag 'By appointment to Her Majesty the Queen.'"

I pointed out that his wife was an optometrist, not a tradesperson; not a manufacturer of biscuits or saddles.

"Optometrist to the leader of the free world? There'd be a fookin' line around the block."

I said, "I'm sorry, but this whole thing sounds fishy to me. I don't see why I should help you get divorced. Go find the accident report. Go find the bystander who called 9-1-1 or the EMTs who scraped me off the street."

"Is that so? Let me ask you this: are you looking forward to a check from Veronica's solicitors?"

I managed, after an offended gasp, "That sounded like extortion."

"I resent that! Did you or did you not have two conversations about potential compensation?"

"That's gone nowhere. I'm not affidaviting. I'm not your ally. Your wife almost killed me."

"Fan of your old employer Donald Trump, are you? Did he fancy you, too?"

Having been taught that you don't engage with a bully, I ended the call with a loud, derisive *Ha!*

Had I been hasty? Would a more experienced journalist have stayed on the line and teased out the rest of whatever insults he hurled? Had either one of us ever said "off the record?" No. On the other hand, what a wanker! What a son of a bitch!

Mr. Champion's first question in my debriefing was, "When is she planning to bring out the knickers?"

"Only if Trump calls his wife a liar. Go figure that one . . ."

"Whose side is he on? I'm not getting that. Does he want his wife back? Is that what exposing the affair is going to accomplish?"

"The only one who mentions love is Mandy, the girlfriend. Simon talks as if it's a business deal. Maybe he's hoping for hush money."

"Do you know if his wife was there when you two talked?"

"Didn't think to ask that . . . doubt it. Then again, so odd . . . the calculations. And he'd checked her phone for calls made right after the accident."

"Are they still living together?"

I said I didn't know/didn't ask . . . sorry.

"Look. You're new at this. You'll get better. You'll learn to ask rude questions, to get down and dirty."

"With him?"

"Absolutely. Call him back. Tell him you've thought it over and you'll write the affidavit."

"Meaning I will, or just *saying* I will?"

"Both. You'll never get around to it. Or you'll sign one that says you were involved in an accident, hit by a car driven by his wife, with the location, time, date — diddly-squat, in other words. In the meantime, you'll get answers to all your questions, because he'll think he flipped you."

"How about if I call at the end of the day so it looks like I gave some serious thought to the affidavit?"

"Fine. But do it before he gets those knickers defrosted."

Back at my desk, as I was fine-tuning my call-back script and perspiring, Mr. Champion knocked on the flimsy frame of my room divider to ask, "Does she know what you look like?"

"Who?"

"Doctor Veronica!"

Did she? Had she Googled me? "If you count my body hurled against her windshield, and, if she jumped out of her car before the ambulance arrived, she saw me lying on the street."

"Face up or face down?"

I said, "Could be either. My concussion felt like it was the back of my head, but—" I lifted my bangs, where there was still the faded yellow remains of a bruise. "Why?"

He took a hammy bow accompanied by a twirl of his wrist. "Sandra got me her last appointment of the day, four-thirty. She had a cancellation! And you're coming!"

Unhappily, this job was getting more collaborative by the minute. I asked if the appointment was under his own name.

"Of course not! I have a medical pseudonym I use, Curtis Champlain, like the lake. That way, if someone recognizes me in the waiting room, and yells, 'Hey, aren't you Kirby Champion?' it's close enough so the receptionist doesn't get suspicious."

"Don't they ask for your insurance information?"

"Of course. But Curtis Champlain pays cash."

I tried again: "I don't understand why you need me there if there's a chance she recognizes me—"

"Let's think this through. If by some miracle she recognizes you, you give her a foggy look" — he demonstrated, squinting — "and say, 'Sorry. I remember nothing from that day.'"

"And we pretend it's just a huge coincidence that of all the eye doctor's offices in Washington, D.C. we walk into hers?"

"None of this is going to come up. She won't suspect anything. I'm sure lots of patients come with relatives or friends."

I didn't want to press my case further, lest I appear a slacker, unwilling to go out in the field. I asked, "Do I bring a notebook?"

"No. We're playing it straight: a second opinion on new frames." He lifted my shoulder bag off its hook and handed it to me. "I'll tell her that I get very nervous during any kind of medical exam, and can't remember what the doctor is saying, advising, recommending, diagnosing, whatever. So I always need an extra pair of ears. Of course she'll say 'no problem.'"

What an optimist. Sandra buzzed me at 4:10. She'd called a car, and it was there. Between front door and backseat, he reminded me that we didn't talk about work in an Uber or taxi. And while he was at it, call him Kirby. Of course when "The Blight" came out, and I might be quoted somewhere as his aide-de-camp, I'd refer to him as "Mr. Champion."

I nodded, tried "Kirby" aloud; said, "sure". But hour by hour, task by dubious task, I was wondering what "The Blight" would cover, and how we'd get there.

15

OFFICE VISIT

A HEAD TALLER THAN I, and barely shorter than the towering Kirby, Dr. Veronica Hyde-White was skinny, narrow-shouldered, not unattractive but severe in every way except for her disproportionately large and suspect bosoms. Her husband had said she was forty-seven, but in person I'd have guessed older, due to the absence of makeup and the inch of gray roots below lank, brassy yellow hair. She introduced herself to Kirby, banished me to a corner chair, and installed herself at the examining room's small desk. There, with her back to her new patient, she asked without expression, "What brings you here today?"

"New frames and an overdue check-up."

"And," with a thumb jerked over her shoulder, "she is . . .?"

Kirby explained that he'd brought along his assistant, due to his white-coat anxiety, which interfered with his retaining the particulars of any medical appointment, thus his need for an extra set of ears.

"You don't mind that we'll be discussing your confidential medical history?" she asked.

"Nothing to hide! Lipitor and Zantac. Surgery on a torn ACL. Oh, and I figured recording was less intrusive than taking notes. Do we have your permission?"

"If you must."

He sent me a look that I interpreted as role-modeling ahead; here's where you watch, listen and learn . . . But what I heard was, "I don't meet many women whose height — how to put this? — would make us look like naturals on the dance floor . . ."

I managed to convert my intake of breath to a cough. The doctor ignored his comment, flipping through the pages he'd filled out.

"I'm looking at your framed diplomas," he continued. "University of Manchester. I've heard that's an excellent institution. Were you happy there?"

"Happy enough." Now standing by the examining chair, she said, "Hold this shield in front of your left eye."

"I'm going to make a wild guess . . . Man United over Man City!"

"Neither. What's the smallest row of letters you can read?"

Kirby bit his lip, pretending to be stumped for whatever cuteness factor he thought that conveyed before reciting T, Z, V, E, C, L proudly.

"Other eye," she said.

After another perfect recitation he said, "I'm noticing you're not wearing a wedding ring."

"No comment," said the doctor. "Now both eyes."

Should I still be recording? Would he ever want to hear himself uttering such epically bad lines? "I can't help it," he went on, now looking inconsolable. "I have this chronic condition . . ."

"Which is what?"

"I'm a hopeless flirt!"

The doctor said, "I'm going to ignore your prattle and carry on."

Kirby held up his hands in mock surrender. "Let me explain. I'm newly divorced. I'm out of practice. That wasn't a very smooth icebreaker."

"You've read the twenty-twenty line perfectly with each eye, which means you have normal distance visual acuity. Now let's test your near vision."

He tilted his head in naughty-boy fashion, then said, "I can't resist a British accent."

Dr. Hyde-White had had enough. "You seem to be confusing a medical office with a dance hall, and me with a willing subject."

"Was I not supposed to compliment your accent? You must hear that from patients all the time."

"Not like that; not preceded by several uncalled-for personal remarks."

"Was I misinformed? You're not single?"

By this time, I'd sunk into the chair and shut my eyes.

"It's none of your business! I have to ask you and your . . . stenographer to leave!"

"At least let me take you out for a drink sometime so I can properly apologize," he tried.

"Do you not understand English? This has gone beyond inappropriate to bloody ridiculous! I'm terminating this appointment." She turned to me. "And you! Abetting and, and, and enabling him! I only hope he behaves appropriately towards his female employees, because this makes me wonder."

I picked myself up, intending to lead the way out the door, but stopped, suddenly flashing back to my own optometric state of affairs. "Do you have a minute?" I asked her.

"I do not."

"Thirty seconds then? It's medical. I suffered a concussion—"

"In a bad accident," Kirby volunteered. "Straight to the hospital, unconscious."

"Where the doctors and nurses kept looking in my eyes—"

"To see if your pupils were reactive rather than fixed," she finished impatiently.

I pushed my bangs up and opened my eyes wide, a silent request for a second opinion. Her mouth twisted this way and that, her #MeToo indignity at war with her Hippocratic oath. Finally, with a sigh, she took a penlight from her pocket and made some gesture to Kirby, which he eagerly translated to "dim the lights". She raised my chin with one unsympathetic finger. Right eye, not even five seconds; left eye, the same.

"Everything appears normal. You wouldn't have been discharged if anything was amiss."

"Except that my head doesn't feel totally back to normal."

"How long ago was the accident?"

I hesitated. Should I say something vague, such as "two months ago," or be specific and risk blowing whatever puzzling mission we were on? Kirby settled it by prompting, "It happened the day you left your last job, correct?"

"September seventeenth," I told her.

Would that make the doctor step back with a gasp? No. Not at all. She asked if I'd suffered or still suffered: double vision, nausea and vomiting, dizziness, ringing in my ears, memory loss, fatigue, sensitivity to light and sound?

I said, "Some of those. But better every day."

"From what I see, you're fine. Do you have your own doctor?"

Kirby asked, "This doesn't count?"

"I mean as follow-up, with an ophthalmologist. I'd recommend six months."

"Six months," Kirby echoed. "Do you mean from now, or

six months from the accident? What was that date again, Miss Klein?"

I repeated, "The seventeenth of September," wondering if this was the moment we'd come for. *Spill the beans! Out yourself as her victim!*

I resisted with a tight shake of my head, and turned back to the doctor. "I really appreciate your checking my pupils."

"And I appreciate you slipping me in today," said Kirby, managing to make even that sound sexual. "I hope our paths cross again."

"Out," she said.

As soon as the door closed behind us Kirby said, "That date registered, believe me. Did you see her face? Wasn't that fun?"

I didn't say aloud what I was thinking: *no, it was excruciating.*

Though we weren't supposed to talk business in the backseat of the Uber, I had to ask, "Was all that flirting your plan from the get-go?"

"No! It was a last-minute brainstorm!"

"To what end? I don't get it."

"Call it going with my gut." He pointed at the driver, and then put his finger to his lips.

I said, "C'mon. If people have sex in the back seats of Ubers, you can tell me what the flirting was all about. He doesn't care."

He said, "Klein, I think you're getting gutsier. I saw it there in her office and I'm seeing it now. I like it!"

I played with the window control . . . down a few inches, then back up. I checked my email. I returned the wave of two lovebird tourists atop a red double-decker bus. Finally I said, "It would've been nice to know ahead of time that you were going to put the make on her."

"Here's the problem: When and what to tell you? I take the

EEOC guidelines very seriously. It could've been grievable to confide to a female employee that I was recently unmarried and consequently taking advantage of every opportunity. How would that have sounded? I'm not that kind of clueless male boss. I have daughters! I hope I haven't crossed a line right now."

If sincere, he was the most painfully sensitive supervisor I'd ever known. But didn't he have the bad taste to like Veronica Hyde-White? I said, "I appreciate all of that. But I had no idea what was going on, whether it was real or fake. And I hope *I'm* not crossing any line to say *Really? Her?*"

"Imagine what I could glean if she and I had even one drink together."

"After today's visit, speaking as another woman, I wouldn't get my hopes up."

"Did I blow it? I'm rusty. And I apologize for catching you off-guard. I caught *myself* off-guard. You surprised me, too, Klein, with that check-my-eyes bit. Very inspired."

"Not really. I was just thinking *eyes . . . eye doctor . . . might as well ask . . .*"

"You'll call the British embassy and get the name of the top limey restaurant in the city, Yorkshire pudding and all that, and I'll write her a thank-you note—"

"Who will? Kirby Champion or Curtis Champlain?"

"Good point. Maybe I'll send flowers and sign it 'Your contrite patient, the wanker.'"

"With the goal of . . . ?"

"Dinner!"

This time I lowered my voice. "But she's dating the you-know-what, plus she's married. She's not going to complicate her life any more." *Or*, unstated: *say yes to you after the most ridiculous advances ever uttered.*

"Do you think a drink is out of the question for a woman in a screwed-up marriage? Imagine if I could get a one-on-one with the latest person to shag you-know-who! And can I share a little secret? She's an unhappy woman. She gets an audience with him two afternoons a week, for, what, thirty minutes when he's not off at a rally. She may be flattered into giving me a go."

It was 5:15. Yasemin would be home soon, all ears as she prepped and cooked something exotic and delicious. Elizabeth would weigh in on EEOC guidelines and quiz me, as I was quizzing myself, on whether I should be working for a man who thinks my job description covered accompanying him on the prowl.

I asked Kirby if the driver could drop me at my Metro stop, a few intersections ahead.

"Which stop?" the driver asked, guaranteeing that he'd heard every word of our conversation.

"Rhode Island."

"Nah. We'll take you straight home," said Kirby.

"Not necessary. Not in rush hour. I'll get home quicker underground."

When we'd pulled over at my stop, Kirby said, "See you tomorrow. Don't let today dampen your enthusiasm. I know right from wrong. You're my lucky charm, and we're on a mission."

Which mission was that, I wondered: his love-life or his next book? Because so far, our only storyline seemed to be my unlucky, ever-expanding collision with the awful Hyde-Whites.

16

I'M A JOURNALIST NOW

WALKING HOME FROM the subway stop, I had ten minutes before my parents' store closed. Because they wasted no time locking up and heading home, I'd get away with the briefest of rose-colored job reports. I called the landline, which Mary-Jo answered, then proclaimed, "It's Rachel, everyone!"

My mother was on in seconds. "How's the job? We were going to call you last night but we restrained ourselves. Can I put you on speaker?"

"Not if there are customers there, Ma."

"They're not paying attention."

In as general and impersonal detail as this public airing deserved, I said only, "Mr. Champion has been showing me the ropes. I'm doing some writing, and I'm accompanying him on interviews."

"Already?" asked a distant male voice.

"Hi, Murray. Yes."

"An interview with anyone we might have heard of?" my mother asked.

"Doubt it."

"But interesting? And a challenge? I mean, you're not doing clerical work, or whatever it's called these days?" my dad asked.

At this point "clerical" sounded preferable to accompanying Kirby on dubious social pursuits. I said, "Definitely doing real journalism."

"Anything you can tell your biggest fans?" asked my dad.

"I'm sworn to secrecy," I said. "But we're getting along really well."

"How's the living situation working out?" Mary-Jo asked.

"Good. Really good. Elizabeth's girlfriend moved in and she made me a welcome meal."

"Girlfriend?" my mother asked.

"Yes, like that," I said.

"Fine with us," my father called.

I almost slipped and mentioned my room-mates' matchmaking efforts, but thought no, too soon. Bev and Ken would be looking for romantic advancement every time we spoke. I said, "That's about it. Everyone good there?"

"We're fine. How are you feeling?" my father asked.

What made me elaborate other than a throwback to childhood obedience? Why did I have to announce that an optometrist had checked my eyes and everything looked good?

"Optometrist?" said my mother. "With a hyphenated name, by any chance?"

"Ma. I shouldn't have said that much. Everything is off the record, even a visit to an optometrist. Forget I mentioned that."

"A medical examination in your private life is off the record?"

I told them I'd reached the apartment and needed both hands to find my key. Nice talking to everyone . . .

"Snap a picture of the office so we can see where you work," Murray said.

"Will do."

"And try to get the people in the photos too."

"There's only Mr. Champion and his sister. Oh, he wants me to call him Kirby, so I started that today."

I heard Mary-Jo laugh. "Maybe one day I'll start calling Murray 'Murray.'"

I didn't comment, but thought to myself *I think those two just went public.*

Yasemin and Elizabeth arrived home together, one carrying two bags of groceries and the other a knapsack, a pocketbook, and a briefcase. I helped unpack rotisserie chicken, flour tortillas, onions, pepper, avocados, salsa in two colors. "Something Mexican?" I asked. "D.I.Y. fajitas," said Yasemin. "How about cutting up the onions and peppers? That would be a big help." I agreed, and said blithely, "You two should put your feet up, have a glass of wine. I can handle the onions and peppers"— which was exactly when a text arrived from Kirby, advising me to check @realDonaldTrump's newest tweet.

I did. **U.S. presidents have to be born here, can't be immigrants. Maybe should apply to 1st Ladies. #MAGA**

Just below that, twenty minutes earlier, a more reasoned one had said @FLOTUS needs "a rest." **She's the hardest working FIRST LADY in history. Anything else is FAKE NEWS.**

I texted back to Kirby, **What do you think it means? She's outta there! She knows!**

Did I have to answer? Texts from my boss might be confidential, but presidential tweets certainly weren't. I showed them to Yasemin and Elizabeth.

Turn on CNN came the next directive from Kirby.

I told Yasemin I'd have to do the onions and peppers later. The boss wanted me to watch TV.

"Go," she said. "Work before fajitas."

I went to the living room alcove we facetiously called the media center, turned on CNN and sat down on the Persian carpet that had arrived with Yasemin. Wolf Blitzer was moderating a panel of pundits, but the topic was farmers and pork, despite the news ticker below the screen repeating Trump's tweet asking if immigrants should be first ladies.

A new text pinged. **My WH source helped her pack EVERY SINGLE THING**.

"Can you guys come watch for a few minutes?" I called towards the kitchen.

Elizabeth appeared first, managing a bottle of wine and three glasses. I told her I was waiting for Wolf and company to address what was scrolling beneath them: the president's marital tweet.

Yasemin joined us and plopped down next to me. "Yikes! She's bolted! We could get a really ugly divorce! Yay. Go, Melania."

"That gold digger," said Elizabeth. "You're not taking pity on her, are you? She married him! She deserves him!"

I said, "She does seem to be a devoted mother. And that 'Be Best' stuff looked sincere."

"Then where's the kid? Is she leaving him behind with his sociopath father?"

"Something must've finally gotten to her," said Yasemin. "Something worse than Stormy."

"She hates him! She wanted to leave him after Pussygate."

Pussygate. It was getting a lot of traction this week. If only I could confess all: that I'd been told Donald Trump was having sex with his optometrist, who'd been speeding to meet him when she'd hit me. And by the way, I'd been to her office, an excruciating half hour during which my boss, there on the pretense of choosing new frames, had hit on her. Oh, and further? I'd been harassed by her husband, who didn't know which way the wind was blowing in terms of his cheating wife, marriage, separation, or divorce, and was using me in some way I hadn't figured out yet.

I had my phone in one hand and the TV remote in the other. I said, "I'm switching to MSNBC. They should be all over this."

Better than that. Better than a reporter standing on the south lawn of the White House filling in the gaps, there was an aerial shot of a highway, with the breaking news underneath, *First Lady Melania Trump heading north on Route 95*.

"Holy shit," one or all of us said.

"She's still the freakin' first lady. I hope Homeland Security doesn't shoot down the news copter," said Elizabeth.

MSNBC's regular programming had given way to a panel of anchors, and one was saying, "NBC hasn't independently confirmed this, but the Associated Press is reporting that a moving van is outside the First Lady's parents' house in Potomac, Maryland, generally regarded as her — to put it diplomatically — home away from home."

"Maybe she's heading there to get her parents and kid," said Yasemin. "They all want out. And this was no spur-of-the-moment escape."

"But I just saw an exit sign that said Wilmington. She's almost in Delaware," Elizabeth said.

An ex-senator-turned commentator was saying, "The First Lady doesn't drive herself anywhere. She's not driving! There's a Secret Service detail! She's in the back seat of the middle car!"

Kirby's new tweet asked **R U watching? Do we think she's heading for NYC?**

We. Had I become, overnight, Kirby's pal and confidante? Was I now the person he texted with news, ideas, feelings and innermost thoughts?

His next text: **Call the real estate agent???**

I emitted an involuntary "Oh God."

"What?" asked Elizabeth.

"The boss again . . . He's asking me to call a source who might know what's causing . . ." I flicked my hand at the screen, ". . . whatever this is."

"They're going to hit traffic in Jersey, let alone the Lincoln Tunnel," said Yasemin. "I'll do the onions and peppers. Yell if something more exciting happens."

"Who's the source you don't want to call?" asked Elizabeth.

"Can't say."

"Works for the First Lady?"

I shook my head.

Gray bubbles on my phone turned into **?????** from Kirby. Hearing my groan, Elizabeth instructed, "Shut your phone off. You don't want to reinforce a twenty-four/seven workday."

I said, "It's only my first week. I don't think I should ignore him."

"Then make the call, for crissakes. Get it over with. He or she probably won't pick up and then you can say that you tried."

I checked numbers under "recent." There she was, Mandy Cullinane, my old call to her car.

Elizabeth leaned over to sneak a peak. "Mandy Cullinane. Aren't I the detective! Is she your source?"

I said, "Please forget you saw that. She's only a source several times removed from anyone major."

"Even if she doesn't work in the East Wing, I bet she works in the White House."

With my finger pointed, I drew an imaginary line around the

alcove. "Cone of silence, never to leave this room: she works for Cornwall Parker."

"Oh the intrigue! A real-estate agent! I bet she keeps bottled water and a box of Kleenex in her shiny deodorized American car!"

I silently reviewed everything I couldn't say, that she was the girlfriend of an obnoxious schemer, who'd had a possible green-card marriage to a woman allegedly having sex with the president of the United States. What I *did* say was, "If I stay in this job, you'll have to respect that everything is off the record until Kirby's book comes out."

"No problem," said Elizabeth.

I hadn't noticed that Yasemin had been watching from the doorway, wine glass in hand. "Look," she said, pointing at the TV.

The convoy had pulled off the highway at a rest stop. Mrs. Trump, in a white shirt, sleeves rolled up, black pants, no coat, large sunglasses, baseball cap, got out of the middle car, quickly surrounded by — my best count — three men and three women. Other travelers were gaping, pointing, snapping pictures.

Yasemin said, "You have to give her credit — stopping like a normal person to pee."

"They'll clear the ladies' room first," said Elizabeth. "Melania Trump isn't going to wait in any goddamn line."

We watched. The talking heads were thrilled to have something besides northbound traffic to discuss. After at least ten minutes, Melania and her detail were back on the road, behind the tinted, presumably bullet-proof windows, merging without signaling. Blitzer noted that her stop had been at the Biden Welcome Center.

"Another fuck-you to her husband," said Elizabeth. "She probably didn't even have to pee."

Abandoning texting, Kirby phoned me. I answered, despite my advisors shaking their heads *no*. He was his usual optimistic and enthusiastic self, unfazed by my failure to do anything.

"This is unbelievable," he gushed. "You're too young to remember O.J. and the white Bronco, but this is the closest thing to it. This could go on for her entire trip. Fox is saying she's headed for New York, and this is no shopping trip."

I handed the remote to Elizabeth and whispered, "Find Fox."

"Can't wait to hear what the real-estate agent tells you!" said Kirby.

That again. "I'm thinking I should learn more before I call her . . ."

Kirby was enthusing, "I just had a brainstorm: call the husband! You have his number, right? Why waste time with the middleman?"

Was it too early in my journalistic career to say, "No, *you* do it. You're the muckraker." I offered an anemic version of that: "Do you think I'm the best person for this pretty critical follow-up, with the presidential marriage falling apart? I'm not a reporter—"

"You'll do fine. Just ask this: surely you're aware that the first lady of the United States has absconded from the White House. Was it precipitated by her finding out about his most recent affair?"

My nerves wouldn't let me retain half of that. I said, "Can you hang on? I have to write that down."

"I'll wait. In the meantime do you want to hear my theory?" Without any prompting, he said, 'I'm good at reading people. She was in a mood—"

I'd darted in and out of my bedroom for a notebook and pen. "Who was?"

"Veronica, today. And now I'm thinking it wasn't just my

social overture. Who throws a patient out of an office for being a little playful? Something else was going on. I think she knew either who I was or who you were."

"But I didn't mention the date of the accident until, like, two seconds before she threw us out." Desperate to end the call, I added, "Shouldn't we be watching the news? They're starting to talk about how this will affect the evangelical vote."

"Don't you want me to repeat the question you should hit Mindy/Mandy/Candy with? Isn't that why you got a pencil and paper?"

I said, "Yes. Shoot."

He repeated: "Ask her if Donald's latest affair was Melania's last straw." I thanked him and said, "I'll try to call during the next commercial."

"I think we should prepare ourselves for Melania Trump giving it all up because of something we set in motion. Bye-bye, third wife! Bye-bye, second term!"

I had to remind myself that I hadn't caused the breakup of POTUS and FLOTUS. I was merely an innocent bystander, if stumbling into traffic could actually be called bystanding. Why was I feeling that I was in the middle of a big story that involved the president of the United States? Oh that's right: because I was.

Maybe the glass of wine had made me braver because I found myself asking, "What was your book going to be about before you hired me?"

"Trump, of course. 'The Blight'!"

I said, "But then the Hyde-Whites came along. They're seeming pretty front and center."

"They'll be one chapter! That's it! And in interviews when the book comes out, I'll tell them the story of us."

I waited. I knew his chatty mood — no, his entire effusive

personality — would lead to his elaborating without a prompt.

"It's a great story! I have a contract for a second Trump book. My assistant quits. I need to hire a replacement. And who do the gods send me? An ex-Trump employee! What channel do you have on? We'll synchronize. Are you on Fox yet? Lou Dobbs just said that the First Lady is speeding, going ten miles over the speed limit. And sources told him that her driver's license may have expired. She's not even at the wheel! That had to come from Trump!"

I said, "Yes, I'm watching, but I have to get off. Supper's ready. This could go on for hours, given rush-hour traffic. I've driven that route between D.C. and New York City."

"What's for dinner?" he asked.

If I weren't 100 per cent disinclined to do so, increasingly worried over his divorce-induced buddy-buddiness, I might've said, "Fajitas. Do you want to come over?" I didn't.

A thornier question: was I in over my head, professionally? I knew that if I posed that question to my room-mates, they'd tell me that everyone feels like a fraud. They'd lecture me: I'd brought sources to the future book, so take ownership of them! Call, interview, cross-examine, challenge! Don't be a girl. Don't wimp out. Run with it, unless you want to go back to selling paint.

I wouldn't confide in them tonight; wouldn't admit that I felt unqualified to muckrake as an equal with Kirby. Too much too soon. Maybe I'd even dial that back and revert to calling him Mr. Champion. You never know what's around the corner, literally and figuratively. It was bad enough getting knocked unconscious by a speeding car, but why did it have to be driven by a woman who was having sex with the president of the United States?

17

THE PURSUIT OF HAPPINESS

"WE'LL NEED MORE WINE if we're going to be up late watching the Trump marriage disintegrate," Yasemin said, pouring the last ounce into my empty glass.

"Don't we have a bottle of something in the fridge?" I asked.

"We both think you need a break from breaking news," she said.

"And some fresh air," said Elizabeth.

I pointed out that I'd had enough to drink. If I showed up at Varsity Wine & Spirits every night I'd look desperate or alcohol-dependent. Plus, I have Kirby texting me every few minutes.

"Let's analyze this," said Elizabeth. "How long has it been since you bought those two bottles of vermouth?"

"Correction," said Yasemin. "How long since you *paid* for one, since the other was a loaner?"

"Two days, and are you familiar with the word *yenta*? Or in this case, plural, *yentas*?"

"Is it flattering?" Yasemin asked.

"It means busybody, often in the context of matchmaking."

"We're impervious to insults in any language," said Elizabeth. "Besides, I don't want the sweet vermouth, and I don't think you want to be seen as someone who defaults on a pledge."

"Let me remind you," said Yasemin, "that the very pleasant heterosexual behind the counter took your contact info, right?"

I admitted, yes he did and put it in his shirt pocket.

"Who writes things down on a piece of paper any more? It speaks volumes about his good intentions."

I said, "Maybe two lawyers don't consider watching TV to be work, but—"

Elizabeth stood up, left the kitchen, and returned with her parka and the unwanted vermouth. "What's his name again?"

This time it was Yasemin raising an objection. She said, "If you do this errand, it'll look like Rachel is avoiding him."

I said, "I'm going to start calling you two Bev and Ken."

"I think that means we're being parental," said Elizabeth.

"*Jewish* parental," I corrected.

"I'll take that," said Yasemin.

"You were almost killed!" said Elizabeth. "I mean, when had your parents ever called me at work? Never. I didn't even know they had my number. And they weren't exactly reassuring about your coming through the accident alive. It made me wonder if my parents would care if I got run over and would they track down Yasemin at work. So it brought up all kinds of stuff. Who wouldn't take up your cause after that?"

I said that was so sweet of her, but I hoped she didn't view my main cause in life as boyfriend acquisition.

"We took oaths to uphold the Constitution, and that includes the pursuit of happiness for ourselves, our posterity and our straight room-mate," Yasemin said.

"In other words, I'm on my way," Elizabeth said.

Yasemin stood up and planted a kiss on Elizabeth's closest cheek, very obviously a decoy.

"What are you two whispering about?" I asked.

Yasemin said, "Just reminding her to say something along the lines of 'Rachel would've brought this back herself, but she's monitoring breaking news.'"

"I'm not an idiot," said Elizabeth. "I was going to convey exactly that."

"I'd offer to go with Lizzie," Yasemin said to me, "but it'll look like an intervention. I mean, how many people does it take to return one bottle?"

My phone was chirping, and re-chirping: Kirby texting, **Someone on Twitter said he changed the locks at Trump Tower.**

I cleared our plates, scraped them into the trash, gave them a hasty rinse then said, "I'd better go back and watch. Leave the dishes — I'll do them during commercials."

"I'll join you after I wrap up the chicken," said Yasemin.

I wondered if I should supply Elizabeth with a greeting for Alex that would improve upon whatever awkward sentences she might blurt out.

Too late. She was out the door.

I worked up the gumption to call Mandy Cullinane, landing in her cheery saleswoman voicemail on the first ring. "This is Rachel Klein calling," I said. "I need to talk to you." I hesitated for a few seconds, then added, "I've been watching cable news since

I got home. I have a few questions regarding the First Lady's apparent . . . exodus. Thanks. Please call me back."

Cross-legged on the floor, phone on one thigh, notebook and pen next to me, I texted Kirby: **tried the r.e. agent. No answer. Still watching.**

Turn to Fox! the next text commanded.

I did, landing on *Tucker Carlson Tonight*. It was quickly apparent, thanks to the chyron beneath the picture, that the president was on the phone. The first fragment I heard was ". . . luckily, the stingiest pre-nup in the history of pre-nups."

"But you're not saying . . .?" Carlson asked.

"She never wanted this job! I didn't know I was going to be president until it happened! She didn't sign on to be First Lady!"

I yelled to Yasemin, "Trump's on the phone with Fox."

She appeared within seconds, making me laugh with her stagy sock-slide into the alcove. "Saying?"

"He's already talking about their pre-nup."

Carlson, reminding the audience how he, as a father of four, felt obliged to ask where the youngest Trump son was.

"He's with her. He liked that school up there. I gave them a million bucks for a gym when we didn't know where he'd go."

I almost felt sorry for Tucker Carlson. "Fine, tall lad, your boy," he said. "And I know you're proud of him. It can't be easy living in that fishbowl. From what I've seen, he's never uttered a rude word . . . No reports of misbehavior or insolence . . . Heh heh. Wish I could say the same about all of mine—"

Trump followed with a bored *ya, ya, good kid*, then announced that Ivanka's daughter was fluent in Chinese.

"Mandarin, I believe," said Carlson. "I understand it's one of the hardest languages to learn. All those foreign characters, no ABCs."

"Smart as a whip."

"Like her parents." Carlson seemed to be getting guidance in his ear, which brought him to, "I hate to bring up politics at a time like this—"

"Those Obama girls? Do you think Obama and his wife didn't give a million dollars to Harvard to get them in?"

Carlson said, "Mr. President . . . that isn't something we ever reported on."

"You think they got all 'A's? That's what you need to get into Harvard. Well, maybe not if you're black."

"Harvard, if you're listening..." Yasemin yelled.

Carlson asked, "Can you stay with us to the other side of the break, Mr. President?"

"Isn't Hannity coming on?"

"Soon. Top of the hour."

Not meant for the television audience was the president growling, "I said one scoop chocolate and one vanilla. Take it back!" to whichever poor soul had delivered his bedtime snack.

I switched to MSNBC, already replaying Trump's Obama defamations. Their panel was making no apologies for discussing what effect the First Lady's escape could have on the president's popularity.

Yasemin said, "I can answer that: he'll blame her for whatever this is — separation, divorce, breach of contract. He'll give her a nickname. He'll deport her parents. He'll start dating, so the headlines will be who's on Donald Trump's arm."

I turned back to Fox. Carlson was reading, with obvious distaste, a statement that gave the Obama daughters full credit for their college acceptances, the younger not to Harvard but to the University of Michigan, presumably earned on the basis of grade point averages and (this with an eyeroll) recommendations, followed by an explanation for Fox viewers as to what "grade point average" meant.

Most gingerly, even psychiatrically, he continued. "Mr. President? Perhaps you'd want to take a break? It's been a trying day . . . good . . . that's good." With a pained smile, he added, "I'm with you on that: ice cream can cure a rough day."

The president's audio returned. "Thank you, Tucker. You've heard me say that you're the most important pundit in America," and, with a laugh, "on most days". He asked if it was the top of the hour, because on Sean's show he was going to tell the country that Melania took stuff that doesn't belong to her.

"Mr. President, you're not saying—"

"She cleaned out the whole damn place."

"That can't be possible," said Carlson, "considering *how* many rooms?"

A production assistant was clearly on the task because Carlson within seconds supplied, "One hundred thirty-two rooms and thirty-five bathrooms."

"Many knickknacks and many very beautiful objects that belong to the American people! Some were gifts from . . . maybe I'm not supposed to say where her favorite one came from or who gave it to us." With further prompting he said, "I guess it doesn't give anything away if I say without naming the brand or the country: a jeweled egg. An antique."

Carlson went to a break of his own now. Yasemin and I waited through an odd number of commercials. When he returned, he announced Fox News had spoken with the White House communications director, who said that the president had only been kidding about the reigning First Lady taking *quote-unquote* beautiful objects. And further, gifts that the president and Mrs. Trump received from world leaders were transferred to the National Archives and Records Administration, except for the porcelain dinnerware purchased from the government for the appraised value, which they liked to call "china from China".

"Reigning!" Yasemin scoffed. "How perfect is that!" She stood up, saying she'd brought tons of work home and at this rate will have to pull an all-nighter. "Yell if anything more outrageous happens," she said on her way across the living room. A few minutes later I heard, "Elizabeth sent me a thumb's-up emoji. Want me to call her?"

I said, "She might still be in the store. I'll wait."

Elizabeth must've texted from our block because it was only minutes later that the front door opened and I heard, "Success!"

"In here," I called.

First there was a clank of bottles going into our crowded refrigerator, then a shout to Yasemin about being low on milk. Coyly, especially for Elizabeth, she joined me in the alcove, sat down on the sofa, folded her hands in her lap and smiled.

I said, "You're looking very pleased with yourself."

"I should be."

"Because?"

"Okay! Got to the store, went to the counter, introduced myself as Rachel Klein's room-mate for whom she'd bought the vermouth, and I was now returning the one I didn't want. Then I said you would've brought it back *yourself*, but some big political shit hit the fan, so you were back at our apartment, glued to the television, taking notes, texting with your boss. Then I said you thought he was very nice, which evoked a smile."

She's on the spectrum, I thought.

"I bought two bottles of wine that weren't from the bargain table," she continued, then pulled out her wallet and from it a punch card. "We're now members of the Varsity Vino Club. When you've bought a dozen bottles, the next one is buy-one-get-one-free. Here, it's yours."

Yasemin, back in the doorway, was making strangled noises.

Elizabeth said, "I thought you wanted a play-by-play. Okay, I paid for the two new bottles and I told him that he should 'ask you out.'"

What stopped me from cringing, whimpering and rebuking was the victorious smile on her face.

I asked, "What did he say to that?"

"I believe his exact words were 'I intend to.'" She exchanged a high-five with her fellow in-house cupid. "Oh, and I didn't leave it there. I told his father, who helped me pick out the Sancerre and the Muscadet — which are in the 'fridge, on the door — 'I have a nice girl for your son.' And to sweeten the deal, I told him that you and Alex had a lot in common because your parents also owned a retail business and sometimes you worked there. That's it, the whole visit, word for word."

Could I ever again show my face at Varsity Wine & Spirits? "Well done," I said.

I switched between Sean Hannity and Rachel Maddow. Hannity was furiously covering Trump's exemplary marital and parental role-modeling, without mentioning the First Lady's O.J. Simpson-like vehicular getaway. Maddow, as ever, was trying not to rehash what the three previous MSNBC shows had been covering to death.

Approximately fifteen minutes after the store would've closed, an email arrived, its address leading with Alex. There was no mention of Elizabeth's visit, her matchmaking, or her questionable social skills. It said, *Hi, Rachel. Alex from Varsity W & S here. Random question: do you like jazz?*

How soon could I answer without appearing overeager? It was brave of him to have jumped in, so why play hard to get? Though jazz-challenged, I wrote back after a nonchalant ten minutes, *Yes! Was it JUST a random question?*

He answered immediately, *Nope. An invitation.*

I wrote back, *Except you forgot the invitation part.* Was Alex the kind of man who found emojis to be juvenile? I took a chance and added a winking smiley face.

I'll get back to you as soon as I know time, place, etc. How's Saturday?

I wrote back, *Yes to Saturday* – affirmative, but without revealing the full extent of my relief and delight.

18

SOME THINGS
YOU'D RATHER NOT KNOW

My phone rang at 1:35 a.m. — not Kirby but Mandy Cullinane calling.

I turned on my bedside lamp, picked up the prescribed scratchpad and pen and said, "Give me a sec," meaning *as I try to remember what I wanted to ask you.*

"Are you alone?" she asked.

"I'm in bed."

"That doesn't answer my question."

"Yes, I'm alone."

"I couldn't talk before — a lot was going on, to say the least."

Before I could ask my first question — do you know who or what prompted Mrs. Trump's escape? — she gushed, "Amazing, isn't it? This soon?"

I asked where she'd been watching the Melania drama unfold.

"With Simon and Veronica, of course."

Of course? "With both of them, in person?"

Instead of expanding on that, she informed me that Melania had wanted to run away, solo, drive herself to New York, but she couldn't. "No way the Secret Service lets her go anywhere on her own. Besides, the Escalade is registered to Donald."

"How do you know all this?"

With labored patience she said, "I told you. I was watching with Veronica and Simon, and she was getting texts from you-know-who."

"Does Veronica know about you and her husband?"

"She does now. It's not as big a deal as you think."

How was that possible? How were tandem adulteries not a big deal?

"Are you there?" she asked.

I said I didn't get the "no big deal" part, since Simon had sounded furious when he and I had talked.

"I find that hard to believe because both of them are proud of how well they manage their open marriage."

I wrote "open marriage" on my scratchpad and underlined it three times. I wish I hadn't emitted a mousy "oh, dear," because it inspired Mandy to ask if I was reacting like that because ninety-two per cent of open marriages end in divorce? Simon and Veronica were the exception!

I said, "You and Simon are dating, Veronica's allegedly having sex with Trump, and they both want a divorce. How is that an exception to an unsuccessful open marriage?"

"Everyone's playing it by ear," she told me.

"I'm sorry to be so literal, but playing what by ear?"

"Everything! Simon has a flow chart: guilty, not guilty, defeated, re-elected, drops out, arrested, not arrested . . . Lots of ifs in there."

I asked, "Does anyone know if Melania's just taking a break?"

"It's a break all right; the big one. It's over."

"What about the rumor that Melania was being paid to stick with him?"

"Right, but the deal was she doesn't have to stay if he's indicted or impeached, or if he cheated on her *after* the inauguration."

"So she found out about his affair with Veronica?"

"She found a prescription that told the story."

"A prescription for a *drug* told the story?"

"Ha! Viagra would've done it, given their non-existent love life, but no, not for E.D. It was for reading glasses."

"Melania left him because she found a prescription for *glasses*?"

"Yes and no. The prescription, which he left lying around — we think on purpose, because they share like zero space — told the story in two words."

Trying to sound girlfriendy, I asked, "Wow, that must've been some major X-rated notation!"

"It wasn't a notation."

I waited. After a pause she said, "Remember, this is not for *The New York Times* or *Washington Post* or CNN."

"Got it."

"I probably shouldn't be saying this on my cell. I sometimes think Amazon is listening to every conversation I have. But okay, here's why Melania went ballistic: the president has a nickname for his penis. And apparently all his wives knew what he called it. So Veronica, figuring she'd be filling the prescription herself, made it out to Herman Trump, which could only mean one thing. And Melania knew *exactly* what."

As I scribbled furiously, Mandy asked, "Are you writing this down? Because I meant it to be off the record."

That was one journalistic principle I'd learned in my first

week on Team Champion, that pronouncing "off the record" couldn't be applied retroactively, as a P.S.

I said I'd better get back to sleep. Big day at work tomorrow.

"That's right. What do you do?"

I said, "I'm a research assistant. In Georgetown."

"Sounds interesting," she said, already bored.

I found Kirby in front of the office TV the next morning, watching Democrats and Republicans discussing Melania's retreat and its upshot. Every network seemed to have a star reporter outside Trump Tower, behind its cement barricades, traffic diverted, bystanders galore, some waving insult-signs from earlier marches.

"Can we talk?" I asked him during a commercial.

"Uh-oh," he said. "What's wrong?"

"Nothing—"

"I have a bad association with 'can we talk?'" He muted the audio. "Before you continue, let me apologize for dragging you to the optometrist's appointment. I thought it would be Interviewing-101, but I know every minute of it was torture for you as soon as it turned personal. You're not going to quit, are you?"

I'd been shaking my head throughout, which he seemed to be misinterpreting as, *be quiet; I don't even want to hear your excuses.* I said, "I'm not quitting. I wanted to tell you I finally heard back from Simon's girlfriend last night."

He put his right hand over his heart and said, "Whew! Now remind me . . .?"

"Mandy Cullinane, the real-estate agent. Cornwall Parker. If the Trumps broke up, the Hyde-White marriage would be kaput, and Mandy would get Simon in the deal."

Because he was writing something down, I sensed he thought that was all I had to report. I peeked and saw **follow-up, order flowers**. He put down his pen, picked up the remote, reclaimed the sound, smiled, and said, "I'm so glad you're staying."

"Flowers?" I asked.

"Yup. Following up with the optometrist, revisiting that drink offer I made."

"You don't think, given all that's going on, she'd be . . . busy?"

"I'll find out!"

Should I remind him that he wasn't supposed to have any dirt on the Hyde-Whites and their respective paramours? No; not necessary. She'd never accept his invitation, no matter how beautiful his flowers or how charming his note.

He seemed happy and engaged enough, channel-surfing, drinking in the First Family's drama, dogging Veronica for a date.

I'd type up my notes and save Herman Trump for another day.

19

THE AWKWARD REALM
OF THE PERSONAL

THE PRESIDENT SET A one-day record of tweets — half name-calling members of the Intelligence, Judiciary and Oversight committees, plus Joe Biden, Hunter Biden, Hillary Clinton, Barack Obama and various generals, and the other half bullying "Mad Melania."

TV panels featuring marriage counselors and divorce lawyers agreed: the third Mrs. Trump was the mother of his fifth child. Very bad parental and presidential form!

I was sitting across from Kirby's desk during what he liked to call our morning summit. Today's sport coat was a replica of newsprint, black and white, with blaring headlines that weren't actual words. The first worry on the agenda was his failure to reach his major White House source. What if she'd been fired?

"Can't you call her?"

"She calls me from a phone booth. In the old days, I might've put a red flag in a flowerpot like Bob Woodward did to signal Deep Throat that he wanted to meet. Did you see the movie? Those two had a view of each other's terraces. Maybe with binoculars, but that wasn't shown. I need to find out how far Housekeeper One lives from here."

I made a half-hearted note: **Hskeepr's address?** then asked why he thought the woman might've been fired.

"She's a maid! She probably helped Melania pack."

I said, "I'm pretty sure that would be an unlawful termination."

"Who's she going to sue? Trump? Good luck with that!"

I pointed to his hand-written list and asked, "What else?"

He grinned. "Hold onto your hat . . . I heard back from the optometrist!"

"And . . .?"

"We're meeting for a drink, tomorrow at six-thirty . . . Remind me how much I'm supposed to know about her personal life — husband, separated, divorce, Trump?"

How was such a get-together possible? Very reluctantly, I said, "She thinks you guessed about her marital status because she wasn't wearing a wedding ring. You *do* know Melania bolted, because anyone with a TV knows it. You *don't* know that Veronica and Trump are having an affair, or that she's his optometrist, or that she drove the car that hit me."

"That's what I had up here, in my noggin," he said, with a proud tap-tap to his temple.

I couldn't say what I was thinking — that he must've gotten something wrong, that Veronica couldn't possibly have agreed to meet him after our disastrous faux appointment. I watered that down to, "Amazing that she's giving you another chance after throwing us out of the office."

"No question: that phony patient act got me nowhere. She

ignored the flowers and the masterpiece of an apology that went with them. So I called and introduced myself as . . . me. The name Kirby Champion does open doors."

"Even after posing as a patient?"

"I haven't told her yet that the guy who came for new frames was me! It was just Kirby Champion, calling out of the blue."

Out of the blue except that her boyfriend's wife was in headlines all over the world. "But she'll know the second she sees you that you were the guy who did all that phony flirting."

I waited for him to say *Yes, true, the flirting was all an act,* but instead he said, "I explained that to you, didn't I? How I don't have my bearings yet as a single man?"

We were back in the awkward realm of the personal. But he needed a flashing yellow light. I said, "Just in case you're thinking this is a drink *drink*, don't forget that she's still married to one guy and has her sights set on the president. I wouldn't get my hopes up."

"She agreed to meet me, didn't she?"

"You just said it yourself: you're Kirby Champion! She thinks she's next in line to be First Lady. Either she's wondering what dirt you have on her, or how to win you over for future worshipful coverage."

"As if Trump is going to marry her! Like a guy with two ex-wives, going on three, wants to get hitched again? Trust me, that romance is doomed. Soon enough, probably it's hit him already, he's gonna realize he can meet new women, go out on dates. I don't know why her husband doesn't tell her she's living in a fantasy world."

"Are *you* going to tell her?"

"I certainly am not. Not tomorrow, at least."

I said, "I admire your confidence. I hope it's rubbing off on me."

"You? You're coming along nicely. You speak truth to power — I've noticed that, and I like it."

I said, "As long as that's the case, can I say that I think you can do a lot better? There are tons of women out there who aren't shagging the president of the United States and who'd appreciate a successful professional, who lives in this beautiful townhouse, whose kids are grown" — I pointed to the array of photos behind him — "and ..." what else to add? "... is a sharp dresser."

"Thank you, Klein. Not every woman I could meet has been close to the president of the United States. Does that sound like pure ambition on my part? Maybe she did file my invitation under 'I'm meeting Kirby Champion to find out what he has on me,' but I'm pretty good at making people come around after we get off on the wrong foot."

I'd already expressed in six different ways that Veronica Hyde-White was a lost cause, journalistically, temperamentally, and romantically, so why should I keep nagging? I said, "Well, more power to you if you can wipe the slate clean and start over as Kirby Champion, author or suitor, after — no offense — the disastrous appointment."

"You know what I'll say if she leads with that? I'll explain that it's the downside of being famous. I'll say 'I needed new frames. My assistant Googled optometrists, found you, saw your five stars on Yelp, and made the appointment. Yes, I use a pseudonym so I don't have to sign autographs in a waiting room. Or worse, sit next to a woman whose daughter wants to be an investigative reporter and what advice do I have for Samantha or Madison?"

"How will you explain the assistant who tagged along and taped the conversation?"

"That's no lie. You *are* my assistant. I should probably tape tomorrow's get-together so you can see how to reverse a wrong turn with the right dose of apology and flattery."

"She didn't strike me as a woman who'd be susceptible to flattery."

To his credit, he winced before asking, "Do I have your permission to explain something personal? Well, not so much personal; more like cultural."

"To me, you mean?"

"Yes. I'm always careful, employer to employee."

I barely nodded, hoping he'd read that as *please don't*.

"Okay . . . Very tall women — and the doc must be a six-footer — consciously or unconsciously are drawn to tall men. That might sound conceited, but it's not. Guys my height get a second look and a second chance that short guys don't. It's biological. They want to put their head on a guy's shoulder when they dance, and they don't want to walk down the street or down the aisle with a shrimp. Plus, they want the tall gene in their kids' DNA. Even if their child-bearing days are over, the preference still kicks in. And if it's not about the genes, it might be — how to put this politely — what's *inside* the jeans."

I'd been bracing for exactly that narrative landing place. But what assistant in the second week of a three-month trial period was going to scold or sue? I forced what I hoped was a congratulatory smile. "And you're even taller than Donald Trump," I said.

20

NIGHTS AND WEEKENDS

MY ROOM-MATES WERE expressing increased disapproval of Kirby's after-hours tweets, diagnosing him as boundary-challenged.

"It's only going to get worse," Elizabeth insisted, as we three were waiting, dressed for work, briefcases by the door, for our commuter coffee to brew. "You have to nip it in the bud! Tell him you work Monday through Friday, nine to five, not twenty-four/seven. Do you have a contract?"

I didn't. I pointed out that a trial period wasn't the best time to debate fair labor practices. I didn't admit that there was timing of another sort at play: as much as I shrank from his calling/texting/brainstorming after hours, I didn't want to wait until Monday to hear about his drink with Veronica. "What if I ease into it?" I asked.

"Define!" said Elizabeth.

"Okay . . . He has a meeting tonight with someone who's

pivotal. I could tell him to report on just that when he gets home."

"Still bad," said Elizabeth. "That's giving him a creepy green light to call you when he's home alone — who knows, confiding in you from his bed or bathtub."

"How's this?" asked Yasemin. "Tell him you'll make an exception to the rule about nights and weekends being sacred—"

"He'll say, 'What rule? We have a rule?'"

"He's scattered enough that he'll think somewhere along the line you codified that," said Elizabeth.

"Tell him to email you about that big meeting, but not after five or six, or whenever, on Saturday" — and with a sly grin — "it being date night."

"Forget 'easing into it,'" said Elizabeth. "Tell him you have a private life, and it starts when you leave the office."

Yasemin said, "Rachel's not going to say that and you know it."

"Ladies! I'm perfectly capable of texting back, 'Can't answer now. Turning phone off.'"

"Along with 'please respect my embargo,'" Elizabeth amended.

From the other side of the kitchen, I mouthed to Yasemin, What embargo?

She said, "Lizzie and I expect bulletins from the jazz club — just a few words when Wine Boy goes to the loo."

"Emojis will do," said Elizabeth.

"We're very invested in you two," said Yasemin.

"How did I end up living in Yentaville?" I asked.

They'd approved my outfit — black pants, black boat-neck sweater, soft, part cashmere — after swapping my discreet gold hoops for louder, bigger, silver ones of Yasemin's. As for what Alex was wearing and what he looked like, I was waiting to describe him only when I sensed there was more than platonic patronage of Varsity Wine & Spirits.

But he had come through. Thus: his hair was brown, his eyes light brown/maybe hazel. His black eyeglass frames I knew to be hip, having seen the latest in eyewear at a Royally Warranted optometrist's showroom. He wasn't a thin fellow; there was a bit of a belly that his apron hid, but hardly worth mentioning. He picked me up at my door like a suitor of old. If we'd been classmates at White Plains Senior High School, I may have overlooked him. Then, at our fifth or tenth reunion, as we'd talked about what we'd both been doing in the five or ten years since never knowing each other in school, I'd have thought *how was I not friends with this boy who has grown up to be attractive in a non-flashy, five-foot-eightish way? How did I not invite him to the Sadie Hawkins dance junior year? He seems not only smart but, well, nice. And if I went back to our yearbook I'd probably find under his photo a line by Shakespeare or Fitzgerald that was compatible with my Judy Blume quote: "Our fingerprints don't fade from the lives we touch."*

We drove to the jazz club, a fifteen or twenty-minute ride in a car that served as a conversation-starter because it was electric, my first such vehicular experience. I asked the whys and wherefores of charging, of charging stations, of charging time, of how far a charge took him — hoping to sound genuinely interested in his Bolt. Just like our two exchanges at the store, he'd answered in an amused, indulgent fashion.

I knew from my homework that the club was a jazz landmark — brick-walled indoors and out, and a framed 1933 front page announcing *Dry Amendment is Dead*, an homage to the club's speakeasy past. Once we were seated, the topic turned quickly from prohibition to wine, not occupationally but because the menu listed only beer and cocktails.

When asked, the waitress said, "We have a red and a white."

With a wry tilt of his head, he asked, "The red is...?"

"Pinot Grigio."

He smiled and said, "Maybe Pinot Noir?"

"Meant that," she said. "Long day. Brunch this morning. Two seatings plus dinner, and the show."

"I'll have the red, too," I said.

She pointed to the italics at the bottom of the menu. "The twenty-five dollar minimum can be for food or drink or any combination."

"Maybe we'll just start with the wine," said Alex.

"Perfect," I told the waitress, "but don't go too far away."

Alone again he asked, "And the new job? Still excited about it?"

I didn't want to sound like a complainer, so I said only, "Not quite what I expected."

"In a bad way?"

I lowered my voice. "My title is research assistant. I knew I'd be listening in on interviews and transcribing them, but I was shocked when he said I'd be turning those interviews into, essentially, a book. His next one."

"Can that be bad — ghostwriter to a celebrity author?"

It felt great to speak bluntly about Kirby to someone who wasn't going to urge me to file a grievance. I said, "It's just about how we're going to get there. He's impulsive. He gets an idea in his head and runs out the door, dragging me along. Or he gets a big piece of news—"

"Such as . . .?"

Once again, the question of what was confidential. I said, "He's a muckraker and he's not a fan of Donald Trump."

"I think I just heard a non-answer answer."

I said, "I'm not supposed to talk about stuff that's going into the book."

"Then I won't press you. I'll read the book when it comes out."

"Working title: 'The Blight.'"

Alex laughed. He asked if I'd read Kirby's other books.

"I skimmed the most recent one on the train, heading for my interview. I'd only had one day's notice between applying for the job and meeting him."

"Obviously nailed that interview — that's what the Prosecco was for, right?"

I said, "I'm impressed — remembering what a customer bought two weeks ago for, I think, $14.99."

"Fifteen-ninety-nine," he said. He took off his glasses, cleaned both lenses with his napkin, reinstated them, then said quite deliberately, "Not that I remember every customer's purchase."

"Probably just because I chatted you up."

He smiled. "Are you fishing for a compliment?"

I said, yes, I was; no question.

"You told me you were celebrating a new job, who you'd be working for, that you had two room-mates, lesbians, to be exact, while you yourself were straight."

"Awkward. But helpful, no?"

"Very helpful." *He gestured: here we are, after all. On a date.*

The waitress returned and asked if we'd decided.

"Anything not to be missed?" Alex asked.

"Crab cakes, made here. Shrimp and grits are popular. I don't eat meat, but everyone says the burgers are awesome."

After a fast speed-read of the burger lineup, I said I'd have the Ella Fitzgerald.

Alex said, "In that case, I'll have the Herbie Hancock, medium, with the truffle fries."

"Medium for me, too," I said. "With the vegetable of the day instead of fries?"

"Because she'll have five of yours," the waitress said with a wink.

Waiting for our food, I launched into a history of the Klein family business: originally hardware, founded by my paternal great-grandfather on the Lower East Side of New York in 1925.

"Still family-owned? Still in the same location?" Alex asked.

"Yes to family-owned. But *Upper* East Side now, on Lexington. And exclusively paint and wallpaper since my dad took it over."

"And who takes over after your dad?"

"Not me. I have no aptitude for it. Or maybe no patience with the customers agonizing over four shades of the same color that look identical to me. When someone says 'This red doesn't have enough blue in it,' I say, 'You'd better talk to my mother.'"

Alex said, "No kidding. How about people who assume I've tasted every wine in the store?"

"Don't you want to say 'how the hell do I know? I'd have to be drinking twenty-four hours a day!'"

"Yup. But I say, 'I haven't tasted this exact cheap New Zealand Sauvignon Blanc, but I'm a big fan of the expensive Sancerre one section over.'"

"No you don't!"

"Not in so many words . . . just practice . . . doesn't take a genius."

"Okay to ask the same question you asked me: what happens when your dad retires?"

"I have two brothers, one older, one younger, both on different tracks."

"That leaves you?"

"That leaves me."

"Is that what you want?"

"On some days."

Maybe he was being modest; maybe he didn't want to sound overly enthusiastic about succession when I had spurned a parallel path. Was some positive reinforcement called for? I said, "From what I've seen, you enjoy the work. Didn't I tell you how good you are at customer relations?"

"I believe the term was 'good client facing,' which I've gotten some mileage out of since I heard that. I found that . . . never mind. I shouldn't say."

"Stiffest compliment ever? Biz-speak?"

"No. Just the opposite. Sweet. I could tell you wanted to keep the conversation going, but didn't want to come across as over-friendly, hence the jargon."

I said, "I have to do better."

The first song sounded like repetitive randomness in search of a melody, at least to me. Had my face given my jazz apathy away? I suspect I was guilty of that because Alex whispered, "If you don't like it, we can slip away during their break."

I said, "No. I'm enjoying this" — true, in the big picture. The Fitzgerald and the Hancock, as high as triple-decker sandwiches, arrived mid-set. Holding the burger in both hands, the first bite imminent, I whispered, "This isn't going to be pretty."

"I'll be the judge of that," he said.

*   *   *

After we'd eaten most of our burgers, after I'd asked him if he wanted to see a movie next weekend, the pianist announced, "Next up, a song by Jimmy McHugh and Dorothy Fields, debuted by singer Adelaide Hall in 1928. We have Artie Steinberg on tenor sax."

The jazz-savvy all around us clapped and whistled. Was it possible that the trio was silently dedicating this to us? Of course not — with composer, lyricist, and chanteuse's names at the ready. What a narcissistic, loopy thought. Surely 'I Can't Give You Anything But Love' was their standard fare, and had nothing to do with blushing patrons holding hands under their two-top.

21

THREE'S A CROWD

As I walked past her desk Monday morning, Sandra said, eyes on her screen, "He'll be late."

I stopped, back-tracked, and asked, "And how are you?"

"Me? Why?"

Had no assistant ever addressed her in friendly fashion? "I just thought that was overdue. We hardly ever see each other during the day."

"I'm quite well, thank you." And then, with what sounded like a reach into some rusty can of manners, "And you?"

I said, "Good. Really good."

She sighed. "I suppose you want to elaborate."

I said, "I don't want to jinx anything, but I had a very nice weekend."

"How so?"

"A date."

"Which night?"

Odd question? It seemed so until I realized why she'd asked: She must've known her brother was stepping out Friday night with an unnamed companion. All innocence, I asked, "Saturday. Why?"

"Just wondering. Do I know him?"

I answered with a murmur that deliberately gave nothing away.

"Did you meet him — if it *is* a him — online?"

"No. In real life. At his workplace."

I could see she was steeling herself for her own next question. "And is that workplace here?"

I pretended to be both startled and appalled. "You weren't thinking — I don't even want to say it — that I had a date with Mr. Champion?"

"Can you blame me? All of a sudden you stop and tell me about a date, as if it somehow related to me."

"Because it's the first date I've had since I started working here. And you're . . . a fellow woman."

"How nice for you," she stated so primly that I knew she meant just the opposite.

I said, "It won't happen again." I headed for the elevator, pressed the button, then called back — "I mean the conversation won't happen again, but the date will."

What had gotten into me, chatting up the inscrutable Sandra, who might still have a say in my upgrade from trial to full-time? I made a note when I got to my cubicle: bring Sandra cookies next time Yasemin bakes.

I heard the elevator ping, then a not particularly cheery "Morning." I waited the customary interval it took Kirby to settle in, then went to his office, notepad in hand.

When he didn't look up, I coughed.

"Yes?"

"Friday night! Veronica! Did it happen?"

"Yes, it did."

I helped myself to the visitor's chair and said, "I'm dying of curiosity."

He shook his head.

"No? Not good?"

"Not good and — sorry — can't talk about it."

"That bad?"

"No. Just that I had to promise our conversation was off the record."

"But I'm not *on* the record. I'm on the *project*."

He answered with a look I recognized, his eyebrows raised: *give it a try*.

"And aren't I the one who brought the Hyde-Whites into this enterprise?"

"True..."

"How's this: I'll ask you softball questions."

"Maybe. Like what?"

"Where did you meet?"

"Let's leave it at 'a hotel bar.'"

"What was she wearing?"

"A suit? Black? A big pin here," pointing to his shoulder.

"Did she talk about Trump? Did she say what's happening between them since Melania ran away? Will that speed up her own divorce?"

"Those aren't softball questions. The answers are all no. We didn't talk about any of that in front of him."

"Him who?"

"The husband. Simon."

Aye! "There were three of you at the bar? Simon came with her?"

"He met us there. I didn't tell you that?"

No, he had not! I told him I was officially gob-smacked. And he must've been, too, since he was viewing their meeting as — sorry if this was overstating it — a date.

"My first impulse was to leave when he showed up, but then I remembered *grist for the mill. I'm writing a book, for crissakes.* By the way, he's no princely specimen. You'd never put the two of them together. He's shorter than she is; has kind of a mafia vibe I wasn't expecting from someone with a hyphenated name."

"Mafia vibe as in threatening?"

"Not exactly. Hard-nosed. Aggressive. Well-dressed but shifty."

"But you stayed."

"It only took me a minute to figure out he wasn't there to mark his territory. This was no jealous husband. This was her self-proclaimed manager there to interview me."

"About . . .?"

"What sells. I was set up!"

I said I didn't understand. Set up how? Sell what?

"She figured out that the reason I came for new frames was because we knew about the affair, thanks to his big-mouth real-estate girlfriend. They were there to pick my brain!"

"About what you'd put in a book about her?"

"No! She wants to write her own goddamn memoir!"

Was that shocking news? No. Hadn't everyone who'd left the employ or embrace of Donald Trump written a book? I asked, "What if she and the president *don't* break up? What if things work out and he marries her?"

"Believe me, she's keeping her options open. She thinks she has a title for the book that'll fit any outcome and will write both endings in advance."

"Did she try the title out on you?"

"She did. And it stinks."

I waited.

"It'll never see the light of day."

"Tell me!"

"Would you believe: 'The King and Eye.' E-Y-E, the organ."

"Are you sure she wasn't kidding?"

"She's not kidding. She thinks Donald will love it, the good version, the happy-ending version. Especially with the word 'king' in the title."

"And Simon just sat there listening?"

"Listening and asking me questions."

"Such as?"

"Who's my agent? Would I introduce them? How about a blurb? At this point, I stood up, said I had to be somewhere else, and slid the check across the table to that twit."

"Good for you. I hope you ate and drank a lot."

"One cocktail, 'The Postmaster General,' twenty-four dollars. Did I mention that we met at Trump International? Her choice."

"Yikes. Something's seriously wrong with those two!"

I thought I was being dismissed, but he asked, "Remind me. What was it that Simon wanted from you? Some favor, right?"

"An affidavit. And they wanted me to go to the press and tattle on Veronica and Trump."

"To what end?"

I said, "So he'd be the injured party in a divorce? So he and Mandy could be together? So she'd have to pay?"

"D.C. is a no-fault jurisdiction," he told me. Then, "It's all so depressing."

"I hope you don't mean depressing because it was an informational interview and not a date?"

"No. More like . . . I thought we had ownership of the bombshell you brought to the operation. It was driving the story. Now it's *her* story, her book."

One of us had to be aspirational. I said there would still be plenty to write about Donald Trump; more bad deeds to uncover, possibly even more affairs. Buck up! Surely Team Champion would find other muck to rake.

22

PERSONAL MATTERS

SANDRA KEPT A JUNGLE of plants on the third floor, which I viewed as a pretext for spying on me. She'd made it clear that horticulture and its ministrations were her province; that I should never be tempted to pinch back a little green shoot, or, on my way to the recycling bin, empty a water bottle into soil I deemed dry. She serviced her indoor garden at hours that coincided with my comings and goings, as if expecting late arrivals or early exits.

Since I liked to confound her with congeniality, I said, "It's really nice to work among greenery. What's that one called?" I pointed to something tree-like in a giant planter, hogging a window.

"Chicken Gizzard Aralia."

Laughing at its name was apparently another offense. Her whole face registered disapproval. I added, "It has such beautiful leaves. I wasn't making fun of the plant."

"It takes a lot of care. I want her to think she's still growing in Polynesia."

Hearing that touch of humanity and anthropomorphism, I tried expanding on the topic. "Does that mean keeping it warm and . . . humid?"

"Obviously," she snapped.

Why didn't I ever learn? She reminded me of certain Klein customers, first-timers, who spoke down to my parents and to old pros Murray and Mary-Jo as if they were temps who couldn't possibly know anything about color or wall adornment.

Sandra's combination of cold shoulder and condescension was harder and harder to ignore. I waited to discuss her antipathy with Kirby until she'd left our floor with her set of dainty gardening tools and long-spouted Swedish watering can. I knew I was taking a chance, that he might say, 'Sandra? She's never anything but pleasant to me.'"

I knocked on the door frame and asked if he had a minute to discuss a personal matter.

"Is it about me?"

"No, Sandra."

"Ahhh." He put down the fresh cup of coffee she'd just delivered. "It often is."

"Really? With whom?"

"Former assistants. My ex. The accountant. The UPS guy."

I told him that was a relief because I thought it was me, that I couldn't say anything right.

He motioned *close the door*. "I'll let you in on a secret, if I'm not crossing a line—"

That again — personal matters he feared would be labeled sexual harassment when I eventually ran to the EEOC. I said, "We've covered that. Permission granted to tell me the secret."

Long exhale, then: "She's in love with me."

I said, "I'd better sit down." Only somewhat recovered, I whispered, "Isn't she your sister?"

"Oh that! Nah. We're step-siblings. Her father married my mother at some point."

"When?"

"Ages ago. I was in college. She was at some boarding school in Connecticut. And I was stupid."

"Stupid how?"

"Stupid for thinking I was doing the high-school girl a favor, dancing with her at our parents' wedding. Do they still call it 'cheek to cheek'? I had had too much to drink—"

"That's it? You danced with her, like forty years ago?"

"I wish that was it. There was a room in the hotel, like a green room, where the bridesmaids dressed, undressed, their hair and makeup, whatever. So it was empty after our parents left for their honeymoon. Sandra and I fell asleep on the same bed, which she thought meant something. Her girlfriends kept enabling her: write him, call him, invite him to the prom."

"You never had the talk with her?"

"Which talk?"

"The one about how you weren't her boyfriend; how that night, the champagne, the music, the dancing, how pretty she looked . . . it was just what happens at a wedding."

"You know what she's clung to? That we slept together. Literally, slept. Together. Not in the bed, *on* it! Not a polite word for having sex. Just slept. Who knew she'd turn it into . . ." He waved his hand dismissively toward the door. "Forever."

"Did she ever marry?"

"She did! A fraternity brother of mine, whom she met at *my* wedding. I thought, well that'll take care of that. I had to be the goddamn best man. I probably didn't help matters by saying in my toast what a beautiful bride she was and how lucky Bruce was. And back in the day, as kids, at her prom we were the king and queen. Why the hell did I have to bring *that* up?"

"So you *did* go to her prom?"

"My mother bribed me. Prom, homecoming, some dance in a barn with hay. Who the hell remembers?"

"*Was* she beautiful?"

He shrugged. "All brides are, right?"

The sour, severe, heartless Sandra that I knew today made it impossible for me to picture her as a glowing bride, let alone a prom queen. I asked, "Was it a love match — her and Bruce?"

He shrugged. "Turned out he was gay. Not that she knew at the time, nor was he admitting it to himself."

"Did your wife know about her crush?"

"She knew, and it was a standing joke: Sandra's carrying a torch for me. And it had its usefulness."

I asked what that meant.

"She had a better relationship with my mother than her own. She visited her at the nursing home, the hospital; hired and fired the aides — daughter-in-law stuff that my wife wasn't good at."

"And that's why you hired her?"

"It just evolved! I didn't need an assistant or a bookkeeper or an office manager. Back then, she had this big house, rooms going begging. It started with an innocent-enough, 'You'll use the third-floor den. I'll answer your calls so you don't have to be interrupted.' She thought an answering machine sent the wrong message: that it said 'I'm not successful enough to have help,' plus what kind of source leaves tips on an answering machine?"

"You were married then?"

"Married with three kids, writing at the kitchen table. Who'd resist a free office?"

"But you live here. You have the famous living quarters with the elevator button I was told never to touch. Why aren't they *her* living quarters?"

"Because it's the size of a subway car! She owns another house! Bruce put his money in real estate. Every time I get a new book contract, I try to buy this place, but she won't sell."

I said this was a lot to digest, starting with Sandra being his landlady rather than his sister. I asked if things got sketchy after his divorce.

"Meaning what?"

"That she got her hopes up."

"Believe me, I was careful! I was a monk! I never even asked if she'd like to have a drink after work or sandwich at my desk to discuss health aides for our parents."

I said, "Well this sheds a lot of light . . . on everything."

"Her bark is worse than her bite. Don't let her get to you."

"What about her vote?" I asked.

"What vote?"

"Whether I make it through the three-month trial?"

"Three-month trial? There's no trial period. She *told* you that?"

"Multiple times."

"Forget about that! She has no say in who I hire or fire! I'm going to tell her she has to be nicer to you."

Would that work? Incontestable evidence that I'd come crying to Kirby? I said, "Better not."

Yasemin texted me at work: **Count you in for dinner? Nothing special. Could u pick up skim milk lettuce ripe avocado?** I wrote back **Yes & lots 2 report**.

I didn't wait more than sixty seconds after the embellished lentils had been served before saying, "Wait'll you hear what I found out today!"

"Don't tease us if you can't give specifics," said Yasemin.

"Especially if it's who's fucking Trump," said Elizabeth.

"No! Better than that! The awful Sandra not only owns the building where we work, but" — I waited a beat; took a cool, calm sip of wine — "she's been in love with Kirby for forty years!"

Their reactions were identical, a most gratifying incredulity. "Sandra the dungeon master? Sandra who's never said a pleasant word to you? They're having an affair?" asked Yasemin.

"No! A one-sided crush that started when she was in high school."

Elizabeth said, "Wait. Aren't they siblings?"

"Step-siblings! He never bothered with the prefix!"

"Who told you this?" she asked.

"Kirby! Today."

"Unprompted?"

"No! I went to him like a baby — 'Sandra's so mean to me, boo-hoo. What's her problem?'"

"Please tell me you didn't actually cry," said Elizabeth.

"I did *not* cry. I interrogated him."

"And he told you, just like that — 'blame her nastiness on the fact she's in love with me'?" asked Yasemin.

"You know what this means, right?" asked Elizabeth.

"I hope you're not going to say I have to file a grievance somewhere."

"No! You're going to stop worrying about her! She's jealous and she's a case — nursing an unrequited crush her whole adult life."

"Is there anything that man won't discuss with you?" asked Yasemin.

"Here's the good news," I said. "There's no three-month trial. That was completely bogus."

The two legal minds wanted to know why I thought someone who sorted the mail, ordered supplies and made coffee was my judge and jury.

"Because she held that over me. Because she's intimidating! She watches me like a hawk."

"Does she think Kirby has a thing for you?" asked Yasemin.

"Of course she does," said Elizabeth.

"She'd think that about anyone; she'd think that if I had two heads and warts on both chins."

"I bet they're having sex," said Yasemin.

"No! He's been avoiding her except in an office-management kind of way."

"But you hear about these crushes that go on for decades and finally the one resisting gives in. He's divorced, right?" asked Yasemin.

"Recently."

"And she's what?"

"Widowed. She inherited the townhouse."

"Why is he such a wimp?" asked Elizabeth. "He can't afford his own office?"

I said, "By putting up with Sandra, he gets impressive Kirby Champion world headquarters, plus his bachelor quarters."

"Let's review," said Elizabeth. "She's no blood relation, has nothing to say about your tenure, so she's just an asshole. Agreed?"

"Agreed."

"She's a bully," said Yasemin. "A big, territorial bully."

"Starting tomorrow, you're going to give as good as you get," said Elizabeth.

Instead of mealy-mouthing my way to the elevator, I planted myself in front of Sandra's desk the next morning. When she didn't look up from doing nothing, I said, "I had an enlightening talk with Kirby yesterday."

She put down her pen and folded her hands. "And you're telling me this why?"

"I learned a lot."

"Such as?"

"That you were married, and your husband died."

She held out her right hand, wrist tilted downward, fingers splayed. "You never noticed these rings were on my *right* hand, in the widowed position? He died eleven years ago. So it's a little late to be expressing condolences."

"Then I won't."

"I'm busy," she said. "And surely you can find something to occupy yourself."

I said, "Speaking of work, I also found out that there's no three-month trial period. You made that up . . . AKA lying."

Her face became a cartoon version of furious. She hit four numbers on her phone. An annoyed "Whaat?" came through: Kirby's.

"I have Miss Klein here, being brazen and disrespectful," she sputtered.

In just the right tone of weary, fake indulgence, he pleaded, "What do you want me to do?"

I said loud enough for him to hear, "Sandra's offended that I mentioned her widowhood and that I was feeling more optimistic about my tenure here."

"Sandra?" he asked. "What am I missing?"

I didn't say, *Same as ever. She's in love with you.* But the look I fashioned, the clued-in nod I bestowed on Sandra, made her mumble, "Nothing."

23

THE WRONG RACHEL KLEIN

My phone rang as I was walking from the Foggy Bottom-GWU stop to work, dutifully listening to Kirby's first book, *A POTUS Can Get Lonely*, mostly about the Lincoln bedroom. When I answered, a male voice announced he was from Buzz-Feed, was following up on a tip left on their tip line, and had he reached Rachel Klein?

I said, "You reached a Rachel Klein, but I didn't leave any tip."

"Not *by* you. About you, in part."

"No, sorry. You must have the wrong Rachel Klein."

There was a pause, then, "Aren't you the Rachel Klein whose job was terminated by the Trump Administration?"

I left the flow of foot traffic and stopped in the doorway of a closed café. I said, "Is that what the tip says?"

"We can't reveal content. We guarantee the tip line is secure and anonymous."

"But you call someone and ask her to explain why she's in a tip you can't read to her? I mean, why call me at all?"

"I'm obliged to ask: Did you leave the tip yourself?"

"Haven't I already said that? I did *not* leave a tip. And how did you get my number?"

"I Googled you. I found a Rachel Klein, Duke alum, who'd worked at the White House until September of this year." Then, in a rapid-fire cataloguing of my recent life: "You were terminated, then hit by a car, then hospitalized, which generated a get-well wish, televised in a White House press briefing."

"True. I'm *that* Rachel Klein, but—"

"So it's not a giant leap to think you might have suffered professionally and legally?"

I said, "Well, I did land on my feet. I have another job." Then asked, "Is the tip about the president?"

"Once again, I can't say."

Next I tried, "How about if you don't actually *say* it. I'll give you my email so you can forward it."

"Even if I wanted to, I can't. It's a voice message."

I said, "Well, now you've heard my voice. Did the tipster sound like me?"

"I'd have to listen to it again."

"You do that. I'll wait."

"You mean now?"

"Now."

It took a few minutes, during which time I tried to remember whether a panic attack was avoided by breathing more or breathing less.

Then he was back. "I listened. Twice."

"And?"

"It's not you."

I was tempted to ask, "Did she have a British accent? Or did she sound like a perky real-estate agent?" but I refrained.

Should I consult Kirby? Better not. I'd handle it myself. And/ or check with Attorneys Elizabeth and Yasemin? No, not that either. Both would surely counsel, "Why get involved? You told BuzzFeed you didn't leave the tip — you didn't, did you? So just drop it. You've said enough already."

In my cubicle, before I even took my coat off, I called Suspect Number One, Mandy Cullinane. She volunteered that she was in her car, removing "for sale" signs at two locations that were under contract. A very good week! Then volunteered, "On the personal front, things have gotten complicated. But it makes life exciting! Any minute I could turn on the news and find out what was ahead for me and Simon!"

"Really? Is that why you called BuzzFeed's tip line and . . ." What? I didn't know one word of it — ". . . mentioned me?"

Rather persuasively she yelped, "Whaaat?"

"It's so obvious! Didn't you beg me to leak the news of Veronica's affair with the president!"

"A long time ago! How would that help us now? Okay, maybe we *used* to think it would break up the Trump marriage so Simon and I could be together, but at this point, no one knows if her affair with Forty-Five is on or off. He hasn't called her since Melania left!"

"He's the president! He's got a lot on his plate!"

"Bullshit! He's on the phone all day! I don't have five minutes between appointments, but I talk to Simon whenever he calls, *and* my mother, *and* my sister. *And* you'll notice me taking your call right now, with an open house in fifteen minutes!"

Pointless to argue that she was merely Mandy the real-estate agent versus the leader of the free world. Instead, I asked, "Is everything okay with you and Simon?"

"Why wouldn't it be?"

"Because if things don't work out with the president, Veronica and Simon might not split up."

There was a pause, then, "I didn't call any stupid newspaper or leave any goddamn tip, okay?"

I said, "I believe you," and I meant it.

I was on his payroll. Information and intel I gathered was presumably on his behalf. I decided to tell him. "BuzzFeed called. Someone left a tip with my name either attached or implied," I dutifully reported.

"What does 'either attached or implied' mean?"

"The reporter said the tip was about me in part."

"Sit," Kirby said, then, "I hate to ask, but I have to: *did* you leave a tip?"

"Of course I didn't."

"Do you have it? The transcript of the tip?"

"No! All tips are confidential."

"But if you had to guess . . .?"

"Something like 'An optometrist named Veronica Hyde-White is having an affair with Donald J. Trump. And maybe you should ask Rachel Klein, who was nearly killed by said doctor of optometry as she was rushing to the White House to have sex with her patient.'"

With a coy smile he asked, "Did you consider *pretending* you were the tipster?"

"No! Why would I?"

"So you could tease the content out of him."

"I'd be terrible at that."

"You'd be playing along with it until you weren't. Wanna give that a try? It might be fun."

Not for me it wouldn't. I said, "It's too late. I asked the reporter to listen to the caller again, once we'd talked, so he knew it wasn't me."

"Oh. Too bad."

No, not too bad; a relief. I told Kirby I thought the obvious tipster was Mandy, the real-estate agent, because of our history, but—

"Great! Call her! Or do you want *me* to?"

"I already did. She swore she didn't call the tip line and why would she want to at this point?"

"Of course she'd say that!"

I reminded him that his drink with Veronica had left him feeling that we'd gone too far down a rabbit hole with the Hyde-Whites, and it was time to find something new elsewhere, something original and juicy for "The Blight."

I'd learned in my short few weeks that he was more distractible than any adult I'd ever met. His face brightened. "Any ideas?"

"I'm going to sit down and start working on new areas of focus."

I was already backing out of his office, my hasty exit prompted by my phone vibrating. I picked up the call, luckily outside Kirby's range.

I say "luckily," because those few yards saved me from explaining the incredulity on my face as the BuzzFeed reporter asked, "Is there any reason why Ivanka Trump's Hebrew coach would know your name?"

24

BETWEEN THE LINES

I LEFT THE TOWNHOUSE, coatless, and called BuzzFeed from the sidewalk. Pacing, I asked the reporter how he'd confirmed it was Ivanka's Hebrew coach.

"She left her phone number."

"On an anonymous tip line?"

"Some people do that. They feel that it gives the tip gravitas. Did you know her?"

I asked again what was in this sacred tip, especially the part that roped me into it.

"We've been over this. No. We have to preserve the integrity of the tip line."

"What if we Woodward-and-Bernstein it . . . like I'll guess what she said, and if you're still on the line after ten seconds, it'll mean I was right? Or fifteen seconds if—"

"No thanks."

"Then I withdraw that offer. I shouldn't be leaking dirt anyway."

"Dirt?" he repeated.

"Excellent dirt. What I might let slip if I took my best guess at what was happening at the White House . . . especially since it's stuff that'll be going into my boss's next book."

"Who's your boss?"

"Kirby Champion."

This name was met with a terse, "I see."

I said, "Aren't you wasting your time, calling me, not telling me anything? I never met Ivanka or Ivanka's Hebrew coach. You're not one of those people who thinks that all Jews know each other? Is that all you have?"

"No! Certainly not!"

It was good psychology on my part. BuzzFeed called back the next day, this time a reporter named Lorna. She told me that my situation had come up at an editorial meeting where a majority of those present felt I had a right to know the gist of the tip I'd been consulted about.

"The *gist* of the tip? How about word for word?"

In a tone suggesting *don't be greedy*, she said, "We sensed that your take-away was that the tip had presidential sexual content."

"It doesn't?"

Her brisk non-answer was, "You work in Georgetown, right? On O Street?"

Of course, having looked up Kirby's address, she named the closest Starbucks.

I asked, "Can't you just tell me now?"

"Not over the phone. How's three today?"

I hadn't so far taken an off-site coffee break, a holdover from worrying about Sandra's monitoring my every move, but now I could say, "I'll be there."

"I'm six feet tall with sleeves," she said.

She'd chosen the remotest table, maximum distance from any other patron — most of whom, I guessed, were GW students. Her short hair was either blue or purple depending on the light, and running between her elbow and knuckles, tattooed in beautiful old English script, was the First Amendment and accompanying artwork. She slid one of two grandes to my side of the table and said, "I took a chance that you drink coffee. It's black. I'll wait while you fix it."

I said, "I can do black. What can you tell me about the tip?"

She didn't have a notebook, pen, pencil, or paper in sight; just a phone. She handed me one end of an earpiece, and placed the other in her own ear. After some swiping on her phone's screen, she signaled *ready* with a nod.

The voice was a woman's, best described as posh papered over a nasal, Bernie Sanders' Brooklyn accent. I heard: "President Trump is going to announce on the first night of Hanukkah that this was a special holiday for him because his grandparents came to America to escape persecution by the Nazis." Lorna hit pause and said, "Note: they emigrated in 1885." Then the rest, with the caller sounding angrier and eventually choking up: "Though he's being tutored in reciting the blessing in Hebrew, it's a total waste of that tutor's time because he'll read it from the teleprompter anyway. If you're wondering why he's telling such a huge, vile, insulting lie, it's because he doesn't like being called anti-Semitic or being blamed for shootings at synagogues and rabbi's houses, and thinks people will say, 'How can he be an anti-Semite if his grandparents were running from Hitler?' He doesn't know any history so why would anyone else go look it up? And while you're at it, check White House employment records to see who's been fired in the last few months, whether there was a religious bias. Thank you. Shalom."

Lorna asked me what I thought.

Not wanting to sound insensitive, I sputtered, "Couldn't be any more despicable!" Then, "But . . . I didn't hear my name."

"It's there, between the lines. She's hinting that someone was recently fired because he or she was Jewish. And not that you can tell someone's religion by their name, but there was only one that fit the bill in recent months: Rachel Klein of the White House Office of Records Management."

Should I bother to say, "Except I was fired for cause"? I didn't. I winced in a way that could mean either *ouch, yes, the sting of anti-Semitism*, or *what a crock*.

"Did you file a complaint?" Lorna asked, having fished a reporter's notebook and pen from an NPR canvas bag.

I said no, I hadn't.

"What if she's on the right track and you were fired based on religious discrimination?"

She must've taken my shrug for embarrassment and shame because she said, "I think it's a badge of honor to be fired by the Trump White House. Think: McMaster, Tillerson, Mattis, and every chief of staff from day one."

And Rachel Nobody Klein from the Scotch Tape squad. I asked, "Do you know if this coach ever met me? Maybe when I was in Correspondence or Records Management, or saw me eating matzoh in the White House mess?"

"We did ask if she knew you personally."

"And?"

Lorna flipped backwards in her notebook. "No, she did not. But she kept an unofficial head count of Jewish employees, just for her own . . . I guess you'd say 'fun.' Or as she put it 'for her own edification.' Apparently, before you were terminated, you were on a guest list for the next White House Seder."

I said, "Patently ridiculous. They must've been desperate." But what I was thinking was *wait till I tell my mother*.

Was it too early in our fledgling relationship to stop by Varsity Wine & Spirits on my way home from work? I told myself no; it was where I bought my alcohol, regardless of who was on duty. Not to be discounted: only Alex was Switzerland in terms of my job and my boss. My room-mates were skeptical of Kirby and no fans of his methods or his books. On the other side of the Kirby equation, my parents were overly proud to have me on Team Champion, and especially enthusiastic about my getting a paycheck.

When I arrived at the store, Alex was ringing up a magnum of something red for a man wearing a Nationals cap and a pin-striped suit, with three customers queueing up behind him. I squelched my retail impulse to ask if I could help; instead I made my presence known with a wave and a smile that I hoped signaled *no hurry; I'll browse*.

After the customers had been rung up and their bottles bagged, Alex joined me. "What good timing," he said. "I was just going to set up a tasting with a nice . . ." he looked at the display I'd been studying, ". . . Beaujolais Nouveau."

I said, "I'm going to put Thursday wine tastings on my calendar."

"They float. They're often . . . spontaneous."

After uncorking the prettiest bottle, its label a pastel land-scape, he produced two glasses, gave me a generous pour and an on-duty taste for himself.

"Delicious," I said, my glass raised.

"It's called 'the wine without rules.' "

"Because . . .?"

"You can chill it. You can serve it on the rocks. And if no one's watching . . ."

The unspoken rest of that sentence would be ". . . you can kiss a customer." He did. On the lips, fast, then a few seconds longer after a quick check of the front door.

I said, "Exactly what I needed after the day I've had."

"Recap, please."

I would've summarized my unnerving exchanges with BuzzFeed, but in walked a couple with a toddler in a stroller and a papoosed infant on the man's chest.

"Can you hang around?" Alex asked me.

I said "Yes, take your time." I sipped my wine, photographed its label, checked my email; found nothing work-related or nerve-wracking. One neglected voicemail was from my mother, the usual *Call when you get a minute or two. Nothing special. Love you.*

I did have a minute or two. Alex's customers were asking questions in front of the single-malt scotches and appearing to ponder every answer. I called my mother's cell, reached her, and went straight to "I had an interesting phone call—"

"From who?"

"BuzzFeed, but no need to go into the gory details—"

"I love gory details!"

"Not necessary. Just the main thing: someone who works for Ivanka Trump keeps a head count of Jews who work in the Trump administration just for fun, and allegedly I was going to be invited to the next Seder!"

"Whose? Where? The Kushners'?"

Alex was heading my way. I said, "Ma, I'll call you later. Gotta run." But just as he returned to my side, another customer arrived, an elderly woman pushing a walker, a large alligator handbag weighing down one wrist. Alex murmured, "Won't take long. Johnny Walker Black, like clockwork."

I said, "I'll meet you up front because I'm buying a bottle of this flirty wine."

He stuck the cork back in the one we'd sampled. "No you're not. You're taking this one home."

"Are you sure? I'm happy to buy one—"

"You can do that when my dad's here. He encourages me to exchange the merch for cash."

I smiled — apparently for the whole length of his return to the scotch section, and in a manner conspicuously fond, because the customer whispered something to him.

"What gave you that idea?" he asked her, grinning.

More whispering by her, accompanied by an unapologetic stare at me.

I waved, fingers only.

"Come closer!" she instructed.

When I did, she took my left hand, inspected it, dropped it, asked my name.

"Rachel. And you're . . .?"

"Norma English. Mrs. Conrad English. Have we met before?"

"You mean do I work here? No. I'm just a customer—"

"A steady one," said Alex.

Finally the woman smiled. "I have two good eyes. You think I'm buying 'steady customer'?"

Did I need to respond? Alex took care of that by slipping his arm around my waist.

"I knew it," she said.

On the walk home, buoyed, socially optimistic, feeling chatty, I called my mother back. Her greeting was "Whose Seder?"

"The one at the White House, except, well, obviously, I didn't last long enough."

"How'd you find this out?"

"A reporter told me?"

"I thought they were finally leaving you alone."

I said it wasn't about the old stuff, not my accident.

"About a Seder you won't be at?"

I said, "About other stuff, and then it got around to me."

"What other stuff?"

Should I tell her who? I couldn't resist. I said, "This is totally off the record, okay? It was about something Ivanka's Hebrew coach left on a tip line. They figured out who it was—"

My mother said calmly, "Shoshana Gottlieb. Everyone knows that. She was raised in Flatbush but you won't find that on her website. She's quite the self-promoter. She has a waiting list for Bar and Bat mitzvah coaching — people are signing her up when their kids are in kindergarten. She's become quite the *frum* diva." And finally, impressed: "You got mentioned in a tip she left?"

"Not by name. And don't worry, it's going nowhere. Gotta run. Love to Dad."

"Wait — Thanksgiving! You're coming home, of course."

"It depends."

Very coyly she asked, "By any chance, does it depend on someone else's schedule?"

"If you mean the person I've had one date with, Thanksgiving week is probably one of his busiest of the year."

"Not that I know what he does . . ."

"He's a clerk."

"Clerk! I'm not falling for that one," she said.

"Which one?"

"That your mother the snob won't like 'clerk,' so she'll stop asking about him."

"Pretty close."

'Is he a clerk for a judge?"

"No. He's a clerk in his father's wine store."

"Nothing wrong with that," she said, then adding gleefully, "You know who's the snob? You are!"

When she called me at work the next morning, I answered with a brusque "Hi, I'm kind of busy."

"I'll be quick! I told Daddy about the Ivanka-coach thing and he insisted I tell Murray and Mary-Jo."

"Why? I told you not to say anything—"

"Listen! Murray and Mary-Jo have been confiding in us."

"About?"

"First, I can assure you I have their permission to break their very big news. I mean, it's about time—"

"Ma, what?"

"Murray proposed with a gorgeous cushion-cut diamond!"

When I let out a happy squeal, my mother said, "That's not all."

I instantly worried: was his proposal prompted by a doctor's visit, by illness, by cancer; a marriage having to do with hospital visitation rights? "Tell me," I whispered.

"It's a hundred per cent her decision, no pressure from Murray; none! She's converting!"

I said, "Yikes! I didn't see that coming."

"None of us did. But then her mother passed, and — who knows how these things metabolize? — Mary-Jo decided to embrace everything! You remember — who liked latkes more than Mary-Jo?"

"Don't you have to promise to keep kosher and move within walking distance of a synagogue? She's willing to make that pledge?"

"Oh my God, you're a mind-reader!"

"Why? What did I say?"

"'Synagogue!'. . . You won't believe it but Mary-Jo's taking conversion lessons at Ivanka's shul! Do you have a pencil?"

Unmoved, I reached for a pen, expecting to hear the dates of the wedding, engagement party, or her conversion ceremony. But what my mother dictated were numbers, starting with 9-1-7.

"Whose number?" I asked.

"You won't believe it, but Mary-Jo was at one of her sessions, and the rebbe's assistant pokes her head in, and hands him a Post-it note. She doesn't say a word, but they exchange a look that made Mary-Jo think this must be something either really personal or someone like Bloomberg calling. He puts the Post-it note on his desk. Then, looking very pleased with himself, says something like, 'I have to be careful, have to balance the good they do with the bad. And it's all about Israel, isn't it?'

"Mary-Jo said, 'I didn't catch who the "they" is.' He says 'Oh. Sorry. No one.' Then said something in Yiddish that probably meant 'Me and my big mouth.'"

I said, "So you're saying it was Ivanka Trump's number on the Post-it?"

"Which Mary-Jo texted to herself, just in case."

"Just in case of what?"

"In case it was really Ivanka's cell phone! You know how Mary-Jo feels about Trump. I mean, imagine being able to call her and say, 'Are you having a nice Mothers' Day? How about the babies and children still at the border, separated from their mothers and fathers!' That kind of thing!"

She sounded so triumphant that I didn't have the heart to

belittle her sleuthing. So I said, "Thanks, Mom. If and when the time comes for me to call Ivanka—"

"One thing, hon. If you do reach her, don't say where you got her number, or that the rabbi left it lying around for anyone to copy."

"Promise."

"I'm putting Mary-Jo on. She's standing right here."

Next I heard, "Had you given up on us?"

"No, never! Mazel tov. I'm so happy with your news, all of it!"

"How'd you like the Kehilath Jeshurun part?"

I said, "Listen to you! That rolled right off your tongue."

"It was Kenny's idea. When Murray told him our news, and that I wanted to convert, Kenny said, 'I'll get right on that.' Which meant: let me pick a synagogue that could give two tradespeople the prestige their humdrum lives are lacking. I figured if that's how I get his blessing, I'll let him run the show. I think he was hoping we'd get married there and invite the entire congregation."

"Will you?"

"No! I'm switching to a friendly place on the Upper West Side, Reform. Lesbian rabbi. I won't have to keep kosher. And no Kushners need apply."

"You're going to make a stellar Jew," I told her.

"And you're going to make a stellar bridesmaid," she said.

25

TOWARDS A BETTER "BLIGHT"

I DIDN'T OPEN THE FIRST two emails from a floundering Democratic candidate, assuming they were fundraising appeals. But when a third email's subject line said *Personal for Rachel Klein, formerly of WHORM*, I clicked and read that Candidate X needed my help. Could I send a number and a good time to talk, asked someone named Dale with the title "Chief Innovation Officer."

I hit reply. *I can't do anything, can't campaign or donate. (Journalistic ethics). Sorry. Good luck.*

Can you give me 2 minutes? It's not about campaigning or $$$.

Could it be a job-opening? A job *offer? Is this about working for Senator X?* I wrote back.

It's about an opportunity.

Opportunity, my ass. It was probably a stolen URL and a pyramid scheme. I wrote, *Not interested.*

* * *

Since learning that Sandra had no power over me and no stature other than name on the deed, I asked Kirby if she might take over transcribing his interviews, freeing me up for more journalistic duties. Perhaps giving her heavier responsibilities than watering plants and signing for packages would whittle down the chip on her shoulder?

I broached the subject with him in person, in his office, reluctant to commit my idea to paper or email, suspecting that Sandra helped herself to all correspondence.

"It's tricky," he said. "She always made it known that she wanted your job."

"*My* job? As in 'replace me'?"

"I mean any time there was an opening, she applied."

"But obviously you never hired her . . ."

"I tried her out once. I mean, I had to. Here I am, reaping the benefits of her largesse" — his hand swept the great room beyond.

"But it didn't work out?"

"Knowing I was lukewarm about the idea, she talked me into giving her a trial period."

"Let me guess: three months?"

"Bingo. But I knew after one month that I had to lower the boom."

"You fired her?"

He pointed to his phone with its full screen of text messages, presumably from Sandra, "Does she *seem* fired?"

I asked if he could sum up what she'd been doing wrong. I should know. I wasn't exactly tenured.

"She was a perfectionist in a way that drove me crazy. She wanted me to go back and check quotes, double-check facts. She wanted the finished book to have an index!"

I said, "I'd like to think I'm careful, too."

"But you know what works, what sells, and you know your place, which I hope doesn't sound *lord of the manor*. You don't yell at me to do this or do that or call this one or stop harassing that one."

I felt obliged to say, "And I appreciate that you don't lose your temper—"

"Or drop dead like that one up in New York where you ended up a person of interest!"

Not quite, but I said, "That too."

"Big mistake, hiring her. And then the firing — I've been paying for it ever since. And I know what you're thinking, which is what everyone else wonders: do you really need a whole townhouse as an office, and do you really have to live above the store?'"

"And what do you tell them?"

"Inertia! Plus divorces are expensive!"

To dodge that topic I returned to, "Worth a try — Sandra doing the transcribing?"

"Sure. Let me know what she says."

"I can't ask her. It'll look like I'm trying to palm off work. It has to sound like your idea."

He grinned. "I hit the jackpot with you, Klein."

"You did?"

"You have initiative. You're not afraid to give me an assignment, which is a relief when I'm under deadline pressure."

I didn't argue with "deadline pressure," didn't point out that he'd never mentioned it before. "Shall we give her a call? Like now?" I asked.

"And it's my brilliant idea, right?" He winked. "I'll cop to that." He hit four numbers on his desk phone, nodded when she picked up, then announced, "Your very thoughtful co-worker asked me if you could contribute in a more meaningful way. And I said, 'I think Sandra would be an outstanding transcriber of my interviews. That woman could write a book on punctuation!' "

He probably shouldn't have hit "speaker," because after a distinctly frigid pause, Sandra asked, "And if I do the transcribing, what does that leave on *her* plate?"

I said, "If you mean *my* plate, Sandra, I'll be turning the interviews into copy, and copy into chapters."

"We're an assembly line!" Kirby crowed.

More silence.

He took her off speaker and, with his chair facing the window, asked, "How does this strike you?" He listened, nodding unconvincingly. "No," then "Yes," then "That could be help-ful . . ."

He hung up, swiveled back to face me, shrugged.

"Not thrilled?"

"When is she ever thrilled? She said fine, okay; had to remind me that she'd paid the price for being a perfectionist. Was that going to be an issue? And what if she had opinions and questions about what she was transcribing? Could she jot notes in the margins?"

"And you said yes?"

"Look. She's no dummy. She might think of a follow-up question I should've asked but didn't. Maybe she'd even call the source back if I was too busy."

Too busy. Sure. Busy on OK Cupid, Hinge, Bumble, Match, and Our Time.

The first completed assignment she tossed on my desk contained a readout of a phone conversation between Kirby and a couple who'd sat behind the Trumps at his inauguration. I opened the folder, trying to look supervisory. The pages smelled like Sharpie due to heavily blacked-out words in every paragraph. "What's this?" I asked. "What's been redacted?"

"Names."

"Whose names?"

"Sources. I was protecting their identities."

"From who? Me?"

She pursed her lips, cocked her head, then asked, "Did you study journalism in college?"

I hadn't. I'd taken one creative writing course with a visiting poet. I said, "Well, Sandra, as the person who vetted me, who asked me to jump on the next train to D.C. for an interview, you'd know that my last three jobs had to do with words on the page."

"Words on the torn-up page that you taped back together? How could I forget?"

I didn't say anything while she was by my desk, but as soon as I heard her murmuring to the farthest potted plant, I spit out a suppressed *Fuck you, Sandra.*

Did I outrank her now? If so, why not lower the temperature? Why not be the grown-up? I texted her an hour later, complimented her on the typo-free pages, adding with a winking emoji, **Hmmm. A donor couple thought Trump paid more attention to Ivanka than Melania when he was sworn into office. Quelle surprise!**

She texted back immediately, just a wide-eyed emoji that could mean either yes to the so-what-ness of Kirby's interview or amazement at my comradely overture. I answered that with a thumb's up.

Would she see my sisterly sarcasm as disloyalty to Kirby?

If she did, and tattled on me, I'd say it was all in the spirit of workplace peace and toward a better "Blight".

Senator X's staffer, the fast-talking Dale, called me at work. I asked if someone at BuzzFeed had given him my name, number, email, everything.

"BuzzFeed? No. Should they have?"

I said no, no, of course not. Was it my mother?

"Hardly. We've been talking to your representative."

"My congresswoman?"

"No, your rep . . . press agent . . . manager. Whatever."

I said I didn't have any of those.

"Apparently you do. Hang on."

I waited while he presumably scrolled down for the answer. "Got it. A Douglas Feinberg. Way. W-A-Y exclamation point. He's convinced you have a story to tell."

Which of my stories? I'd told Dougie some things, but couldn't remember if I was yet in possession of Trump intel — adultery and optometry — when I'd met with him. "Did he expand on that?" I asked.

"He said you worked for the president and you made him look like an idiot."

"Did he say how I did that?"

"You recorded stuff."

"No I didn't. I never recorded the president."

"Wait. He told me you did that all day long."

"Did he say 'recorded' or did he say 'taped'?"

"Does that make a difference?"

"Yes it makes a difference! My taping was with Scotch tape, as in Trump tears everything up and other people put it back together."

When Dale didn't answer, I asked if he was expecting I had some bombshell recordings that would help his candidate?

"Your guy said you were fired for exposing some really embarrassing stuff."

I said, "Okay, listen. I wasn't. The embarrassing stuff is that the president can't stop ripping things up as if everything that crosses his desk is a crooked real-estate deal. Poof, no records, no record-keeping. I doubt if they even had file cabinets at Trump Inc."

"You must've seen some embarrassing stuff — memos, emails?"

"I didn't stop and read the stuff. Some of it was confetti when it got to me."

"Still, we're all on the side of 'He's not equipped. He's unfit. He's an idiot.' Don't you feel it's your duty to expose it?"

I said, "It's already out there. It's not news. I'm sure your candidate is a fine man, but I'm not interested—"

"Maybe you and your manager should get on the same page," said Dale.

Manager! I'd never signed anything, never agreed to call attention to myself, my embarrassing job at WHORM, the fact that I was fired, run over, or before that questioned for the possible murder of my cardiac-arrested first boss. I emailed Dougie, *Call me.*

He did. First, he proudly pointed out that he, the founder and CEO of WAY!, was calling me back himself. Not a junior consultant. Not Jace. Did I know whose calls he took himself? New York Yankees! Red Bulls! Rockettes!

I said, "Then let me get right to the point — I'm not newsworthy. I'm not a whistle-blower. I'm not going to write a book about taping paper back together. And I don't remember signing up with W-A-Y exclamation point."

"Hey hey hey! You're selling yourself short. You'd go on TV and remind people where their tax dollars are going. And as far as your hideous job being in the rear-view mirror, it's not a negative; it'll read as *fired for telling the truth*."

Should I argue and resist? In a neutral and nearly agreeable tone, I asked, "Why this candidate?"

"Can I be honest?"

I said, "As opposed to lying?"

"Don't be a smart ass. I contacted them all. This campaign is the one that got back to me."

"Would I be endorsing him? Because no one's going to care what Rachel Klein thinks."

"I bet you expect me to say, 'That's not the Way!-way; that's stinkin' thinkin'. But we're all about confidence and high self-esteem projected as modesty. You're totally in that groove."

Was it worth any of my battery life to argue whether my modesty was real or fake? I said, "I have a job now. You know that, right? Because when I met with you I was just out of the hospital, still black and blue."

He asked the who/what/where of it.

"D.C."

"Doing what?"

"Research assistant for Kirby Champion, the author."

"Maybe I knew that. Remind me what his shtick is?"

"You mean, what does he write about?"

"What's his platform?"

"Presidents, the seamy side."

Dougie must've been Googling Kirby as we spoke because within seconds he said, "He's controversial. Critics hate him. They think he makes things up."

"They don't hate him. They just think he doesn't . . . dig very deep."

"Looks like he's already trashed Trump in a book two years ago. How'd it sell?"

"Well enough that he's got another one in the works."

"Another hatchet-job? Will it come out before the election?"

"Doubt it."

"Doesn't matter. Your exposure will be good for the Champion brand and good for turning the screws on Trump. And I think you'll get it when I say 'not bad either for Klein Wallpaper & Paint.'"

I said, "The *store*? Are my parents behind this put-Rachel-on-the-map campaign?"

"Not exactly. We had dinner—"

"When?"

"Last week. With my dad and Mary-Jo, like two days after she came to work wearing the rock."

"And the topic of me came up?"

"Now I remember: your mom and Mary-Jo were talking about some overlap with Ivanka Trump — top secret, my lips are sealed. Remind me: did you sign an NDA when you worked at the White House?"

"I had to. But I have no overlap with Ivanka Trump except for the flowers she sent me in the hospital."

"For a head injury, right? If you violate the NDA we can claim — what's that thing called?"

"Amnesia? No, thanks."

He said, "I'm sending Jace down, okay?"

"To D.C.?"

"Yes to D.C. Send him a selfie. We may have some work to do before we put you on TV?"

I said, "I haven't agreed to anything."

"Don't be a baby. You have nothing to lose. *Nada*."

I repeated: "I have a job. I'm a journalist now. I can't run around endorsing candidates."

"You're not endorsing anyone. You'll be telling the world how stupid the current occupant of the White House is. By the way, that's what you're going to be calling him instead of using his name — 'the current occupant of the White House.' Subtext: Buddy, your days in the Oval Office are numbered."

"I wouldn't necessarily take you for an ardent Democrat," I said.

"I'm whatever my clients need me to be."

"Is this guy's campaign paying you?"

"No." Then, minus any enthusiasm, "No one is."

"You shouldn't have to work for free."

"Sometimes you do favors, and favors go under 'pro bono.'"

"Favor for whom? Not me."

"For my dad, okay? I've given him plenty of grief since the divorce. He's a loyal Kleiner, and it's not as if he has another cause to promote. You're it. He's still worried about your head, your spine, your brain, whatever. He was freaked out by that accident."

It was time to sound appreciative, even if I disapproved of the mission. "Am I going to be the new spoiler, the next Stormy Daniels?" I asked in jest, every syllable awash with irony, or so I thought.

"If only," he sighed.

"Dougie . . . I appreciate your wanting to help and your dad's devotion to the Klein brand, but there's nothing here. I don't want to go on TV and rehash my getting fired. I have no book in me."

After an uncharacteristic silence, he said, "My dad's gonna think my pitch stunk."

"It didn't. Do you want me to write him and tell him how helpful you tried to be?"

"No, I'll do it. I'll tell him I tried but you're . . . how should I frame it? Too humble?"

"That'll sound right. He knows me pretty well."

I could hear the tapping of keys. "I'm sending you an email that says 'Don't hesitate to call or write me any time if Way! can be of help in the future.' I'm copying Dad on it. And feel free to tell any high achievers in need of branding about Way! — assholes or not."

"Sounds good," I said.

26

SATURDAY NIGHT

MY MOVIE DATE WITH Alex began with dinner at his place, a freshly painted one-bedroom carved out of a tall Victorian on Irving Street. Off-street parking, yes; landlords Dominican, nice couple, on the premises and handy; room-mates, none.

He seared steak expertly in a cast-iron skillet, narrating at my request: "Salt in the pan, as hot as you can get it. Cook one minute; flip; another minute; flip; four minutes total" — smoke alarm going off but handled with aplomb.

He'd made a salad with what I considered advanced ingredients — pears, blue cheese, walnuts, homemade vinaigrette. 'Impressive," I said.

Mid-tossing, he pushed back on that: no big deal.

"Why so modest?" I asked.

He pointed to the oven window, to the crinkle-cut French fries baking inside. "See. From a package. Nothing to brag about. Frozen."

I said, "Steak frites. Perfect. And by the way, I grew up on Tater Tots. I loved them. Did you know that the name is trade-marked?"

"I did not. Interesting."

I sat down at the round table, silently vowing to do better at small talk. His place mats made me smile: plastic, white on black, giant spiderwebs. One iris in a tall water glass. Black linen napkins. There were candles in brass candlesticks. He brought the steaks to the table on an oval platter commemorating the hundredth anniversary of the Wright Brothers' flight at Kitty Hawk. "They should rest," he said, back-tracking for matches, then dimmed the overhead light, returned, and lit the candles. The wine, of course, was red, served without fanfare, without swirling it in his glass, without inhaling pretentiously, without lecturing about notes of this and notes of that. "Italian," was his only comment when I said, "Delish."

The rested steaks were served. As I cut into mine, I paused, suddenly reminded of a blind date with an unhappy outcome.

"Everything okay?" Alex asked.

I told him: I'd suddenly flashed back to a regrettable dinner where my date cut everything on his plate into little pieces before he took one bite, probably like his mother used to do for him.

"And did that mark the end of him?"

Was he asking how judgmental I was? "Nothing was good," I said. "We hardly talked." I skipped that we'd accidentally chosen a cash-only restaurant and only I had cash, which would've been okay if he hadn't reacted as if he'd just scored a free ribeye.

Alex volunteered that he'd dated a woman who always had to ask the waiters if the Szechwan chicken or the Kung Pow chicken or the Moo Shu chicken or the chimichanga was made with white meat. If the answer was no, she'd change her order.

Or worse — she'd offer to pay an upcharge for the preferred white meat. Excruciating.

"Even the chimichanga? Very bad. She was *not* the woman for you."

"Plus . . . I hate to even say it . . . she claimed she was allergic to wine."

I took another sip, pronounced it the best red ever, and the steak delicious, just the way I like it.

"I know, medium."

"Always a safe guess."

"No. I remembered our burgers."

How many men would remember what someone ate on a first date, let alone its internal temperature? I said, "They were memorable — named after the chanteuses. I think I had the Billie Holiday."

"There *was* a Billie Holiday, but you had the Ella Fitzgerald and I had the Herbie Hancock."

"Let's toast those greats," said I, the jazz ignoramus.

We did, pausing between clink and sip to exchange smiles that felt to me like declarations.

I'd brought dessert, a lattice-topped apple pie. When he claimed it was his favorite pie, I asked, "Are you being polite? Because if you invite me back, I want to bring what truly is your number one pie."

"You're definitely invited back . . . but . . . Okay. If under oath: lemon meringue. My mother used to make it, and it looked like it could go on a magazine cover. She was a really good baker."

Was. No wonder his tone had gone from teasing to solemn. "Is your mom . . . no longer with us?"

"She died in June."

"June! Last June? That's practically yesterday. I'm so sorry."

"It wasn't sudden."

"Cancer?"

He nodded.

"What was her name?"

"Alice. Why?"

I said, "That's the kind of question girls ask."

"Better than most questions I get."

"Such as?"

"How am I doing? Is your dad going to keep the house? Is he down-sizing? Moving to Florida? And how about this: a so-called good friend of hers asked if she could keep, i.e. get back the earrings she'd given my mother on her last birthday."

I put my fork and knife down. "Someone actually asked you that?"

"A neighbor she played tennis with."

"Okay to ask how your dad is doing?"

"He gets up. He goes to work. He goes home. He goes to the cemetery. My older brother has two kids that my dad is crazy about."

He changed the subject back to the pie; asked where I got it because the crust was excellent. I told him about the non-profit bakery on Grace that helped veterans. I should've picked up ice cream—

He cut off my apology by going to the fridge, came back with a half-gallon of supermarket vanilla, and a metal ladle. The scooping seemed to dispirit him. I said no, just pie, neat. He helped himself to another slice, neglecting to ask me. I knew what was distracting him: thoughts of his mother or, at the very least, her pies, beautiful ones undoubtedly topped in bronzed meringue. I leaned closer across the table and said, "I'm going to kiss you now, okay?"

He smiled, wiped his mouth in swashbuckling fashion and said, "I don't want no mercy kiss."

I said, "Not even close."

He kissed me back, then went straight to the question of whether I had my heart set on seeing *Little Women*.

I said, "Beth dies. Do we really need to go through that tonight?"

"Can't now, not after that spoiler."

"I thought everyone knew that! Maybe it's just girls. We were raised knowing one sister dies. Sorry!"

"Apology accepted. We'll watch something uplifting here."

"Dishes?" I asked. "It's the least I can do."

He didn't say "No, I'll do them after you leave." He said "I'll do them tomorrow."

Most obligingly, he agreed to a romantic comedy after a search under — my suggestion — Hugh Grant. It was after 9 p.m. A movie would end around 11. Not very late. But then what? On and off through *Notting Hill* I wondered, what now? At what point would I confess that I'd thought a sleepover was a possibility and I'd come prepared, contraceptively. Would that be pushy? Or clinical? What if he said, "I'm sorry. There's been a misunderstanding. This is only our second date, and didn't your Southern-Belle college suite-mates drum the three-date rule into you?"

After Julia Roberts found her way back to Hugh Grant and his flat, Alex asked if I'd like to watch another movie. Or an episode of something I'd been binging on?

"If it won't be too late . . ."

He checked his watch. "Maybe midnight. I could order an Uber. Or not order an Uber. Your call."

I asked if he remembered my room-mates.

"Of course. Very subtle, those two."

"I know. Like the Mack trucks of matchmaking. When I was leaving tonight, one of them yelled 'If you don't come home, we won't worry.'"

He asked, "Where's your phone?"

I retrieved it from my coat, on his tightly made double bed, and returned to the couch.

He dictated. I texted, **Having a wonderful time. Don't wait up.**

27

MY FUTURE SANITY

I WOKE TO THE SMELL of coffee and sounds of a kitchen clean-up. When I called to Alex, he returned, barefooted, wearing striped boxers and a T-shirt advertising Tito's Vodka. I touched my head to see what my hair was doing. Was there a brush in my bag?

He lay down next to me, an arm around my shoulder, his left hand landing casually on my left breast. "I only meant to offer you coffee or tea," he said, "but as long as I'm here . . ."

"Give me a sec—" I said, then ran to the bathroom, peed, rubbed toothpaste around my mouth, returned to a now-undressed Alex, who was wearing a look that was arousal-apologetic and so sweet.

I told him not to do any more dishes while I showered and got into last night's clothes. He asked what I liked for breakfast.

"Such as . . .?"

"Eggs. I can do scrambled—"

"Any pie left?"

"Definitely. I'll warm it up. I like a girl who eats pie for breakfast."

I said, "I noticed."

I took inventory while in his bathroom: the black and white tile, the Soft-Scrub with bleach sitting on a sponge where tub met wall; the just-unwrapped bar of soap. His towels were a flattering shade of red, so with one wrapped around me I popped my head into the kitchen to say, "Nice bathroom. Brand-new soap. I'll be dressed in a sec."

When we sat down to warmed-up pie, he said, "Tell me about work. Tell me what you do every day."

Had I realized how much I needed a sounding board who wasn't a boss, a litigious attorney-room-mate, a parent, a publicist? I said, "I'd really like to tell you what I do, but I'm not supposed to."

"Because . . .?"

"I signed something that said, essentially, what happens at work stays at work. No leaks."

"Not to anyone? Not even" — he gave my bare foot a nudge under the table — "close personal friends?"

Didn't my mother believe that a secret whispered to her could be shared with my firewall of a father? Her loose confidentiality rule was all the green light I needed. I summarized: I'd signed a piece of paper without thinking it through. Yes, I'd read it before signing, in front of hawk-eyed Sandra, wanting to look like a smart, analytical, cautious future employee. "Transfer of intellectual property" sounded reasonable, even fair, merely asking that I wouldn't help myself to what Team Champion covered.

"Is everything you do there so hush-hush?"

"No. A lot is . . ." Should I say it? *Worthless? Mundane? Past its sell-by-date.* I settled on, "pretty dull".

"If this helps: I'm trustworthy. And discreet. I have to be."

He refilled our coffee mugs and returned to the table. "What do you have to be discreet about?" I asked. "Do you mean at work?"

"Okay . . . I know this sounds puritanical . . . Let's say a customer comes in with a woman, and they're all over each other, and they're buying Sancerre as if it's the cutest thing two people ever bought, like I don't know it's straight out of *Fifty Shades of Grey*. Then, maybe a week later, the same guy comes in with his wife and two kids. I don't look confused" — he cocked his head, feigning a puzzled look — "I don't say, 'Hey, weren't you just here with a woman young enough to be in your Introduction to American Literature seminar?'"

"Not even a raised eyebrow that says 'I'm onto you'?"

"Nope. None of my business, and bad for customer loyalty."

I wasn't sure how retail diplomacy squared with the type of secret-keeping I'd need. I started with the merely historical. "Did I ever tell you I was hit by a car, leaving the EEOB?"

"No! When?"

"September."

"Holy shit. No, you never told me! Were you hurt?"

"I was. Not that I remember anything, because I was knocked unconscious, but I bounced off the car with several broken ribs and a concussion. Police, ambulance, hospital, the works. I'm fine now." Out of habit, I lifted my wet bangs to show the ghost of former bruises. "Anyway, here's the part that's going into Kirby's next book: the car that hit me was on its way to the White House."

"For?"

"Sexual relations with Donald J. Trump!"

"Wait. What? A prostitute hit you?"

"No. An optometrist."

That earned me a most gratifying near-spit-take, after which he managed to ask, "How do you know all this?"

"Oh," I said as airily as I could, "from the driver's husband's lover."

I was officially, at long last, enjoying the topic. I'd been telling half the story to various parties, but now, adding the presidential sexual sub-plot was not only liberating but, for the first time, bordering on fun.

"Was this a one-off or an affair? Do you know?"

"An affair."

"Also learned from the girlfriend? If the lover *was* a girlfriend."

"Correct. Mandy Cullinane, girlfriend and real-estate agent. She called me at my parents' store, filling me in and asking me to go public with it."

"Why couldn't *she* go public with it?"

"Because I was nearly killed by Veronica — that's the driver's name, Veronica Hyde-White, O.D. — so people would see it as the angry accident victim speaking out."

"And Champion has your scoop under lock and key? Is he contributing anything himself to this alleged book?"

"So far, not much. He talks to quote-unquote sources, but there's nothing new. Blah blah POTUS is an idiot, fighting and yelling in the West Wing . . . a big fat baby, apoplectic, vindictive beyond belief. Separate bedrooms, steak and ice cream, same old same old."

"He's using you," said Alex.

"I know! But I was so happy to get the job! When he asked me to write a summary of the whole weird thing, accident plus adultery, I never thought to say, 'No, that belongs to me. Hire me or don't hire me, but it's my story.'

"You don't think voters should know Trump is having an affair in the White House, maybe in the Oval office? You don't think evangelicals should know? And faithful husbands and wives and priests and rabbis?"

"But it's second-hand! Maybe third- or fourth-hand. I can't just pick up the phone and call the *Post* or the *Times* with hearsay. What could I offer as proof: 'Mandy Cullinane of Cornwall Parker says her alleged boyfriend's wife is shtupping the president?'"

"Do you think she could be making it all up?"

"The husband claims to have proof."

"What kind?"

"Clinton kind of proof. On his wife's knickers — they're British — stashed in the freezer."

"What a world," Alex said. He left the kitchen, came back with his phone, sat down, opened his email. "Tell me what I need to know."

"Is this for therapeutic purposes? For my future sanity?"

"No."

What was left? "For patriotic slash moral reasons?" I asked.

"Yes."

"But why? We know Trump will deny everything. *Fake news! All lies.* He'll say, 'I don't even know this optometrist! And my vision is perfect! Melania didn't leave me. She's up in New York, shopping for her next inaugural ball gown.'" I pushed some pie around my plate and mumbled, "Plus I'd lose my job."

"No you wouldn't. Your boss sounds incompetent. He needs you."

When I still hesitated, he tried, "What if this is the affair that gets him defeated? What if the anonymous leak checks out . . . Think of the possibilities . . . It could mean clean water, clean air. You could flip the senate. You could pass gun control . . . You could reunite families at the border."

Did he know me that well already? . . . *Babies at the border.* My face must've been signaling *I could be convinced* because Alex put his hand over mine. "What if *you* didn't leak it? What if someone else tipped off a reporter?"

"Like who?"

"Like me," he said.

28

INCREASINGLY UGLY

WE WERE MAKING THE BED together, straightening the over-worked sheets and AWOL duvet. Neither of us commented on the tangle of bedclothes, but we were both smiling. While giving one of the dented pillows a shake, Alex returned to the topic of duty to country. "The summary you wrote for Champion about the accident and the optometrist? Do you have a copy you can access from home?"

I most certainly did, having saved every draft. I told him how I'd started with a few sketchy paragraphs, about which Kirby had said, essentially, "nothing here". So I filled in the holes, uncovered the redacted names, and emailed it to myself. Would he need that?

"It'll help to have it when he shows up."

"When who shows up?"

He named a reporter who was Pulitzer-winning, TV-familiar, and Trump-allergic.

"You know him? Personally?"

"Nice guy. Modest. Usually buys from the $15 and under table, but that's fine."

"And you two talk?"

"I read his column, so I usually have a compliment in hand." He lobbed the pillow at me. "How's that for good client facing?"

"Too good. I'm nervous."

"Don't be. He wouldn't have to quote you unless you want to be quoted."

Did I want my name in the *Washington Post*? Might using an actual name help him write an exposé? Democracy dies in darkness, doesn't it?

I asked, "What if I lose my job?"

"That job that keeps you up at night? You won't."

When I kissed him goodbye I said, "I'm going home to take a nap . . . Didn't sleep very soundly."

"You're welcome," he said.

But before the prize-winning reporter ever dropped by the store or heard about Rachel Klein, before he could bring down the presidency, Melania stepped up. There was no official notice on White House letterhead; no Rose Garden or East Room statement, just @POTUS's ugly tweets confirming the marital rupture.

Gleeful hell broke out when the First Lady was spotted dining well outside her milieu, in a small Greenwich Village trattoria, with a tall, swarthy, forty-fivish-year-old man whose one martini and two glasses of wine ruled him out as her Secret Service protector. Within minutes of the first sighting, Twitter identified him as Mohammed Riley, private wealth manager; straight, never married, a supposed old friend who lived in Trump Tower too. Was she making a statement with her alleged date, trying to inflame her husband's Islamophobia? — notwithstanding Mr. Riley's regular attendance at Park Avenue's Church of Saint Ignatius Loyola? The majority of opinionistas said without a doubt, yes.

The President called into *Fox & Friends* the morning after Melania and Mohammed's dinner, where they reportedly shared orders of both fried calamari and seafood risotto — things that never touched the president's lips. He ranted that *she* didn't leave *him*, no she did *not*. "I fired her," he said. "And believe me, it was overdue." When the hosts changed the subject to the newly installed golf simulator in the White House, Trump returned to the topic of his soon-to-be ex, calling her "mad Melania," "mad, *mad* Melly," and accused her of "marital treason." After an awkward silence, Kilmeade asked, "Do you mean she was mad in the sense of angry? Because of the impeachment hoax? Because we can all identify with that!"

"No," said Trump. "Mad as in crazy as a bat! Did you ever see a bat get into a house? They don't know what they're doing. They fly this way and that way and bump into the wall. They're blind! And they have rabies! They caused bat flu!"

As if it were a logical follow-up question, Doocy asked, "Doesn't the First Lady speak several languages?"

"So? She's lived in a lot of places. If I lived in a lot of places I'd speak their foreign language better than she does! I graduated from the Ivy League!"

All that followed was awkward non-recovery from the hosts. Finally the blonde-tressed Janice Dean said, "Mr. President, as a woman, I have to say, with all due respect, that you're talking about the mother of your child." Neither co-anchor walked it back, nor was there an abrupt cut to a commercial, suggesting that a voice in their earpieces was prompting them to express support for the still-standing, anti-bullying First Lady.

Those ninety seconds were endlessly repeated on networks that Trump disparaged every chance he got. Would Melania respond? Did she still have East Wing access to the minions who wrote her press releases and her tweets?

Apparently, she didn't need them. The tectonic plates of the presidential marriage had clearly shifted. Mrs. Trump stopped before a throng of reporters and cameras on Fifth Avenue, speaking over the cement barricades, triggering live, breaking, leading news as soon as she said, "The Donald is a little boy who thinks name-calling, using words like nasty and nervous and shifty for people he's afraid of, is good. He thinks it's how you get votes, how you make friends, how it makes him a big man, but only makes him a small bully."

Shock waves! Every Democratic passerby posted photos and videos of Melania, in black pants, a fur cape and a black baseball cap bearing the word "Stonewall". Had the reporters been tipped off? Their presence and her leave-taking from the front door of Trump Tower rather than the family entrance and exit on East 56th, was proof they'd been alerted.

LIES! SHE'S NOT WELL! tweeted @POTUS, followed by two dozen increasingly ugly Melania tweetsults. As ever, retweeting with abandon, he failed to notice one that closed with #OnTheRag. Though expunged minutes later, it still had time to make the news, with commentators using the euphemism "a dated and disparaging synonym for menstruation".

I was in my office, closely following the tweets and replies on my phone, when Kirby texted me: **R U following POTUS attacks on FLOTUS? Can u write a tweet 4 me?**

Must I? It was a slippery slope, ghost-writing his alleged work, let alone thinking aloud for him on social media. I wrote back, **Don't you want to use your own voice?**

I thought you'd be better at the woman stuff.

Woman stuff?

2 b discussed in person.

I took my time getting there, announcing myself with only "What?"

"I'm being careful," he said. "I didn't want a written record of me using the expression 'on the rag' to you, a female employee. You know how careful I am."

I did, tediously so. "I'm not going to sue you for sexual harassment. And by the way, discussing a retweet by Donald Trump is business." I flopped down into the upholstered visitor's chair, opened the notebook I'd brought, and said, "I assume you want to sound outraged?"

"Exactly! I want women to know it offended me, too."

"*Did* it?"

"It should've, right? Isn't 'on the rag' a horse-and-buggy term? Have millennials even heard it?"

I wrote a half-sentence, crossed it out, tried another. "How about 'I was greatly offended by a hashtag that is antediluvian and so misogynous that I can't repeat it here'?"

He was shaking his head.

"Not good?"

"Too wordy. I want a certain follower to read it as *Donald Trump is a pig and I'm not.* But dignified."

When I asked who the certain follower was, he confessed a woman he'd had a drink with and wanted to see again.

"So we're writing this for her?"

"For all women who buy my books and will buy the next one. Is that so bad?"

I tweaked a few phrases then said, "Then how about 'No man should ever disparage' — insult, attack, trash-talk, you pick — 'the mother of his child'? Does this woman you met have kids?"

"I didn't ask."

"You should ask, and you should look like you're hoping the answer is yes."

"Can I be honest? I'd rather date someone without kids so she can be spontaneous." He leaned forward and said, "Well . . . as spontaneous as you can be when you're, shall we say, keeping time with a woman of child-bearing age, if you catch my drift."

I did, especially since it was accompanied by a wink. "Back to the tweet," I said, adding, "I'd rather not discuss your personal life."

"Sorry! I take responsibility for anything I just said that was inappropriate. I'll tweet what you wrote. And if I use a hundred-dollar word — nothing wrong with that, right? Kind of professorial," which he followed by the gratuitous, "After all, I was a genius to hire you!"

Was this a good time to ask a favor? I decided yes. "You know that T.I.P. I signed?"

When he leaned back in his chair, squinting, I reminded him, "Transfer of Intellectual Property? The day you hired me?"

"Okay, sure. What about it?"

"It doesn't apply to my accident, does it?"

I could tell he was trying to look legally introspective, but was stumped. I helped him out with, "When I was knocked unconscious by a speeding car as I was leaving my last job?"

"Of course. *That* accident. Wham! By the Brit. Remind me: was it hit and run, and did she settle?"

"No and no. But what I'm wondering was whether the T.I.P. covered things like my hospital stay or my work at Klein Wallpaper & Paint." This supposition, deliberately inane, playing to the dimmest of Kirby's brain cells, had been rehearsed with Alex over the weekend.

"That's what you're worried about? Don't be! By intellectual property I mean what happens here, stays here." He grinned, proud of his TV-commercial-retention.

"Can you give me an example, just to be safe?" I asked.

When that didn't prompt an answer, I tried, "Maybe like what the White House housekeeper told you about the tanning bed, and the ex-Pence aide who didn't like saying grace over the donuts and coffee at staff meetings?"

"Yes!" he said. "Yes! Things like that. Razor-sharp memory."

I put a star next to the first-choice tweet, ripped the page out of my notebook, handed it to him, and said I'd better get back to work, such as it was.

On a drizzly morning, a week after Melania referred to her husband as a little boy, dressed this time more formally in a black suit, ruffled white blouse, sunglasses and a red fedora — inspiring much speculation as to what message a crimson hat was sending — the First Lady met with a high-profile Manhattan divorce lawyer, famous for her mendacity and her press conferences.

The lawyer wasted no time appearing on the *Today Show*. Would this be as bad for Donald Trump as the *Access Hollywood* tape had been for him, two months before the 2016 election, the lawyer was asked.

She tried not to smile. "Do you mean the (bleeped) quote? We don't concern ourselves with possible political fallout." She also managed a straight face when answering the question about her client's financial wellbeing. "Ms. Knauss isn't the slightest bit worried. She can support herself again in the kind of lifestyle that had attracted Donald Trump in the first place."

The anchor noted that the future first lady had met her husband at the Kit Kat Club in Times Square. "That kind of lifestyle?" she asked, eyes on her clipboard. The lawyer continued, unfazed, "If she had to go back to work, to modeling or fashion or moisturizers or using a new skill set gained at the White House, such as planning state dinners, she is ready, willing and able to make her own way."

Next anchor question: "Does that mean the pre-nup is not going to provide much of a cushion?"

"I'm allowed to say that Mrs. Trump's pre-nup was redone by my firm in the run-up to the 2016 election."

"Rumored that she was paid to stay until the 2016 election when he'd lose for sure?"

"Surely you don't expect me to breach attorney-client confidentiality?"

The anchor said, "No. Understood. Let's move on to custody."

"Full custody, since the child's father has no interest in fatherhood."

There was no mention of adultery; no mention in that particular interview of the fatal prescription made out to Herman Trump. Yet someone had decided that the front page of the *Daily News* was the most fitting way to let the world know that the Other Woman was Veronica Hyde-White, O.D. I woke up to a text from my mother that was the *Daily News* front-page, its headline screaming: **OPTOME-TRYST!**

It was accompanied by a photo of Veronica, from her website, showing her in a white lab coat, standing before a display of frames labeled Dolce & Gabbana, looking enough like Ivanka to inspire daddy-love ridicule. Also on page one of the *Daily News*: a photo of the president squinting myopically.

The doctor, reached at her office, neither confirmed nor denied the affair, but insisted she did not leak a word to the *Daily News*. Only an idiot would position herself as a homewrecker. "Ask yourself this," she said. "Who gets to hold her head up high as the wronged woman? Who's chuffed now? Who's wearing the halo? Not me."

Three days later, the first lady herself explained what she knew, how and when. On *Fox News Sunday* she told Chris Wallace what "Herman Trump" meant, using the Slovene slang for penis — hardly a euphemism since the word was "dick." Yes, she'd been the contractually obligated Good Wife who'd stomached the porn star, the Playboy Bunny, and the fourteen other accusers and plaintiffs. She'd had to put a public face on those relentless, post-partum humiliations. But this, at 1600 Pennsylvania Avenue, the people's house? Enough! *Dovolj!* Dr. Veronica Hyde-White was — translated from Melania's "*kurba!*" — a whore too far.

29

AN EXCELLENT IDEA

I'D HAVE CHARACTERIZED our Saturday night dinner with Elizabeth and Yasemin as "casual" — merely pizza — except for their self-congratulatory toasting of the relationship they believed to have micromanaged.

Alex said, "I might've gotten it wrong, but I'm prit-tee sure I asked Rachel for her number before—"

Yasemin, shaking her head, eyes closed for emphasis, said, "Which never would've happened if I hadn't insisted we go to the store after she mentioned she found the man behind the counter attractive."

Elizabeth said, "And I was the one who staged the phony vermouth errand."

Alex asked me, smiling, "Are these two your parents?"

I said, "Just my life coaches."

"We have the advantage of being completely objective," said Yasemin, "due to no conflict of interest."

"Being lesbians," said Elizabeth.

Alex said, "I recall that."

I gave my room-mates a look meant to convey, isn't there anything else to discuss besides the fruits of your matchmaking sideline? Yasemin caught it, because she said, "Boy, what do we think about Melania calling it quits thanks to the woman who ran Rachel over? How many degrees of separation does that make us from the affair?"

"Two," said Elizabeth. "Rachel is one."

"Do we think the optometrist will be the next Mrs. Trump?" Yasemin asked.

I said, "No. A fourth wife? A fourth pre-nup? Doubtful."

"But a wedding in the White House is a good look. Didn't Nixon marry off one of his daughters there?"

Elizabeth picked up her phone and in seconds reported, "Tricia. 1971, to Edward F. Cox. In the Rose Garden."

"And meanwhile, another aspiring bride is shopping for—" I stopped. "Sorry, forget that. It's about a related couple having an affair that's supposed to be off the record."

"Related to whom?" asked Elizabeth.

"C'mon," said Yasemin. "You want to tell us. Out with it!"

I said, "Okay. Have I said, 'cone of silence' yet?"

"Not in the last half hour," said Elizabeth.

"You don't know these people, but here goes: Dr. Veronica is married to Simon, who's allegedly in love with their real-estate agent, and vice versa—"

"Man or woman?" asked Elizabeth.

"Woman."

"Named?"

"Mandy."

"Do we think it's payback?" asked Alex.

"His or hers?" Yasemin asked.

"According to Mandy, neither. It was all fine because the Hyde-Whites have an open marriage."

Yasemin seemed to speak for all three with, "I must say, I'm underwhelmed."

"Have you talked to this Mandy since the whole Veronica-Trump-Melania thing blew up?" asked Elizabeth.

I said, "I haven't. She's gone silent. Maybe Simon isn't rushing to divorce court. I'll give it a little time and then call her."

"You're too nice," said Yasemin.

"Not a bad quality," said Alex.

Elizabeth said, "I just had an idea. An excellent one." She tapped her wine glass with the pizza cutter. "I'm just noticing what a good time we're having. It's feeling like family."

Yasemin said, "I think I know where this is heading."

Elizabeth picked up her phone and pointed to the calendar icon. "It's November sixteenth. Is everyone else thinking *let's do Thanksgiving dinner here?*"

Apparently not. Finally Alex asked, "No one's going home?"

"This is home. I'm not welcome at my parents' house," said Elizabeth.

I said, "My parents are expecting me."

There was a kick under the table, presumably Yasemin's, which I translated to *invite him to go home with you, you asshole.*

Alex, seeming to sense a silent negotiation, volunteered, "My brother and his family host Thanksgiving. My dad and I will go there."

I said, "Alex lost his mother in June."

"How awful," said Yasemin. "I'm so sorry."

"But how nice of your brother and his wife," I said.

Alex said, "This is not a judgment, but . . . my sister-in-law is vegan."

"He sounds so sad, doesn't he?" Yasemin said.

"What if you had an alternative?" Elizabeth asked.

"Does your father need you there?" Yasemin asked.

"As long as I can work Wednesday and Wednesday night, I don't think he'd mind if I missed the actual Thanksgiving meal . . . such as it is."

Both my roommates had their eyes open wide, silently petitioning me. Did they not know that a man doesn't want to meet a woman's parents when he's having sex with her in a time frame they'd consider premature?

"Then you'll come here," Yasemin announced, "so you don't have to have quinoa as your main course."

I coughed, meaning *him? Without me?*

Elizabeth asked how big a deal my parents made of Thanksgiving. Big crowd? Aunts, uncles, cousins? Customs?

"The custom is . . . we go out to a restaurant."

"That settles it," said Yasemin. "Rachel will stay in D.C. Alex will come, and so will the Kleins."

I checked to see how Alex was taking that. Quite well, it seemed. I asked him, "Is that too much too soon?"

"She means meeting her parents," said Elizabeth.

"Got that," he said. And to me: "Think they'd come?"

"In a minute," I said.

Obediently, I went straight to my bedroom, called my parents at home and reached my mother. She announced that she and my dad were giving *Game of Thrones* a try.

"Can you pause it? I have a quick question."

"Kenny — pause it!" my mother said. "It's Raitch! Okay, I'm listening."

"Would you and Daddy consider having Thanksgiving in D.C. with me and my room-mates?"

"You don't want to come home?"

I knew her; knew which card to play. "Elizabeth can't go home.

Her parents don't accept her." Yasemin had never mentioned her parents' position on either homosexuality or Thanksgiving, so I improvised. "And Yasemin is first-generation American. Her parents don't make a big deal about Thanksgiving."

"If we still had the house, they could both come home with you."

I heard my dad ask, "Who could?"

"Her gay room-mates, for Thanksgiving," my mother said. "She's inviting us down there."

"Are we saying yes?"

My mother said, "You know it's impossible to get train tickets this close to the holiday, let alone book a hotel."

"We'll drive!" I heard him say. "And we liked that Airbnb we stayed at when Raitch was in the hospital."

And even though my mother hadn't bought or basted a turkey, or even turned on an oven during any Thanksgiving of recent memory, I said, "You wouldn't have to lift a finger. Yasemin's a fabulous cook."

I heard a deep sigh. "If this is how we get to spend Thanksgiving with you . . . then, yes."

It was mean of me not to sweeten the deal, so I added, "If you can make it, you'll meet Alex."

"Alex?" my mother chirped.

"Yes, Alex. You in?"

I could tell she was trying to be as casual as such a maternal windfall required. "Now that I hear that Elizabeth isn't welcome at home — what is wrong with people? — and your dad and I can be the stand-ins who accept their lifestyle, of course we'll come. Does Alex not have a home?"

I said, "He's invited to one of his brother's."

"But?"

"But nothing. His brother would understand."

"What about his parents?"

"A father, widowed."

"Have you met him?"

"Just at the shop."

"He works there too?"

"He owns it."

Was I imagining an added lilt in her voice when she said, "You and Alex must be getting along very well . . ."

"We are."

"I won't ask for particulars because I don't want to be a stereotype. We'll come the night before if we can get there."

"Something tells me you'll get there."

"Kenny! We're doing this."

I said, "Good. Everyone's here. I'll tell them it's a yes."

"Everyone? Alex too?"

"Alex too."

My father yelled, "The screen just did that thing when you're on pause too long. Let her go."

"Love you!" she said. "Off to the ticket counter, metaphorically speaking!"

I returned to the kitchen and announced, "They're coming. Sorry it took so long — lots of questions."

"Such as why the rest of us were skipping Thanksgiving dinner with our own families?" asked Yasemin.

"Exactly."

"Were they cool about meeting Alex?" asked Elizabeth.

"I wouldn't use the word 'cool.' I'm sure they're already discussing how to act, how to treat him like a random buddy of mine."

"Except," said Yasemin, "he's an awful poker-face. They'll know."

Neither Alex nor I asked, "Know what?"

"I'll bring the wine," he said.

213

30

TABLE FOR SEVEN

AS THANKSGIVING DREW CLOSER, Kirby asked daily if I
were covered for the holiday, going home, cooking at home,
and if so, how big a turkey had I ordered? He loved Thanksgiving! He loved stuffing. He loved that cylinder of cranberry
sauce shaped like the can it came in. His mother always made a
Jell-O mold that had one layer clear green and another creamy
white-ish. How did she do that?

What else to do but ask my unhappily single boss to join us.

First, I'd gotten permission from Yasemin and Elizabeth,
who answered respectively and characteristically, yes and no.
I explained about how his daily Thanksgiving inquiries had
made me feel sorry for him.

"Does he know we work at DOJ?" asked Elizabeth.

Had I told him that? I didn't think so. "You're safe," I said.

Elizabeth relented, since it would be Yasemin doing most of
the cooking, with me helping to the best of my ability. I didn't

even have to check with Alex, whom I knew would welcome the opportunity to evaluate Kirby for brains, character and the degree to which he was taking advantage of me. I made a ceremony of the verbal invitation, knocking on Kirby's open door, and saying, "My room-mates and I are wondering if you'd like to join us for Thanksgiving."

His whole face transformed into a blend of disbelief and gratitude. "Really?" he asked. "Your room-mates invited me?"

"I guessed that you hadn't made other plans."

"Is it potluck? Because I'll bring whatever you need. And count on me for the wine."

This was the obvious time to tell him that we were set for wine because another guest, whose father owned Varsity Wine & Spirits, was also invited.

"Is it going to be a big crowd?"

"No. If you join us, we'll be seven."

"May I ask who the seven are? I mean obviously you and your room-mates and the wine guy or girl . . . named?"

"Alex. Plus my parents will be coming down from New York."

"I'll get to meet the parents who produced my ace assistant!"

It would be nice if I could've added, "Yes, and they're big fans of yours," but my mother was making her way through Kirby's canon, and judging it slapdash and banal.

"I shouldn't ask this . . ." he began. "But the guy?"

"Alex? Is he my friend? Yes."

"And friend means what I think it means?"

"Probably."

"What about your room-mates? Are they women?"

"They're a couple."

He said, "The two women are? That's fine. The more people I meet, the better." He made circles above his desk that seemed to denote widening ripples on a pond.

"Socially, you mean? Friends have friends?"

"As long as I make a good impression!" accompanied by a grin suggesting that the opposite was unimaginable.

I said, "You will. Of course you will."

"Maybe your room-mates would want to invite their bosses, too."

I didn't say, doubtful, since that would be the attorney general of the United States, which would lead to Kirby's asking for every last digit of every possible contact number. I said, "We're good with seven. Seven fits around the table."

"Is there anything else you want me to bring?" — asked in such hapless bachelor fashion that I said, "No, we'll be all set." I headed back to my desk, but returned to ask as diplomatically as I could, "Your kids have a plan?"

"Their mother gets them at Thanksgiving." He pointed to a photograph on the table behind him, the girls all in skiwear, snowy peaks in the background. "I take them skiing over Christmas."

I said, "Then it's a date. I'll email you my address."

"Doesn't Sandra have that in her files?"

Did either of us need Sandra wondering why Kirby was asking for my home address? I said, "Better not," then texted it to him on the spot.

Alex offered to pick my parents up at their Airbnb. "Without me?" I asked him. "Without ever having met them?"

"No big deal," he said.

As planned, the three of them arrived well before the scheduled 5 p.m. dinnertime so my non-cooking mother could pinch the ends of the green beans and peel whatever potatoes were on the menu.

I'd made the first lemon meringue pie of my life, which I'd

be serving on a pedestal cake plate I'd found on eBay. It wasn't picture-perfect, and the crust was Pillsbury's, but it was pretty darn handsome, with about half of its peaks the desired bronze.

My parents had brought bagels from New York — too many: a dozen for us housemates and a half-dozen for each male guest — plus cream cheese mixtures of various hues.

Alex, looking more dressed-up than usual, in a blue and white checked shirt, knitted tie, khakis, had brought a half-dozen bottles of wine. As my father the non-oenophile studied each label, I knew he was trying to think of decent questions to ask a wine insider. I helped by reminding him that he'd loved the movie *Sideways*. Hadn't he seen it twice?

"She's right! And let me ask someone who must know — did Paul Giamatti's character hurt Merlot sales?"

Alex smiled. "Only minimally, according to my dad. But it did a big favor for Pinot Noir. In fact, California growers call it 'the Sideways effect.'"

My father looked so delighted with this nugget that I could see him filing it away as a future conversational gambit. Then winking at me, which I interpreted as *aren't I doing great*, he asked Alex if he'd want to watch the Bills play the Cowboys, starting in five minutes. "Sure," Alex said.

Once it was just us women in the kitchen, my mother said, more tepidly than I expected, "He's very nice."

Yasemin, from the stove said, "Mrs. Klein? You can do better than that."

"I'm playing it cool," my mother said. "Besides, it's new ground for us."

I knew what she meant: I hadn't paraded many boyfriends past the parental grandstand.

Yasemin said, "He has our vote. We all find him very appealing, and we're a tough audience."

My mother said, "Definitely appealing. I mean, not by movie-star standards, but—"

I said, "Ma! What a shallow thing to say!"

Elizabeth asked, "Do you think your daughter is a movie star?"

It wasn't a question that would ordinarily make me laugh, but it did — it was so unadulterated Elizabeth. I addressed my mother, "They know Alex. They pretty much engineered it. They don't care if he isn't a movie star." And my room-mates, my voice lowered so I wouldn't be heard in the TV alcove, "She's not usually like this. She has better values than what's on display."

"Let's start over," my mother began.

Within minutes, that opportunity arose. Alex returned for a corkscrew and wine glasses. "Have I adequately expressed my thanks for your schlepping out of your way to pick us up?" she asked him.

"Happy to do it."

"It was my first ride in an electric car," she enthused.

"A lot of New York buses are electric," I grumbled. "But then again, when do you ever take a bus?"

"But a real electric car. It's so . . . clever."

"Clever for sure," Alex said.

Without giving away one syllable of the previous awkward exchange, Yasemin said, "Alex, you're looking particularly handsome today. Is that a new shirt?"

"And tie," he said. "J. Crew. Thank you."

"I agree," I said.

Yasemin walked to the refrigerator, opened it, handed bowls and containers to ally Elizabeth, and then, rather ceremoniously, brought forth my pie. "For you," she told Alex. "From Rachel. Isn't it a thing of beauty?"

"You *made* this?" he asked me.

"I actually did. Last night."

"Gorgeous," my mother gushed. "Who needs pumpkin and pecan?"

"We have those, too," said Yasemin.

Who knew that manufacturers of Christmas-themed sweaters made ones for Thanksgiving, too? And on six-feet-five-ish Kirby, it was an XX-large tableau of pilgrims and Indian chiefs.

Elizabeth asked, "Are you wearing that ironically? I doubt there were tomahawks at the table—"

"Let alone a table," I said.

"I am! I can't even believe I own this!"

As all seven of us had moved to the living room for the wine, the chicken-liver mousse, and the stuffed grape leaves, Kirby put his arm around my shoulders and announced to my parents, "You have quite the indispensable daughter here."

"We think so," said my dad. "And resilient. She gave us quite a scare, but then recovered like a champ from her accident."

"That accident, and holy smokes, who was driving! My mother used to sing a line from an old song, 'I danced with a man who danced with a girl who danced with the Prince of Wales.'"

We waited. Seeing mostly blank faces, Kirby said, "Her accident? Whose resume crosses my desk but the very person who was hit by a car driven by the woman who's sleeping with the president of the United States!"

"Oh that," said Alex.

"New York's all over it," said my mother. "Every move Melania makes is splashed on every cover. And if you ask me, she isn't trying to lay low. I had the honor of breaking the news to Rachel — right, hon? I sent you the front page of the *Daily*

News — that the optometrist who hit you was having an affair with the president?"

I said, "It's true. I woke up to it."

Elizabeth said, "I have zero sympathy for anyone who married Donald Trump. Gold digger! And I think even less of Ivanka and her flavorless husband whose father bought his way into Harvard, both working side by side with Trump, without security clearances. We're supposed to be impressed because they don't take salaries? Do they not realize there's life after the White House and they'll never live this down!"

Which is when my mother said, with a sly, life-of-the-party smile, "Shall we call her?"

"Who?" asked Kirby.

"Ivanka," said my mother. "Rachel has her number."

I'd never seen Kirby's face look less indulgent, more suspicious. "You have Ivanka's phone number?" he asked me. "Since when?"

"I have some random phone number that someone gave my mother, guessing it's Ivanka's. I haven't called it and don't plan to."

Which required my mother to explain that their long-time jewel of an employee, Mary-Jo, was converting to Judaism and taking what could be called Jewish lessons at the Kushners' synagogue, and while in the rabbi's study, an assistant handed him a phone number that made his eyes pop out.

"A number without a name," I pointed out. "It was probably the rabbi's mistress."

"Did you keep it?" Kirby asked.

I had. I shot my mother a look that said *not another word*.

Yasemin said, "The turkey's resting. Let's sit down and have the soup."

I'd figured out the seating earlier, and made place cards, putting Kirby opposite me, between my parents. My mother, as soon as we were all seated, mouthed "Sorry", and winced.

Alex, on my right, whispered, "It'll be fine."

Elizabeth was delivering bowls of soup and I rose to help, despite her protests. In the kitchen, ladle in hand, Yasemin said, "He'll forget about it by Monday."

I put a few bits of chopped chives on each bowl and returned to the table, two vessels at a time, the sight of which caused my mother to rise and retrieve two more.

Kirby said, with what I recognized as an apologetic smile, "Your boyfriend calmed me down."

Which part of that announcement to dwell on? The designation "boyfriend" or what Alex might've said that smoothed Kirby's hackles. I said, "Glad to hear that."

"He pointed out that Ivanka Trump was never going to answer a call or text from a strange number," Kirby explained.

Alex's expression was clearly spelling out, *do you believe he needed me to tell him that?*

I returned to the kitchen where my mother had been stalling, waiting for my return. "It just came out!" she said. "I think I was nervous meeting this famous man who's written so many books. I tend to prattle in front of a celebrity."

I said, "He's hardly a celebrity. And you meet them all the time! Isn't Tony Shalhoub a customer? And Bloomberg's girlfriend?"

"Yes! I'm sorry. Are you going to suffer for this?"

I said no; Alex seemed to have calmed him down simply by pointing out that some random caller — me — wasn't going to get through to Ivanka.

When we were all seated, napkins unfurled, I lifted my glass and said, "To our guests, who came from near and far."

"Some of whom had nowhere to go," said Kirby, and then to

his new buddy Alex, "How about you? Any relatives who'd have taken pity on you?"

Alex said, "I have many relatives, but this was the hot Thanksgiving ticket."

"Let's eat," said Elizabeth. "Yasemin's been cooking for two days."

Kirby apologized for having his phone on and close by. A few spoonfuls later, it was emitting one of his special rings. "Apologies," he said. "I should take this. It's a source calling."

It wasn't any source. I knew that train-whistle ring, and it was Sandra's.

He got his big self out of his chair and into a corner of the room where he paced for added effect. "You're kidding?" we heard. "Can you email me that exact quote, with a phone number? And I'll need another source before that can go into my book. Can you get me that?"

After a crisp good-bye, he returned to the table, smiling, but offering nothing. "Important?" I asked.

"Very."

"Can you tell us?" my mother asked.

Who was he trying to impress — my parents? His hostesses? Still I helped him out. I said, "Was it a White House source?"

"It was."

My mother said, "Imagine someone calling on Thanksgiving? Do these sources ever give you a moment's peace?"

"It's the life I lead," said Kirby.

I let that stand. I passed the rolls. An indispensable assistant wouldn't amend that to "He means the life he *wished* he led."

31

STATE OF THE UNION

WAS OUR DATING LIFE too sedate, too stay-at-home? Alex said no; hadn't we gone to the jazz club twice, to three nominated movies, and visited the pandas? It was a question I asked, especially in front of the TV, as we were this Tuesday in January, watching the State of the Union address.

Watching, yes, but close-captioned to spare us the applause that followed every sentence Trump uttered. Pundits had speculated whether he'd hold it at the Capitol at all, given the impeachment hearings and the fact that Melania would be absent. That night, in her stead, was de facto First Lady Ivanka in a yellow dress from her shuttered clothing line, and Tiffany in plunging ruffled red. Behind Trump, the vice-president was jumping to his feet, leading the standing ovations by the faithful. To his left, Speaker of the House Pelosi sat grim-faced but elegant in white, clapping occasionally for something that aided the poor, the sick, the female, the undocumented.

Alex asked me how political I'd been before working for Kirby. I said, "Not enough."

He said, "I've never asked, but did you *want* to work for Trump?"

I said, "No! I went on the dot.gov website and just kind of applied. To my shock I was hired. I looked at it this way: good benefits, an office in White House office — the office part of course was a pipe dream. And I thought, wouldn't it be interesting to see the hate mail Trump got? I'd be a spy in the enemy camp. And wouldn't 'Correspondence' look journalistic on my resume? Wouldn't there would be holdovers from Obama's correspondence team, just like there were the housekeepers and gardeners who stayed from one administration to the next? We'd be in the same boat. We'd exchange cynical looks." I demonstrated.

It was the most employment detail I'd discussed with Alex, because the Scotch-tape part of my tenure sounded like a job for the unskilled, like a project at an arts and crafts camp. I confessed, adding, "It was presented as a patriotic job — restoring things that belonged in the National Archives under the Presidential Records Act."

"So a typical day meant what?"

"I'd get there in the morning, go to my desk where there would be little or big pieces of ripped-up documents, each in their own plastic bag. I'd tape them back together. That's pretty much it."

Meanwhile, Trump's speech seemed to be winding down because the captions were showing, **God's grace is still shining, and, my fellow Americans, the best is yet to come.** (Applause.) **Thank you. God bless you. And God bless America. Thank you very much.** (Applause.)

And when he was done and every Republican jumped up for

their final ovation, Speaker Pelosi was methodically tearing up Trump's speech, one page at a time, for all the world to see.

"Ha," I said. "In the great tradition of Donald Trump. Finally they have something in common."

Apparently, that shared deed hadn't occurred to the president because one day after a majority of senators acquitted him of abusing his power and obstructing Congress, he told reporters, "I thought it was a terrible thing when she ripped up the speech. First of all, it's an official document. You're not allowed. It's illegal what she did. She broke the law."

Well, no. I knew that law.

In the unanimous take-away by all lawyers consulted by the news media, no one considered Pelosi's copy of Trump's speech an official one, and for sure not the pages headed to the National Archives.

So I tweeted, just for fun — or so I thought — to the followers I accrued after receiving get-well wishes from the White House: **@realDonaldTrump thinks @SpeakerPelosi 'broke the law' by ripping up his #stateoftheunion speech? Well how come I spent all day, every day, taping back together OFFICIAL documents mutilated by @POTUS? #SOTU #RipperInChief #hypocrite #WHORM**

I learned within hours that an efficient way to catch the president's attention, to get yourself branded "nasty" and blocked, is to call Donald Trump a hypocrite, a liar, and a chronic destroyer of official documents.

Did this make me famous? No. You have to be a celebrity or politician or office holder for people to notice or care. If you Googled, "Rachel Klein" you could find a dentist, a theater director, several PhDs, a novelist, a realtor, a judge, dozens of brides and a few obituaries. I was one among hundreds, thus either safely anonymous or utterly run of the mill.

Kirby told me he'd always hoped to catch Donald Trump's attention and be insulted on Twitter as I was. It would be excellent for his brand.

Was this my opportunity to thank Dougie for his good intentions and Klein loyalties? "Do you have a publicist?" I asked Kirby, "because I know a really talented one."

"My publisher has a whole team — marketing, publicity. Is that what you meant?"

I said, "No. I meant an image-maker, a branding expert."

"I've thought of it, but again — inertia. The divorce. Work. And if I can be honest, too much time out there trying to meet someone." After a twist of his mouth this way and that, he asked, "This spin doctor? How much would it cost me?"

I said, "Worth it, whatever his fees. Look him up. His website is really impressive. W-A-Y exclamation point."

He didn't answer; didn't jump on this tip with his usual gusto.

I said, "You want to get under Trump's skin, right? Wouldn't someone who's obnoxiously persistent be great at making that happen?"

"Obnoxious in a productive way, you're saying?"

"Totally."

"You know him personally?"

"Very well. Tell him you're my boss and throw in that you met Bev and Kenny Klein at Thanksgiving. His dad's worked for them my whole life."

Another pause, then "Do you think he has a friend-and-family rate?"

"You can ask, but—"

"Tell me why I need to pay someone to put me out there."

I could hardly say, "Because his father is sure he's doing me a favor, giving me the gift of Dougie. And my mother thinks I could make a name for myself as both an accident victim and an enemy of the president." I said, "He'd be like a motivational coach. Maybe he'd spot something in your life that he'd run with. He's big. You want to be noticed and insulted by Trump? This is a company that gets its clients on" — where? Did I know? — "television."

Kirby exhaled deeply, unhappily. "I have lots of interviews lined up this morning. Could you call him for me?"

I said as ever, sure, no problem. I returned to my cubicle, texted Dougie, **Good time for me to call?**

He texted back an hour later, **K**. After going through Jace, followed by a long, musical wait on hold, Dougie answered with "You're back in the news, my dad tells me."

"I'm not calling about me. I'm sending you a new client, my boss the author."

"You know I was only doing pro bono for you, right? As a hardship case?"

I said, "Right. Ouch. So you'll be glad to be rid of me. It's Kirby Champion. I've told him all about what WAY! does."

"Miss Rachel! You're sounding kinda take-charge. Has 'nasty' replaced 'I'm nobody?'"

Ignoring that, I said, "He's published six bestsellers. Up to now, he's used his publisher's publicity department for books, but I think you two would be a match made in heaven."

"Full fare, comprendo?"

"No problem. Should I have him call you?"

"Tell me something that will amaze him that I know, as if I've read his books or memorized his Wikipedia entry."

What would that be? It took me long enough that I was back on hold. He returned several unnecessarily long minutes later with, "Well? Anything I can run with?"

I said, "He's a patient of the optometrist who's shtupping the president. And they've seen each other socially. She asked him to advise her on her memoir."

"Holy shit! The eye doctor?"

I said, "I know. Pretty good, huh?"

"He's straight?"

"Definitely."

"Do you know if he shtupped her, too?"

I said "It didn't get that far." I added as an unearned testament to his character, "In this day and age a guy, especially a woke guy with a brain, doesn't confide in his female employee about who he's shtupping."

"So not an asshole? Not that I can't work with assholes."

"A big, goofy good guy," I said.

"He makes money writing these crappy books?"

I repeated, "Best-sellers. Big advances." *Or so I assume.*

"Put him on," he said.

I jogged across what I'd begun to call the arboretum, smiling victoriously. Waving my phone, I said, "It's the aforementioned Douglas Feinberg of WAY! He wants to talk to you." Though I continued to stand there in supervisory fashion, he waved me away. "Close the door behind you, please."

Well, that was a first. He'd always been so proud to have me stick around to hear him practice journalism. I returned a look of both surprise and phone proprietorship. What did Kirby have to say that I couldn't be privy to?

Nonetheless, I followed orders. Back at my desk I read the newspapers I scanned every day for potential intelligence. Kirby liked clips, so I read them old-school, shears in hand. What had I ever come up with that was put to potential use? Mostly names of staff fired by Trump, whom Kirby tried and inevitably failed to reach.

He returned with my phone after a longer interval than

I would've expected for an exchange with attention-deficit Dougie. "Smart guy," he said. "I think he's going to take me on. He must've read my reviews because he says I need authenticity."

"Did you tell him you're working on a new book?"

"I would've if we talked longer, or if I had more in the hopper."

More in the hopper? How about next to nothing in the hopper?

I took back the phone, not a moment too soon. Poor Kirby. His authenticity would have to wait. A text from Dougie arrived, only the letters **NFW**.

??? I wrote back.

no fucking way, he answered.

32

CALM DOWN, KLEIN

I USED "BRAINSTORM" as a verb in the email I sent Kirby later that night. "Tomorrow morning, first thing? I have an idea about where to go from here."

He wrote back, "I like those scones you brought from the bakery you pass on your way here. Ginger and apricot?"

I printed my notes when I got to work. It was a less-than-ideal set-up because what I typed upstairs spit out from the printer at Sandra's elbow, an arrangement seemingly designed by Kirby so he wouldn't have to collate anything himself. Though I wrote "Confidential" at the top of page 1, no such heading stopped Sandra from delivering the two pages with something of a smirk.

"'Meta'? That's your big idea? He won't know what you're talking about."

"I'll explain that it's like a movie about *making* the movie.

And he could just sit back and write about process without combing the earth for sources. Finally he'd be his own source."

I then asked the awkward question that was in her lane exclusively: "Will this operation stay afloat, if Kirby doesn't get a new contract?"

"Of course it will! What does he need? He has this beautiful office and a perfectly adequate apartment. His overhead is zero except for food and clothing and your salary."

"That's the part I'm worried about."

Wouldn't most people find something reassuring to say, especially one who controlled the purse strings? Sandra said, "I'm sure you understood that your job is subject to the vicissitudes of publishing. Now let's go take this meeting."

She and I sat across from Kirby as he read my proposal, frowning. When finished, he held the pages up by one corner as if contaminated. "Would this have to be a whole new book? Or could it be folded into 'The Blight'?"

"Folded in. Because it's about process," I said.

"It would be a memoir *about* process," said Sandra.

"Didn't I already cover a lot of details? My last book was over four hundred pages."

I said, "I was thinking of the story behind the story. That's what I meant" — I pointed to my second sentence — "by 'granular.'"

"Where you go, how you got there," Sandra said. "Remember the time you interviewed one of the Watergate Seven in prison, and had to drive through a hurricane to get there? I think it was a Category Three."

"She's like my brain," he told me.

"I keep notes," said Sandra. "I remember things that happened to Kirby that you might not consider pertinent, but I think the reader would find engaging."

"Such as?" I asked.

"Did you know he was a model for the Big and Tall Shops?"

Instead of batting that away, Kirby nodded proudly. "A loooong time ago. Before I got into the writing game. I had a thirty-two, thirty-three-inch waist. Did you know that the ideal waist size should be half of your height?"

I said, "Very interesting. What else?"

"Sandra?" he prompted.

"Junior year abroad in Berlin when the wall was still up."

"Crazy!" he enthused. "I mean scary. You didn't go near that thing. But the best cakes I've ever eaten. Black Forest — if I see it on a menu here, I always say, save me a piece! They tend to run out."

Was Sandra hearing what I was hearing? Did these examples have any merit, or did the scorned-woman side of her want this man-child to publish something asinine?

I asked, "How personal would you want to get? I mean — marriage, divorce, the daughters? A memoir these days is expected to be a tell-all, don't you think?"

"It will be," said Sandra.

That stumped me, until she added, "It's about time he wrote about Nancy's philandering."

Oy freakin' vay. News to me.

Kirby asked, "Is that what my readers want to hear about? Klein? What do you think?"

"I think . . . if you're comfortable writing about your ex-wife . . ."

"I wouldn't say 'comfortable.'"

"How about 'therapeutic'?" Sandra snapped. "How about, 'it's about time'?"

"I wouldn't want to embarrass my daughters, though."

"Your daughters! As if they're not ninety-nine per cent in Nancy's camp already!"

What was wrong with this woman? Was there not one euphemism in her vocabulary?

"Would readers think my marriage and my ex-wife's affairs are what I mean by 'The Blight'?"

"It won't be called 'The Blight'," Sandra said. "The new title is so obvious: 'A Champion Life!' The flap copy will say, 'How Kirby Champion's books get written, and the story behind them. Success, fame, heartbreak, the good and the bad; being alone by choice."

"No one's alone by choice," he muttered.

Sandra said, "I think you know what I'm referring to."

And so did I. I stood up, took a scone from the bag I'd brought, and said, "Maybe you two should discuss the rest, the private stuff, in private."

Sandra said, "Thank you."

Kirby gave me a pleading look, which I matched with a silent, cock-eyed plea to be spared. He pointed to the chair I'd just vacated. I knew why he needed me to stay. Left alone, Sandra might argue her case, remind him of the bond she thought they forged at a long-ago homecoming weekend.

I retook my seat. "So," I said. "Back to 'Blight 2.0'. Let's not forget the goal is process. How Kirby writes, researches—"

"How the sausages get made!" he boomed. "What floats his boat!"

"I myself would be very interested to plumb those depths," said Sandra.

"But I don't want to sound like a bitter, divorced guy. I want to sound like a nice guy who's not going to spend an entire first date talking about his terrible ex-wife. I'd rather write about new stuff. That can be granular, right?"

"What new stuff?" I asked.

"What you brought! If you hadn't shown up, I'd never have met Veronica!"

Which one of us was going to point out that meeting Veronica meant nothing, that anyone who'd ever booked an appointment or paid her bill had more in common with Dr. Hyde-White than Kirby did.

I said, "But . . . what has that amounted to?"

"How many people have sent her flowers and asked her out, like, two weeks before her affair with Trump went public?" Immune to the depressed silence around him he added, "She's still practicing, isn't she? I've decided to stop using over-the-counter reading glasses and get a prescription." He added a happy wink. "From a *doctor of optometry!*"

Usually I just took it in, committing to memory the ill-considered thoughts Kirby spoke aloud. But this time, emboldened by the sheer inanity of his observations, I said, "Kirby! You're forgetting this went nowhere. Worse than nowhere! You acted inappropriately and she threw us out of the office!"

"Calm down, Klein. That rejection happened before she knew who I was!"

Even though Sandra seemed to be recoiling along with me, she said, "I believe this new direction is a really good use of your talents and your memory."

What horseshit. He had neither talent nor retention of anything that would make a memoir interesting, let alone sellable. I said half-heartedly, "I'd start taking notes. A journal could help. Ever kept one?"

"Never was tempted. That's my day job. I'm not going to go home at night and write in a journal."

"Which is what I do," said Sandra quietly. "I could let you read it."

"Me?" I asked.

"No, him."

Kirby said, "I'll do this much: I'll run this idea by my agent. What's the title again?"

"'A Champion Life'. Or 'A Champion Tells All,'" Sandra said.

He asked us if we thought every word of a memoir had to be written by the memoirist himself.

"I could contribute," said Sandra. "I feel in many ways that it's my story, too."

Her story, too. I felt an unexpected wash of sympathy for her and her unfulfilled romantic quest.

And was it me having this aberrant thought, in terms of Kirby's social life, "What about Sandra? Is she so bad?"

33

NEXT SHINY OBJECT

DESPITE BEING ENTIRELY distractible, Kirby remembered that I was in possession of what might be Ivanka Trump's mobile number, cadged from a rabbi's desk. He buzzed me on the intercom, that dinosaur of technology he favored, and said, "The time has come for you to call her."

"And say what?"

"For starters, you mention that you were on the guest list for the Passover thing."

Please, I said silently. *Please no more about Ivanka or her alleged phone number or anything I have to claim because it's Jewish.*

"Klein? Reaction?"

"First — very hard to believe I'd ever been on a White House Seder guest list. No one knew me!"

"What if you called her, all chummy, and were like 'Hi

Ivanka, rabbi so-and-so gave me your number. Is the White House Seder still on?"

How long could I put this off? I said, "I'll do it tonight. Catching her at home will seem more social . . . more chummy. Okay? Bye."

The intercom squawked again. "I'm not the kind of boss who gives an order, but c'mon. What's the worst that would happen? She doesn't answer and doesn't call you back? Nothing ventured, nothing gained."

My dad had supplied the very answer to "What's the worst that could happen?" He'd called me when he'd had a moment alone, worried about my mother's breezy mention of my being in possession of Ivanka's number. He read aloud, then emailed me a paragraph from Wikipedia that said "mobile phone microphones can be activated remotely, without any need for physical access. This 'roving bug' feature has been used by law enforcement agencies and intelligence services to listen in on nearby conversations."

He added, "Not just on Ivanka Trump's line, but on yours! Sorry to bring it up, but you were fired for insulting her father. I don't want the police or the FBI knocking on your door asking why you were calling the president's daughter. Or worse, have them raid your apartment at five in the morning."

I tried this out on Kirby: "I'm not a citizen in good standing. You know how easy it is for the government to be bugging my cell? Well, the FBI might not like me calling the president's daughter."

"As I said, I'm not a boss who gives orders . . . but what's wrong with 'Hello, I'm Rachel Klein, who got this number from your rabbi, etcetera.' And use your middle name if you have one that's equally Old Testament."

In fact, I did have such a middle name — Naomi — but I said "No, no middle name. So let me get off and try her."

"Good luck, Nasty! Lead with the White House Seder, and remind her that you're the injured party, literally; that you were run over as you were leaving the building, too upset to look both ways. Okay. I'm staying on the line."

I said, "You're on the intercom. I'm calling from my cell. I'll report if she picks up."

Within the thirty or forty seconds it would've taken him to get up and jog to my cubicle, he had planted himself eavesdropping distance from my desk, with one finger tapping his lips. "Not a peep," he said.

I pretended to open the page in my contacts that would presumably say "Ivanka Trump," and dialed my parents' apartment where no one would be home.

I nodded with each ring then whispered, "Got her voicemail." "Mrs. Kushner," I said. "My name is Rachel Klein. Rabbi Manischewitz gave me this number. First, I want to thank you for the beautiful tulips you sent me in the hospital. And second, can you let me know if the White House Seder is still on? Shoshana may have mentioned me to you." I dictated my cell and office numbers, ending with, "Thank you. Shalom."

Kirby was grinning. "All bases covered! Good job. Now let's see what happens."

"Okay. Back to work," I said.

He didn't leave. I said, "Speaking of work, I've been meaning to ask you when your deadline is for delivering the manuscript."

"I make my own deadlines," he said. "We're finished when we're finished."

"But you must have an idea when everything has to go out."

If ever I heard him winging it, it was with, "How does Memorial Day sound? Or Flag Day?"

I said, "It sounds close. Are you and Sandra brainstorming?"

"We're not exactly on the same page."

"Literally or figuratively?"

"She wants more memoir and I want more 'Blight.'"

"More Trump, you mean?"

"Yes! Like a Kirby Champion version of *The Final Days*. I get a sense he's yelling and screaming and talking to portraits, post-impeachment."

"A sense from your sources inside the White House?"

Usually the topic of that dry well made him look pained, but not this time. With a grin he asked, "What about the Hebrew teacher? Wouldn't she have some pull?"

"Pull for what?"

"Getting you to the Seder! Wouldn't she be the first person Ivanka would consult?"

"No! She'd go straight to the RNC and ask for the biggest Jewish donors."

He started his retreat, but returned. "Are you and your roommates having a Seder?"

"Doubt it. Why?"

'Here's my new idea and it may be brilliant: If you don't hear back from Ivanka, you invite the Hebrew coach to *your* Seder."

I said, "Kirby, let me explain. Any Seder I tried to pull off would be amateur night, attended by non-Jews, i.e. my roommates, Alex—"

"And me?"

Oh, brother. "Okay, you too . . . But believe me, Ivanka's Hebrew coach is probably going to a Seder at the home of some chief rabbi, where they recline, where their Haggadahs came over from Gdansk. I'm sure she has her choice of hosts — my mother says she's the hottest thing in the whole field of bar mitzvah coaching."

He smiled. "Hottest how?"

"Over-booked. In demand. A waiting list a mile long."

More silent cogitation until he asked, "What's that other thing you do on Friday nights?"

"Shabbat?"

"Yes. How about Shabbat? Like next Friday? Do you think the coach has all her Shabbats booked?"

I allowed this much: "Let's say Ms. Gottlieb *did* accept an invitation to a Shabbat dinner at my apartment — which she won't. What's my goal?"

"Dirt! After a couple of glasses of wine she might let loose about Trump. Maybe he got talked out of bringing up the Holocaust at Hanukkah, but he wanted to! Isn't that bad enough? Maybe he's going to try again the first night of Passover." Kirby was on his phone, presumably Googling, because after a pause he added, "Or at Purim. You never know what she wants to get off her chest. That's my guiding principle: you never know who's disgruntled. You never know who wants to vent. I think an invitation would be appreciated. You and she are both New Yorkers. Sisterhood is powerful, right? I bet she's suffering under the chef syndrome."

"Which is what?"

"No one invites them to dinner parties, and especially never to a home-cooked meal. Their friends are intimidated. What do you cook for a chef? So what I'm saying is that this Shoshana might not get invited to amateur Shabbat dinners because people think she has too many invitations, plus how good are they at being Jewish compared to her?"

I said, "I have to figure some things out."

"Like what?"

"Like how observant she is. She might not eat anywhere that isn't kosher. Plus, who says I can even get in touch with her?"

Then, my usual, guilt-inducing, "Back to work, right? No time to waste."

What I meant by work was Googling Shoshanna Gottlieb, looking up Shabbat protocol, emailing Yasemin about catering such a dinner, and telling my mother to ignore and erase the long-winded voicemail I'd left on their landline. I felt no guilt at all, devoting Champion time to arranging a future dinner party. Wasn't it, after all, Kirby-bidden, 'Blight'-related, eventually circling back to big-fish Ivanka? Pointless and improbable? Sure, but wasn't that what I was getting paid for?

34

COME FOR DINNER

I EMAILED SHOSHANA via her website, with *Rachel Klein thanking you!* in the subject line, followed by a sycophantic paragraph about her kind attentions to my possible anti-Semitic sacking. I asked if she'd known that I'd been knocked down by a big German car, driven by the now-confirmed paramour of Donald Trump, then immediately doubted the wisdom of mentioning Trump's adultery. Why did I think I had to remind a religious woman about broken commandments? Thirty-six hours later, an answer arrived, a mere *How did you hear about that?*

Which thing? I took a few minutes to consider what to say, decided on *Did you mean your rallying to my cause?*

Yes. Who told you?

Had Lorna or anyone else at BuzzFeed sworn me to secrecy? I didn't think so. I wrote back, *BuzzFeed.*

That was on an anonymous tip line!!!!

I wrote, *You included your phone number.*

For BuzzFeed. Not for them to throw around!!!

Should I end this now or challenge it? I reminded myself of the goal — a debriefing dinner. *But your tip involved me. That's why I'm thanking you. After you told BuzzFeed to look into the last Jew fired by the White House, they came up with me.*

What do you want? she wrote back.

Though feeling way less than hospitable, I wrote, *I'd like you to join us for a Shabbat dinner some time.*

Who's 'us'?

My room-mates, my boyfriend, my boss.

The next morning she named two dates. I wrote back, *Wonderful! Let me check with my people & confirm ASAP. Food allergies?*

She sent a capitalized list: *EGGS, BROCCOLI, DUCK, FRESH (AS OPPOSED TO CANNED) TUNA, VINEGAR, PINE NUTS. NO PORK, NO SHELLFISH.*

I sent the proscribed foods to Yasemin, who wrote back, *What kind of crappy challah is made without eggs?*

I wrote to Shoshana, confirming a date and asking, *A regular challah ok, i.e. made with eggs?*

Her answer sounded like another scold: *Of course regular challah ok.*

One more question: Anyone you'd like to bring?

She wrote back, *No! But if you know any eligible men between 35-60, I'm game.*

Well that certainly didn't sound as pious as I would expect from her. I clicked on "images." She was stunning in every shot, with dark, layered, tumbling hair. She favored a pose where her hands were on her waist, as if to emphasize its admirably small circumference. I knew from Wikipedia that she was thirty-eight, twice married. Her second husband had been a rabbi famous for taking up with married female congregants, of which she was one. She'd coached sons and daughters of movie stars, including a child of Jerry Seinfeld's and a great-grandson of Abe Vigoda.

Did I really have to invite Kirby to this staged Shabbat dinner? I sat at my desk, wishing I worked for a writer who had better instincts, better reviews, whose work had weight, whose demeanor was serious, whose suits weren't loud. Inevitably, and with little else in the way of work, he buzzed me, asking if I'd followed up with ShoShana and was dinner a go?

I said, "Didn't I fill you in? She's getting back to me about a date." And for further dissuasion: "I'm sure you know that at Orthodox shuls the sexes don't mingle, so maybe it's best if it's just me and my room-mates."

No, he did not think that best. He needed to speak to her himself. It's settled: he was coming. "I have a yarmulke some-where, from my ex-agent's kid's bat mitzvah. And I know a few Yiddish words."

"Such as?"

"L'chaim!"

"That's Hebrew, but sure. It'll fit the occasion. Any others?"

"Something might just pop up that I'm not remembering this second."

I said, "Be careful, though. You don't want to look like you're pandering."

A half hour later he texted **Shmuck!**

Who? I wrote back.

Nobody. It just popped into my head!!

I sent back a clapping emoji, hoping we were done.

Elizabeth wanted to know why I thought Ivanka Trump's Hebrew coach should be fed and/or feted.

I said, "Don't mention this at dinner, but she's proven she's not loyal to Trump. Kirby thinks, if wined and dined, she'll sing."

"Disloyal how?"

I told her about the main thrust of the BuzzFeed tip — that Trump was going to inject himself into Hanukkah.

"So? Don't they all do that, pander?"

"Not like this; not just 'I'm wishing my Jewish friends a happy holiday.' He was going to say how much the holiday meant to him because his grandparents came to America, fleeing the Nazis."

Yasemin yelled from the living room, "Idiot-in-chief!"

Elizabeth said, "Wait. Did he actually do that?"

"Someone must've talked him out of it. The math alone is ridiculous — his Lutheran grandparents came over in the 1870s. So BuzzFeed didn't run with it."

"But *you* are?"

"Sort of. Kirby loves it. Thinks there has to be a lot of animosity there if she left a tip on a tip line."

"Kirby loves everything," Yasemin yelled. She returned to the kitchen with her laptop open and resting on her forearm. "Chicken with apricots, caramelized onions and cardamom rice," she announced.

"Sounds great," I said.

"Think it's okay if I found it under Ramadan entrees?"

"Even better," I said.

"You'll get the challah Friday morning before they run out," Yasemin instructed.

Elizabeth, speaking over running water at the kitchen sink said, "I think one of my grandparents was Jewish."

"*Think?* You don't know?" I asked.

"He never said he was, but all his relatives were buried in a Jewish cemetery."

"Which would be persuasive, if only the end result wasn't Ms. White Bread, here," Yasemin said, nonetheless blowing a kiss in Elizabeth's direction.

I asked Elizabeth why she'd never told me this before.

"When have we ever discussed religion?"

"Or had a Shabbat dinner?" said Yasemin.

"What was his name?" I asked.

Elizabeth looked stumped.

"Your mother's maiden name?"

"Coffee."

"With a K? Probably changed," I said. "Kaufman? Either way, it could be a nice topic to bring up at the dinner if there's a lag in the conversation."

"Lizzie's specialty: the non sequitur," said Yasemin.

"Think this woman is okay with" — Elizabeth motioned back and forth between her and Yasemin with a wet hand.

"Meaning gentiles or lesbians?" I asked.

"The latter."

"See what her parents have done to her?" said Yasemin. "She thinks everyone's a homophobe."

"No worries. The vast majority of my people are very pro-gay," I said.

"Maybe *she's* gay," said Elizabeth.

I said, "Married and divorced twice. Hinted that she was in the market if I knew anyone."

"Doesn't sound very holy," said Elizabeth.

"You know what she'll think when we're all seated and paired up?" asked Yasemin. "That you're setting her up with Kirby."

What a thought. I said, "Her last husband was a rabbi. And she's probably twenty-five years younger than Kirby."

"He's a man," said Elizabeth.

"Kirby's kind of charming," Yasemin said. "Am I the only one who thinks that?"

Elizabeth said, "He takes up a lot of oxygen, I'll give him that."

Yasemin had to be Googling Shoshana because she asked, "Did he invite himself? Because I must say, she's quite the knockout!" She turned the laptop around for us to see the smiling line-up of tightly belted Shoshanas.

"Will Yasemin have to cater their engagement party, too?" asked Elizabeth.

Alex said he could get Walter to work for him the Friday night of Coach Gottlieb's visit.

"Have I met Walter?"

"You'd remember if you had. We call him 'the world's greatest authority.'"

"On?"

"On every vineyard, every grape, every bottle. He visits and studies the merch even when he's not working. Big plus: he's retired, so he's free and willing whenever we need him."

"We'll need Kosher wine, but don't go overboard."

"Kosher wine is one of Walter's sub-specialties, along with everything else." Side by side in bed, he gave me a nudge. "Can I give him a thrill and tell him they're for a dinner with Ivanka Trump's Hebrew coach?"

"You don't think he'll ask what that's all about?"

He didn't answer as quickly as usual, and when he did, it was more serious than I was accustomed to. "If Walter asks me why I need wine for Ivanka Trump's Hebrew coach, I'll say, 'I'm in love with a Jewish girl who's invited me to a Shabbat dinner.'"

Was that said in jest? Did the "in-love" part count when embedded in a hypothetical conversation? I hesitated, not wanting to jump the gun with my own declaration, so I asked, "Did you mean *this* Jewish girl?"

"The naked one in my bed? Ms. Klein? Yes."

I said, very carefully, "I hope you know she feels the same way."

C'mon, he was prompting, *not good enough; say it.*

We'd been lying on our backs, shoulders touching. I sat up and faced him. "I think I fell in love with you when you rang up that first bottle of Prosecco, the day Kirby hired me. Isn't that crazy?"

With some laborsaving app on his phone, he made the room go dark. "Come here, you little meshuggeneh," he said.

35

SHABBAT SHALOM

Kirby arrived first, wearing a gray pin-striped suit, a dark tie, a white satin yarmulke. Yasemin took his coat and said, "You're looking très distingué!"

"For a change, you mean? I'm trying to look like a rabbi," and then with a wink, "I know she likes them . . . Is she here yet?"

She wasn't. So far, just fifteen minutes late. Alex had come straight from the store, once again with an over-abundance of wine. At the twenty-minutes-late point, I asked our assembly, "Think she's coming?"

Yasemin said, "What was that movie where the owner of the restaurant cooks his heart out, thinking Frank Sinatra is going to show up?"

"Louis Prima," said Elizabeth, after a quick Google. "*Big Night*. They need him to save their restaurant."

Alex offered to go downstairs and flag her down, should

that car that had circled the block twice, slowly, be hers. As the rest of us waited, I reminded Kirby: easy on Ivanka, at least for starters. Shoshana might hate Donald Trump; hate his turning his back on New York and especially his Hanukkah bullshit, but we should tread carefully.

Kirby said, "Fine with me. I'll follow your lead," earning a look from Elizabeth that said *what else is new?* A few minutes later, we heard voices coming up the stairs, then Alex entered with a comedically wide-eyed look, Shoshana behind him bearing a bunch of gargantuan gladioli.

She wasn't as youthful or as pretty as her posted photos, but she surely knew how to advertise her banner attributes. There were luxuriant false eyelashes, scarlet lipstick, laminated eyebrows, and — after her coat was removed — protuberances above her low neckline that spoke of an assertive push-up bra.

Introductions followed. When we'd circled back to Alex, she said, "I already met your charming boyfriend, but I didn't catch his last name."

"Dekker," he supplied.

I could tell by the narrowing of her eyes that Shoshana was calculating the Jewish content of those syllables.

"It's Dutch," he said.

Kirby volunteered, "I had the good luck to be born into the Champion family."

"Champion of what?" she asked.

"Champion. That's my surname."

"First name again?"

"Kirby."

That landed. Would she run out the door, feeling cornered by a notorious muckraker, or welcome the company of a best-selling somebody? It was clear in seconds. She said, "Well, well, well. Kirby Champion."

I said, "Let's go into the living room. Yasemin left work early to make some beautiful things."

"Without garlic or vinegar," Yasemin added. "Rachel filled me in."

Alex said, "If you're allergic to vinegar can you drink wine?"

"Smart question," Shoshana answered, "and the answer is yes I can."

"He's a pro," I said.

"In what way?"

"My father owns Varsity Wine & Spirits on Rhode Island."

"Do you work there?" she asked.

"I do."

Let me translate: I knew many Shoshanas. Some were from New York, but there was a nagging familiarity to these interrogatory tactics, shared with many of my southern belle college friends, masters of the subtle inquiry into religion, nationality and income.

I said, "I'm Kirby's research assistant. And both Yasemin and Elizabeth are lawyers."

"In private practice?" she asked, running a carrot stick through the baba ghanoush.

Elizabeth said, "No. In the public sector."

"Mere civil servants," said Yasemin.

After more wine and more crudités, I led everyone to the table, its centerpiece a large gleaming challah, and asked Shoshana to do the honors. She closed her eyes, waved her hands, recited the blessing, trancelike. "Amen," I said.

"Amen," echoed everyone else, Kirby's the loudest and most cantorial.

We started with a beautiful ginger-carrot soup. Shoshana stared at her bowl; didn't pick up her spoon until she'd asked what the main course would be.

"Chicken! So no dairy, if that's why you're asking."

"You're kosher?" Kirby asked.

"I *keep* kosher." She smiled. "But otherwise I consider myself a very modern woman."

I'd scripted my toast in advance. First the welcome and thanks for the hard work of this Sephardic feast. Then, "And a special welcome to Shoshana, who knew of me before I knew of her and cared about how I lost my job" — pointing to the challah and candles as if they spoke for all dispossessed chosen people.

Elizabeth added, "Rachel was a wreck. Mentally and physically. That firing did a job on her."

The "physically" required an explanation, so I did a quick summary of the accident, the broken ribs and concussion on my way out the door.

Shoshana turned to Alex, on her left. "Do you know what percentage of men stay with women after they've been disabled or diagnosed with a terminal disease? A shockingly low number!"

I said, "I don't have a terminal disease."

Alex said, "I met Rachel after she'd fully recovered and had started her new job—"

"As my research assistant," Kirby said. "A brilliant hire on my part."

Shoshana said in first-date fashion, with a full-body turn toward him, "Tell me why."

"Because she'd been fired by the Trump White House! I wanted resentment and attitude! I hoped she'd be holding a grudge."

I said, "It's true. My C.V. said I'd left the Trump administration as a matter of conscience."

"Hear, hear," said Shoshana.

"Did *you* quit?" Elizabeth asked.

"It doesn't work that way," Shoshana said. "I serve at the pleasure of the president's daughter."

"Quite the client," Kirby said.

"What's your official title?" asked Elizabeth.

"I like 'consultant.' I think 'Hebrew tutor' or 'Hebrew coach' is limiting, but I'm hardly going to tell Ivanka Trump what to call me."

Kirby leaned sideways, bumping shoulders with Shoshana, and said, "I bet a lot of bar mitzvah boys would love to have you as their coach," he oozed. "I remember being thirteen, and whoa, it was quite the feverish state."

Oh God. Pivot needed. I said, "I understand you have a long waiting list for bar and bat mitzvah prep."

"I do. A lot of it is marketing. I call them 'star mitzvahs.'"

Alex said, "Rachel tells me parents sign their kids up when they're like six."

Her expression indicated that she liked that high compliment *very* much. And liked Alex very much, too.

Yasemin must've noticed the same admiring glance and thought *diversion needed*, because she posed the seeming left-field question, "How are you doing, Kirby?"

"How am I doing? In what way?"

"Emotionally. I mean, is the book in progress the first thing you've undertaken since your divorce?"

"You're divorced?" asked Shoshana. She gave his forearm a pat, then left it there for a few long seconds.

How to answer? I could see he was trying to walk the line between wounded and ask-her-out. He said, "Just about. I'm legally separated."

Shoshana volunteered what we already knew: she was twice-divorced and had been unhappily free for thirteen long months.

Elizabeth said, "Speaking of Ivanka Trump, I'm so repelled

by her values and her failure to walk away when her father—"

Yasemin, who'd been appointed most likely to speak of Ivanka neutrally and diplomatically, said, "She seems smart. Did she pick up the Hebrew quickly?"

"Language takes another part of the brain, which may not be her strong suit. I mean, Hebrew isn't easy, is it, Rachel?"

Uh-oh. Should I tell the truth? That I went to Sunday school at a Reform synagogue, not Hebrew school; can get by on the high holidays, but don't ask more than that. "For sure, not easy," I said.

"How'd you get this gig?" asked Elizabeth. "Did you know her before she drank the Kool-Aid?"

"I knew of her at Chapin," said Shoshana.

"*Knew* her or knew *of* her?" Kirby asked.

"Knew of. We didn't overlap. We had mutual friends, who proved useful."

I remember thinking if I hadn't already sized Shoshana up, the phrase "proved useful" clinched it. "Useful how?" I asked.

"Way back, when she and Jared got engaged, I wrote to her at Ivanka, Inc., pitching myself as a fun Hebrew tutor, explaining why she should learn Hebrew for real, not just getting by at shul."

"Do you think her alleged success in business would've been the case if her name wasn't Trump?" asked Elizabeth.

That seemed to be Yasemin's cue to stifle Elizabeth. "Everyone sit. Lizzie and I are going to clear the bowls."

"Wait'll you see Yasemin's chicken," I said.

"And taste it," said Kirby. "She's a brilliant cook. Being alone, I was very fortunate to have Thanksgiving dinner here, and meet Rachel's charming parents, the Kleins of New York."

"What do they do there?" Shoshana asked.

I told her: Klein Wallpaper & Paint.

She said, "Coincidence?" with a nod toward Alex.

"Coincidence how?" I asked.

Her expression seemed to be asking *What's not to get?* "You and your boyfriend: children of store owners."

I was too puzzled by her statement to answer, but Alex said, "*Exactly*. We met at a store owners' kids' convention last year. I asked her to dance and that was that. We danced every dance together, even when other store owners' sons tried to cut in."

I sensed Kirby had withstood enough attention paid to me and Alex, when he steered us back to, "Obviously Ivanka signed you up for those lessons."

"She wanted to meet me first, which was something I'd suggested. We had tea at the Plaza."

"That first meeting must've gone well," I said.

"At the Plaza? Are you kidding? They danced attention on us."

Yasemin and Elizabeth were making an entrance, jointly holding our largest platter bearing a splayed chicken, laden with fruity embellishments.

After preferences were announced — white or dark meat — and the pilaf and asparagus had been passed, gracious hostess Yasemin said, "Tell us more about *you*, Shoshana."

Her spine went erect as if it were the spotlight she'd been waiting for. "Where to start? I'm on my own, piecing together a living. Bare-bones alimony. That marriage was a mistake, more so than my first. But what good does hindsight do me now?"

Kirby asked, "Is your first husband still in the picture?"

"He's still single, but furious. He was secretary-treasurer of the synagogue where my regrettable second husband was the rabbi. It was quite the scandal. I mean, the *New York Post* got a hold of it. Hirsch had been married three other times, all to congregants."

I asked, "Did that notoriety bother Ivanka when it came time to choose a Hebrew consultant?"

"Ivanka? Things like marital scandals and public divorces don't bother her."

"It's pretty obvious she doesn't say boo to her father . . . unless she *does* and we don't hear about it," said Elizabeth.

"I'm the soul of diplomacy," Shoshana said. "I rarely comment on his politics."

Kirby was coughing out some syllables behind his napkin, which I finally recognized as a guttural "Hanukkah."

With that cue, I asked if she'd be okay telling our tablemates about what Trump had wanted to say to American Jews on the first night of Hanukkah.

That was exactly the right irritant, apparently. Shoshana closed her eyes. "I will, though it sickens me. Believe it or not, he was going to say that the Festival of Lights was so *so* meaningful to him because his grandparents had fled Germany to escape the Nazis." She opened her eyes and blinked rapidly.

Though everyone present had heard this several times, we all gasped. She was holding a drumstick, punctuating her account with small, feral bites. "He asked for my help with learning the blessing. He could've asked Jared. He could've asked any number of people. I mean, why me and not a grandkid or Steve Mnuchin? I wrote it out phonetically, in English, before I knew what he was planning! And before I knew he was a low-functioning reader."

She paused to recover from even that sad truth, and so did I, not out of sympathy but because she'd just held up a figurative cue card that said, "Enter Dr. Veronica Hyde-White." I couldn't let this opportunity pass, but I thought I'd give Kirby the first go. I sent a bug-eyed nod his way, hoping he'd translate it to "ask her about the optometrist! Now!"

"Delicious, as always! Clearly you have a knack for poultry!" he gushed.

"Thank you," said Yasemin. "But let's get back to the president and his offensive use of the blessing—"

"On that topic," said Kirby, smiling, "may I state the obvious?"

"Which is what?" Shoshana asked.

"You said 'why me?' when there were so many others of your faith who could teach him the blessing. I mean, look at you."

Oh God. Well, *Oh God* for most of us, but apparently fine with Shoshana.

Elizabeth asked, "Did Trump flirt with you? Or grope you?"

"I find that refreshing because people don't usually ask me those sort of questions, assuming I live a religious life. The answer is yes."

"To which thing?" I asked.

"It started with him saying 'I didn't know Hebrew coaches could look like models.' I shrugged it off. He's seventy-three. He sees all women as either models or not models. He's not going to change now."

"Did you tell him he was crossing a line?" asked Elizabeth.

"He's the president of the United States. Was I supposed to stay, 'How dare you pay me a compliment?'"

"Did he ever do anything actionable?" Yasemin asked.

"We're off the record, right?"

Kirby said, "Noted."

"Well into the lessons, maybe the fourth or fifth—"

"How many lessons does it take to learn a Hebrew blessing?" Alex asked.

"I told you — he has enough trouble with English. Anyway, next time I met with him, he hugged me, a little too long and a little too close. I tried to pull away but he's big."

"That's assault," said ever-sensitive feminist Kirby.

I asked if she'd reported the protracted hug to Ivanka.

"I certainly did. I was very upset. Supposedly, she charged into the Oval Office and said, 'Dad, that was my Hebrew coach you groped. I thought you weren't doing that any more.'"

Noting what looked like a coy, pregnant pause, I asked, "Is that all?"

"I hate to repeat it."

"Sure you can," said Alex.

"Okay, when Ivanka mentioned I was upset, he just smiled and said, 'You mean the hot Heeb?'"

We five uttered a chorus of "No!" and "You're joking!"

"Unfortunately I'm not. And you might be asking yourselves, why would Ivanka repeat something so hateful to me?"

"Adding insult to injury," said Kirby.

"Or maybe she was saying 'Do something! You have to help, because I can't!'" Shoshana said.

"Then why does this have to be off the record?" Alex asked. "Don't you think she repeated the slur precisely so you'd get it out there?"

"By which he means *here*, among friends," said Kirby, his hand now on Shoshana's forearm.

"But you know how the news cycle works. 'Hot Heeb.' Two words. They'd have been forgotten the minute Melania took off."

"That was big," said Kirby. "I dropped everything to watch her vamoose."

I asked Shoshana if Trump's unwelcome advances were contiguous with his taking up with the optometrist.

"For sure. He probably came on to her the same way he did with me, like 'I didn't know optometrists could look like models,' except she went for it. If you're insecure, you respond."

"You think she's insecure?" asked Kirby. "Because to me, she seemed just the opposite."

"You've met her?"

"I'm a patient," he said.

"Maybe you should explain the circumstances," I said.

"Or *you* could," he said, and then to Shoshana: "Klein's a detail person and I'm not."

I said, "When I told Mr. Champion that Dr. Hyde-White had taken up with Trump, he made an appointment with her to get the lay of the land."

"For new frames," he explained. "Though I have twenty-twenty distance vision."

"It didn't go so well," I said.

"But I did get to spend some time with her. She bears a striking resemblance to Ivanka, don't you think?"

"By design! She wasn't born with blond hair or silicone implants!"

I asked if she'd ever spoken to Veronica at the White House, perhaps diagnostically, since she'd noticed the president's visual issues.

"Whatever it was — vision, comprehension, dementia — I didn't concern myself with that."

"Did you know what was going on between the two of them before it blew up?" Yasemin asked.

"Let's say I suspected."

"And that wasn't creepy enough to make you quit?" asked Elizabeth. "You continued to coach him?"

Shoshana repeated, "He's president of the United States."

"Wasn't there some talk of a Seder?" asked Kirby, sending me a proud nod.

"It was discussed. But Trump was against it because the Obamas had a Seder every year."

"What made you suspect the president and the optometrist were hooking up?" Yasemin asked.

"He's not subtle! Plus he's loud! And she'd come out of the Oval Office looking a little too smug."

"Did you and Ivanka discuss it?" I asked.

"Ivanka saw that quote-unquote romance coming a mile away. Whoever heard of an optometrist who made house calls?"

I said, "I'm going to ask you a question now that you might not want to answer."

"Try me," she said.

"Did Ivanka specifically ask you to leave that tip on Buzz-Feed?"

"No."

"You did it unilaterally?" asked Elizabeth.

"Here's what I was picking up: Ivanka would've liked all the anti-Semitic embarrassing stuff to be in the *Washington Post* and/or *The New York Times*, but I never heard back from either. Only from BuzzFeed. And that went nowhere."

"When was Hanukkah again?" Kirby asked.

"December, right around Christmas," I said.

"And he never actually got to say that his grandparents died in concentration camps or whatever malarkey was going to be his fireside chat?"

"True, he never said it."

"I've found that places like the *Times* and the *Post* don't report things that were only happening inside someone's head," continued Bachelor of the Month Kirby. "If you'd have called me, I'd have run with it. I take chances."

"Good to know," said Shoshana, smiling.

At some point over almond cake and tea, she said she'd arrived by Uber and perhaps should summon one again.

"Out of the question. I have my car," said Kirby, extending his plate for another slice.

"If you wouldn't mind, I'd like to call it a night," said Shoshana. "Shall we?"

We got their coats and said our goodbyes. Once they were safely out the door and down the stairs, Alex said, "As a guy, and at the risk of getting booed—"

"Way to go, Kirby?" Elizabeth provided.

36

NONE OF MY BUSINESS, BUT

KIRBY CAME INTO THE office Monday morning with an unmistakable swagger. I said, "I don't want to know."

"I'm not that clueless, Klein. I only stopped by to thank you for an awesome evening. I'm going to write to your room-mates, too. Or maybe you can ask them if the chicken was made with — what's it called? — Persian lemon?"

"Preserved lemon, and the answer is yes." I didn't ask who wanted to know. I told him I was working, always a safe escape, rarely prompting "on what?" lest it shine light on our marching in place.

"I guess I should get back to work, too," he said, then reluctantly, "I'll be in my office."

Didn't I owe Alex, Elizabeth and Yasemin a follow up? We'd discussed the mating dance after the two lovebirds had departed. I buzzed him five minutes later, and said, "Work-related questions. Do you have a minute?"

"Of course. Everything okay?"

"Everything's fine—"

"But?"

"Re Friday night—just needing a sense of what I should know before I follow up with Shoshana."

He surprised me. "Klein! Nothing happened! She's not even forty and made up like a hooker! I mean, I have my limits. If she threw herself at a much older goy who's not even divorced yet, she's desperate. I don't like that. Did I ever tell you that more than a few women I swiped right on text me naked pictures? I don't answer. I delete them. What if someone with an axe to grind got hold of my phone?"

I said, "But you were so Johnny-on-the-spot when it came to her ride home. As soon as she mentioned calling an Uber."

"You know why? Because I didn't want your boyfriend to make the same offer. I don't mean he had designs on her, but he has good manners and a car. I wanted to get ahead of that."

Was such thoughtfulness out of character, or had there simply never been another opportunity for him to display it? I was confident that Alex wouldn't have made such an offer, nor missed the postmortem, but still, what a sweet and paternal gesture. "Very kind of you," I said. "Really thoughtful."

"Didn't you feel the desperation? The flashing neon sign that said 'looking for my next husband!'"

"The body language! Talk about unsubtle!"

"You don't know the half of it."

Suspecting he'd tell me the whole of it, I waited.

"First thing, she buckles her seatbelt, then tells me that she misses the days of one long bench seat without a gearshift separating the driver and the passenger."

"Uh-oh."

"No kidding. And then she gave me the perfect out, the perfect reason to say, 'not so fast.'"

"Would that be . . . a move?"

"Klein — I can't. I don't want to cross a line."

"Yes you can. We're so past that. Use euphemisms."

"Okay, as long as I have your permission . . . and please know that I'm blushing at this end when I tell you that she reached for me."

"For a kiss?"

"No. To a private place."

"Just like that? No warning?"

"Just like that! I said, 'Shoshana! No! This isn't the right approach for me.'"

"Wow. How embarrassing for her."

"You think so? Well how about 'Don't tell me you're a dinosaur?' I asked her what that was supposed to mean, and she said, 'That you're from a generation who thinks the first move is always the guy's.'"

"And she thought calling you a dinosaur was going to give her a green light?"

"Look. I have manners. I stopped her hand, but didn't bat it away like I was afraid, or offended, or gay. She's a source. And I'm very low on sources."

I said, "Does that mean . . . you went with it?"

"No! She invited me in for a nightcap, which is when my good judgment kicked in again."

"So you declined?"

"I asked for a raincheck."

"What kind?"

"Dinner. That's how we left it."

"Mañana, or on the books?"

"Tentatively set for Wednesday. I'm going to have Sandra book us a table at Pardon My French."

What to do? I said, "Kirby, can I come over and talk to you for a minute?"

"Sure! But if it's about too much personal chitchat and how that's not appropriate, I'll put a plug in it right now."

I said, "No, just the opposite."

Our tête-à-tête, as close as I can reconstruct it:

Kirby: Are you giving notice?

Me: No, no. Don't worry.

Kirby: Sit. Sit. I got nervous. You were looking so heart-to-heart.

Me: It's definitely a heart-to-heart. So let's dispense with all the *is this too personal? Are you going to file a grievance? Are you quitting? Is this sexual harassment?*

Kirby: Because I've been the victim of that. Once burned . . .

Me: Someone sued you for sexual harassment?

Kirby: It didn't go as far as a formal complaint, but it was threatened. And it was a long time ago, before that was a thing. But let me say in advance: It was harmless. And she started it.

Me: She who?

Kirby: I'd rather not say.

Me: Not Sandra?

Kirby: Definitely not Sandra.

Me: Was it a research assistant?

Kirby: Correct.

Me: (Silence, nothing.)

Kirby: Okay, just so you won't build this up in your head to actual terrible-guy behavior: she was always making references to my height, and once, when she asked me what size shoes I wore, I answered in a Trumpian way I shouldn't have.

Me: Got it.

Kirby: I'm a good guy. I have three daughters.

Me: I don't hear that much about them. I don't even know their names.

Kirby: (Points to one of the photos behind him.) Georgia, Becky, Claudia. (Sighing.) They blame me for the divorce. You don't have to be Dr. Phil to figure that one out.

Me: But Sandra said the break-up was your wife's idea.

Kirby: Trust me. Even when the wife wants out, even when she's the adulterous, guilty party and the one who asks for the divorce, she still poisons the kids.

Me: I'm sorry. But you took them to Utah. That was good, right?

Kirby: It's getting better. Claudia, the baby — points to the third in line, who has to be at least eighteen, and six feet tall — is wearing her sisters down. I agreed to take them to the Galapagos next vacation. I could care less about iguanas, but at least two of them are dying to go there.

Me: So maybe you could fill Sandra in on this progress.

Kirby: (Shrugs.)

Me: I've been giving Sandra some thought. Don't you think she was really helpful and supportive at our meeting about the memoir?

Kirby: She's still on that.

Me: Aren't you?

Kirby: I'm jotting down stuff, trying to be autobiographical. It's not fun.

Me: I hope you know I wouldn't feel left out if you and Sandra had private meetings so she could help you recover some memories. Have you read her journal yet?

Kirby: If you were me, would you want to read Sandra's journal?

Me: I know what you mean. But maybe she'd edit it first; take out the really personal stuff, like Hillary Clinton did with her emails.

Kirby: I liked Hillary. Did I ever tell you that I was at a dinner party with the Clintons once, and I asked her if she ever thought she'd run for office herself, and she just laughed. I said, "Like governor of Illinois, or senator. Aren't you from Illinois?"

Me: Practically clairvoyant.

Kirby: I was hoping I could write a book about the first First Husband, but we know how that went.

Me: You could go through Sandra's journal together. That way, whatever needs to be—

Kirby: You're going soft on her.

Me: Maybe just realizing she's not so bad.

Kirby: Not much of an endorsement.

Me: I'm thinking that if you ever gave her an inch—

Kirby: You're not the one she's been in love with for a couple of decades! You're not dragging that behind you! I can't give her an inch. Where do I go from the first inch? Lunch? Dinner? A valentine? When is Valentine's Day, by the way?

So he knew what I was trying to do, to point him in the direction of the not-unattractive Sandra and — win-win — thereby improve the climate at work? I asked the related social question: "Did you really turn down Shoshana's advances?"

"I did. I have a rule: beware of fast women."

When I laughed, he asked why.

"You're having dinner with her. That's not exactly renouncing the fastness."

There was a rap on his door followed by Sandra's unbidden entrance. "If this is a meeting about A.C.L, shouldn't I be in on it?"

"A.C.L.?" Kirby repeated. "I can't even remember how long ago I had that surgery."

"No: 'A Champion Life.'"

In the weary voice he used almost exclusively for addressing her, Kirby said, "It wasn't about the next book. If it were, you'd be in on it."

The unspoken question, judging by the narrowing of her eyes, was, *Then what* was *it about?*

I said, "We were discussing food."

"Whose?"

"Mine," I said. "I was telling him about a recent Shabbat dinner. He likes to hear things about other cultures, right?"

"For sure," said Kirby. "All cultures."

Sandra said, "I'd like to experience a Shabbat dinner. Is this a weekly occurrence?"

Did Sandra think that the way she treated and spoke to me was normal social intercourse; that she'd earned an invitation to a Shabbat dinner or any other form of in-home hospitality?

"Does your silence mean no it's not weekly? Or no I wouldn't be welcome?" she asked.

Was it out of the question? I wondered. My team could meet and appraise the famously cranky Sandra. They'd heard me hypothesize about a Kirby-Sandra detente that could benefit all parties, if only she could defrost, and he'd stop tilting at busty windmills. Wouldn't it be interesting to see her in a setting that might set her on the path to cordiality? And if Kirby were there, the Kirby who flirted involuntarily, might his hand slip onto her forearm to emphasize a point?

I'd roast a chicken myself, buy a challah, a sponge cake, some hummus; not impose again on Yasemin. I found myself saying, "If it's good with my room-mates, how about a week from Friday?"

37

SHABBAT REDUX

I EXPLAINED TO YASEMIN and Elizabeth that dragon lady Sandra had expressed interest in a Shabbat dinner—

"Too bad," said Elizabeth.

"Not again," said Yasemin.

"This isn't a Shoshana-level event. I'd do all the cooking. I'll roast the chicken, mash some potatoes, and buy a challah."

"You'll want some color on the plate," Yasemin advised.

"Carrots?"

"Or green beans. I can coach you through a recipe I make with shallots and lemon zest."

I waited the ten seconds it would take for Yasemin to amend that to, "Or I'll make them."

"When is this dinner?" she asked.

"A week from Friday."

'Do I have to attend?" asked Elizabeth.

"Of course not," I said.

"Agenda?" asked Yasemin.

"Okay. As you know, Kirby can't help trying to win over and charm whoever's on his right—"

"Forget it," said Elizabeth. "He hates her. He went for Ivanka's horny Hebrew coach."

I told them that they might think more highly of Kirby if they knew he'd rebuffed Shoshana.

"Not here, he didn't," said Elizabeth.

"In the car on the way home when she went straight for his crotch."

"While he was driving?" asked Yasemin.

"Probably when he pulled up to her place, because she asked him up."

"Did he tell you why he wasn't game?" Yasemin asked. "Not that we endorse such conversations with your male employer."

"He said he avoids fast women."

"Which he defines as . . .?"

"Hand job instead of a handshake? Or, get this: women send him naked pictures of themselves — and he doesn't answer!"

"How'd we get from there to Shabbat redux?" asked Yasemin.

"It's my own fault. Kirby and I were having the above conversation — Shoshana the predator, the naked texts — when Sandra barged in. She thought we might be talking about the book and were leaving her out. I said um, no, of course not . . . we were talking about food of other cultures."

"And she happened to say 'Just when I was thinking I wanted to experience a Shabbat dinner?'" asked Yasemin.

"Kinda . . ."

"Surely you said no; it was a one-off and it was staged," said Elizabeth.

"You're talking to Miss Beta," said Yasemin. "When Sandra says 'jump,' Rachel says 'L'chaim.'"

* * *

Sandra looked as attractive as I'd ever seen her. Instead of her accustomed velvet headband and pageboy, she'd fashioned an updo with tendrils framing her face. Did she wear eyeshadow weekdays? Her lipstick was a shade that matched bits here and there — some coral beads in her necklace, some flecks of orange in the wool of her sweater. She conducted herself in a state of graciousness that almost made me take her aside and ask, "Is the mean Sandra merely an act?"

She'd brought a bottle of Pinot Noir, modestly announcing that it came from Alex's father's store, not a coincidence; she'd heard me talk about the service there so positively. By the way, a very knowledgeable and attentive sales consultant had helped her choose this bottle, which he described as gorgeously fruity.

"Had to be Walter," Alex said.

"I believe it *was* Walter."

"Has he waited on us?" asked Elizabeth.

Alex said, "A handsome older gentleman? Very knowledgeable. Very big on California reds."

Sandra continued in the role of model guest. She complimented a framed MoMA poster of an Edward Hopper painting, the jasmine hand-soap in the bathroom, and a souvenir ashtray from the 1960 New York World's Fair that held our remote control.

After Kirby finally arrived, and with the oven timer pinging, I led the party to take their seats at the table. Yasemin followed me to make sure I didn't carve the chicken before it rested. When we joined the others, Kirby was narrating what he seemed to think was the met-cute story of the two step-siblings.

"He's wrong," Sandra said, but indulgently. "We already knew each other by the time that wedding happened because it was our parents getting married, my father to his mother."

Elizabeth asked, "How old were you when your parents married each other?"

Sandra said, "I was in high school and Kirby was in college."

"I think I was at my peak," said Kirby. "I was a good-looking fella, wasn't I?"

Who would say that to the woman whose life-long crush had sprung from that very event?

Sandra said, "All my friends thought so."

"She met her future husband at *my* wedding, right?" Kirby said

"Not by accident," she murmured. "They put Bruce and me at the table of the unattached."

Of course it was Elizabeth who asked, "What happened to Bruce?"

"He died eleven years ago."

Condolences all around, a fitting time for me to go religious and introduce the challah. Since the evening had been billed as a cultural exchange, I pedagogued my way through blessings over the half-burned candles that were leftover from the Shoshanafest, over the fruits of the earth and the vine, followed by English translations.

Sandra was looking not only attentive but absorbed. I asked, "Have you never been to any kind of Jewish celebration before?"

"I've been to a Jewish wedding, but probably not a model for the form."

"How so?" Alex asked.

"The bride had converted. The groom's parents were there, but they didn't join the receiving line."

"I think my grandfather was Jewish," Elizabeth said.

Kirby, ever affable and communal, said, "Sometimes I think that too."

I asked, "That your grandfather was Jewish?"

"Just a sense. He looked Jewish, and his name was David."

That caused a bristly silence until Alex said, "Let's all be Jewish tonight!" raising his glass, clinking his against mine.

Sandra said, "Because I live alone, I don't usually drink with dinner. But I'm reconsidering."

Alex said, "We deliver. Six or more bottles. You live in the District?"

Sandra said, "I think I'll be doing my shopping in person. My visit tonight was like a mini-workshop."

"Excellent to hear. I'll tell Walter."

"Is he full-time?" she asked.

Alex said, "No, but he's my number-one back-up."

"A real stand-up guy," said Yasemin, who'd never met or heard of him.

Trying to sound casual, as if it were totally for my own edification, I asked if Walter had a wife or a partner.

"Walter is not currently married," Alex said. "Which is lucky for us because he's often free to fill in for my dad or me."

Less than interested, Kirby said, "I'm the designated driver. Too bad."

"Not 'too bad I have to drive Sandra home' I hope?" she said, in an unmistakably genial, even teasing tone.

"Nope. Just that I'm limiting myself to one glass."

Alex turned the bottle around. "Sandra brought this beauty and I brought back-up. If it's okay with the hosts, you'll take one of the extras home."

"Okay with me," I said.

"Shabbat swag," said Yasemin. "Fine with me, too."

Kirby said, "Then I accept!"

The chicken, thanks to Yasemin's thermometer, was done just right. The mashed potatoes garnered many compliments, prompting me to explain that I'd made them with olive oil instead of butter and milk, which led to a short tutorial on the non-mixing of dairy and meat in kosher homes, which we weren't.

Sandra said, "Everything is delicious. And I'm very impressed that three young ladies sharing an apartment have a dining room."

"We are, too," said Yasemin, "though it's really just a table taking up half the living room."

"Then a dining *area*. Still impressive."

"Do you have a dining room?" Elizabeth asked.

"I had one. I turned it into a gym."

"Wow. How'd you do that?"

"Nothing extraordinary. A treadmill, an elliptical, a recumbent bike."

When no one else followed that up with a compliment, I said, "No wonder you look so fit."

"Thank you. Before my husband died, we had dinner in the dining room every night."

"You cook?" asked Yasemin.

"Very plain food. Not like this," she said. "My green beans would be steamed, and the potato baked."

"Nothing wrong with that!" said Yasemin. "I just saw a recipe in the *Times* where you put yogurt, ginger, onion, cilantro, cumin on the potato after you split it. Voilà, Punjab potato!"

"I'd like that," said Sandra. "It sounds good enough for company."

"For sure," said Alex, and with that excused himself, explaining it was a quick check-in to see how things were at the store.

"He pretty much runs the show," I said. "His dad only works days."

"I'd like a son," said Kirby. "I mean, not now. It's too late. And I love my daughters, but I could've gone for a fourth."

"No guarantees," said Sandra.

"And no interest from the wife, if you know what I mean."

Luckily, Alex returned, smiling. I said, "All good?"

"Unusually busy. We'll have to do a lot of restocking tomorrow." He turned to Sandra. "I hope it was okay for me to tell Walter that coincidentally one of tonight's guests was a new customer."

"Oh my," she said.

"He asked if the customer's name was Sandy. Do you ever go by that?"

"I believe I introduced myself that way," she said.

"I told him I thought you'd be returning for another crash course on another grape."

"I intend to."

"Are you playing matchmaker?" Kirby asked Alex.

"Nonsense. I always call in." He winked at me. "Especially on Shabbat when I can't be there."

"Has Walter always worked in wine?" asked Sandra.

"He's always been a wine buff. Something of an authority. But I believe before that he was a college professor."

Was that true? I thought he'd been a high-school chemistry teacher. Regardless, it had the right effect on Sandra, who asked, "Do you know where he taught?"

"I should know. I'll ask him. Or you could."

Kirby said, "I want to toast what sounds like a productive night at the store." He reached around Sandra to clink glasses with me, telegraphing *We should've had a dinner party with your boyfriend months ago*, "Here's to — what's the name of the establishment?"

"Varsity Wine & Spirits," said Alex, "family-owned and operated."

Elizabeth said, "Months ago, Yasemin and I pushed Rachel

out the door to go make nice to Alex at the cash register. And look where that ended up."

Sandra said, "Let's not get ahead of ourselves."

I said, amazed that I meant it, "I have a very good feeling about this."

Sandra said, "Is Walter of the Jewish faith, by any chance?"

"I think he goes to church," said Alex.

"It just seems so . . . how to say this without jinxing anything, arranged by a higher power — this being my first Jewish holiday."

It wasn't a Jewish holiday, but so what?

No wonder Alex's customers were stocking up. It would turn out that this less-than-sincere Shabbat dinner was our last social gathering in The Time Before the Plague. If I had fully grasped the apocalypse ahead, we'd have dined at as many restaurants as we could afford during the next ten days of unmasked nonchalance. Most of all, I would've hopped on a still-uninfected train to visit my parents, and to bid goodbye to Klein Wallpaper & Paint, for what would be its final, unshuttered day in the city I might never see again.

38

LOVED ONES

I INSISTED ON PAYING RENT at the apartment, an amount easy to manage because I was still drawing my salary, and Alex wouldn't take a penny. Considered essential, Varsity Wine & Spirits was thriving; curbside pick-up had begun the third week in March, and proved to be a boondoggle. Father and son didn't like to say it aloud, given the hard times all around, but business-wise, it was better than Christmas and New Year's combined.

I continued to work, or at least to put my fingers on a keyboard. Alex drove me and picked me up. And since the layout of Champion Inc. was already socially distant, there was no reason to stay home. Sandra didn't leave her first-floor station, even turning the watering of her indoor garden and its accompanying paraphernalia to me. Kirby was speaking his memoir into a digital recorder from his private quarters, in bed. In deference to Sandra's corona diligence, he played his recorded reminiscences over the intercom, which she transcribed, took editorial liberties with, and — thankful for my inadvertent matchmaking — shared some of the most Kirbyesque passages with me.

I didn't have anything to do, but I looked busy, writing down the most farcical exchanges I'd had with the likes of Mandy, Simon, Veronica, Shoshana, and (without naming him) Kirby. Did I have a goal in the form of my own memoir? I did not. But such records might come in handy when headhunters asked what I did in the employ of Kirby Champion and why I was moving on. As my attorney room-mates had implored me, after experiencing Kirby for the first time, "Write everything down."

I worried about the people I loved dying. I came up with reasons — age, occupation, underlying minor or major conditions — for everyone to be high-risk. Varsity was crazy-busy, the orders huge — a case of red! a case of white! a gin, a vodka, a scotch, a bourbon! — so that Alex was working long hours. I worried most about him getting sick, not being able to breathe, getting intubated, me not being able to visit him at the hospital. His father and Walter were also working full-time plus; all hands on deck. Did Alex use sanitizer and disinfectant after every transaction? What about the delivery guys, bringing the merch? Were they, whom I couldn't quiz, in masks and gloves too? Were people trying to pay with cash? Did he wipe the bottles down before stocking the shelves? "Of course," he said, which I knew meant, "if that's what you need to hear."

I had vivid dreams — I was back in the hospital, but this time on a ventilator that looked like a humidifier. My parents were there, resembling their younger selves in their wedding album. My hospital room was a double, and my favorite nurse, the kind, tall man with the shaved head, was in the next bed.

My dead grandparents, one from each side of the family, were praying at the foot of my bed.

I packed myself a sandwich every morning and three more for Alex, for his dad, for Walter — a silent entreaty to dine in place rather than ingest germs from unsanitary take-out places, heretofore not the slightest health risk. Obediently, indulging the worrywart I'd become, Alex took his temperature twice a day, following the example of Dr. Anthony Fauci, who advised me so compassionately from the man-sized TV in Alex's living room. Varsity Wine stayed open till 10 p.m., Monday through Saturday. I waited up for him every night.

I decided to check back at long last with Mandy Cullinane, pretending I was asking from a journalistic perspective, how the field of real estate was coping. Any showings, open houses, sales?

Mandy said she was furloughed and self-containing at her condo.

"With Simon?" I asked.

After some annoyed huffing, she asked "Who wants to know?"

I said, "I'm not working on a Trump book any more. My boss is now writing about himself."

"So you're just being nosy?"

That was true, but I couched it as current-events inquisitiveness. She was the fiancée of the president's paramour's husband, wasn't she?

Another silence, then, "I don't care if you *are* writing a book. I'd like the world to hear my story."

"About you and Simon?"

"No! That I'm suing Trump!"

I reached for my notebook and pencil. "You're suing the president? For what?"

"Alienation of affection."

I was Googling it as we spoke, then broke the news that it was only recognized in six U.S. jurisdictions: Hawaii, New Mexico, North Carolina, Mississippi, South Dakota and Utah.

"I know that! But he's president of all fifty states. I found a lawyer who's willing to take my case."

I asked if she could tell me which end of the alienation she was experiencing.

"Isn't it obvious? As long as Trump is keeping Veronica at arm's length during the pandemonium, Simon is technically a married man."

"Technically, but what about their famously open marriage? Doesn't that make Simon freer than most husbands in this situation?"

"Free? How about deported? How about ICE knocking on their door and dragging him off to jail?"

"Simon's in jail?"

"Only until they put him on a plane back to England!"

I said, "Wouldn't that have made the papers, given Veronica-gate?"

"It should've! I'm working on that. But it was a visa thing. His lawyer couldn't do anything. It ran out. He'd been pretty much in hiding — if you can believe someone like Simon could be considered undocumented!"

I asked if she was planning to join him in London.

"No one said London! He lives in Birmingham. Trip Advisor named it the dullest town in all of Europe."

I said, "You can't go by that. He must like it if he went back there."

"His parents live there. He's quarantining in their basement. The two weeks will be up in another four days."

"Then what?"

"I don't know. It's hard to reach him. He says their Wi-Fi is rubbish."

Or so Simon has convinced you, I thought. "Maybe, when the world is safe again, you'd join him?"

"I can't just pick up and move to England. They don't want immigrants any more! Imagine an American being viewed as an immigrant!"

Sociology thus filtered through the narrow mind of Mandy Cullinane reminded me of being on the receiving end of Kirby's stream of consciousness. What else to say but, "I'm sorry Simon can't be with you during this scary time . . ."

"Now do you see why 'alienation of affection' makes sense? Trump deported my fiancé out of jealousy. So write whatever you want. Or maybe *I* will. I'm bored to death and at the same time I'm furious." There was a long pause. "I'm making phone calls for Biden. You know who thinks that's a good idea? Veronica! She wants her boyfriend to be done with all these national headaches."

"She told you that? You two speak?"

"I designed a virtual tour of their condo, and she had to put in her two cents. How am I supposed to do staging during a lockdown? She thinks the headlines will help it sell — the country's most famous homewrecker."

I said, "So things with those two are still on?"

"They can't see each other right now. Or even speak. But she thinks he's sending her messages from the podium during his press briefings."

"How?"

"Whenever he uses the word 'heat' it's a signal to her."

What to say? Where to go from there? I asked, "Is Veronica still working?"

"She closed up shop, and she's bored. It's not like you can refract eyes remotely."

"Is she answering her phone?"

"Sometimes."

"Do you have her number handy?"

She didn't ask why, but recited it from memory, with gusto.

I didn't call Veronica immediately. I strategized by phone with non-essential federal employees Elizabeth and Yasemin. Yes, of course they'd pretend they were representing me if I needed to invoke the name of an attorney. "Tell her, if she reneges, if she doesn't want to make you whole, you'll go public."

I said, "With what exactly?"

Yasemin said, "That she was speeding to 1600 Pennsylvania Avenue to fuck the president without regard for human life and public safety!"

"Got it."

I didn't mention the dollar amount I'd be settling for. Ten thousand dollars had been mentioned — $10,000 more than I had in the bank — and if that was still on the table, I'd take it.

It was seven months almost to the day since Veronica had put me in the hospital, and I was a more assertive person now, having assumed the unofficial role of the brains behind Champion Inc.

When I finally called, pen in hand, coffee mug refilled at a six-foot distance from Sandra's desk, Veronica answered with a sharp "Dr. Hyde-White."

"It's Rachel Klein. I don't know if you remember—"

"I know who you are. Still working for that author?"

"I am."

"I hope you know I rarely pick up. I'm under siege. I have paparazzi outside the front and back doors of the building. I don't know what they want from me!"

She didn't? Being the co-respondent in the divorce of the POTUS and FLOTUS wasn't enough?

"Why didn't he call me himself?" she asked.

"You mean Kirby?"

"It's insulting that he had his assistant or girlfriend or whatever you are contact me."

I said, "I'm not calling in my journalistic capacity, or his."

"Which means what?"

"It's a terrible time. We're all hurting. I'm calling because your lawyers once offered me $10,000 as an out-of-court settlement for the accident."

"And you want that now?"

"I think it's a fair request. In fact my lawyers want me to ask for more—"

"But that didn't get you anywhere, I was told . . . Hold on," she said. "I have to take this."

I waited. Was it the president? One of her lawyers? Simon? When she returned she said, "I don't know why I even answer these."

I said, "It could be your real-estate agent with an offer on your flat."

"And then what? I go shopping for a new place? I don't buy property based on a virtual tour."

We were off-topic and it was my fault. I back-tracked with, "If I filed suit, instead of accepting your last offer, it would be front-page news, given the timing of the accident and where you were speeding to."

After a disparaging, "Ha!" she said, "Then let's just call this what it is — extortion."

I looked at the notes I was supposed to consult if accused of blackmail or extortion. I said, "Blackmail for chickenfeed? That's laughable. I'm accepting an offer made by the firm of Alden, Winslow, Fuller, Billington and Schwartz. All I'm asking is that I be made whole, in the most discreet and thoughtful possible way, for damages and injuries, some of which are recurrent."

"You ran in front of my car. Anyone would've hit you, so don't bring up that bullshit about driving on the wrong side of the road. That's rubbish."

Wrong side of the road? Was that in any report?

She continued, "How do I know this will be the end of it, and you won't keep coming back for more money, with more threats, more shake-downs?"

I said, "I resent that. And if I'm being completely honest, until this moment I was unaware that you'd been driving on the wrong side of the road." I pretended to be muffling the phone and whispering to the hard-ass lawyer who was advising me. I came back and said, "With that huge added violation, it's worse than my lawyer thought, so she says I have to receive double what's been discussed so far."

"This is an outrage! Twenty thousand dollars? For what? You're fine. I looked at your pupils!"

It was risky, and I was starting to regret the chutzpah I'd reached back for. But then I heard: "Spell your name for me."

I did, slowly, then added a docile, "Thank you."

"Anything else?" she snapped.

I said, "Actually, I have one more question."

"I bet you do."

I forced myself to strike a compassionate note. "How *are* you? This can't be easy."

"Which part?"

"Being in the headlines. Being blamed for breaking up the Trump marriage. Hurting his re-election chances."

"Of course it isn't easy. But do you know how I see it? Some people aren't cut out for being heads of state, and they know it. Are you familiar with the Duke of Windsor's love story?"

While I was thinking *Duke of Windsor? Duke of York? Camilla?* Veronica said, "I've been identifying with Wallis Simpson, who was also married when the future king took up with her."

Near-speechless, I said only "Wallis Simpson . . . It was a very painful thing for your country, wasn't it . . . the abdication . . . ?"

"He was very popular, just like Donald. I know his abdication speech by heart. 'Without the help and support of the woman I love . . .' It gives me chills every time."

I asked, more delicately than she deserved, "Has the president expressed his love aloud?"

"Verbally?"

"Correct. With words."

"In his own way. He has a limited emotional vocabulary, which is why we're going to make it and his other marriages didn't."

"Meaning the other wives expected time and attention, but you don't?"

"I have a career and a thriving practice. Or *will* have when normal life resumes."

I was writing furiously. "When do you think that will be?"

"On the twentieth of January."

"He thinks that too?"

"When the pandemic is over, Donald's going to start divorce proceedings."

"Didn't Melania do that already?"

"He's going to counter-divorce. You know his style is to hit back."

"And you'll be divorcing Simon soon?"

"He's carrying on," was her non-answer. Then: "I'm a scratch golfer. Donald and I will have our own quarters at Mar-A-Lago."

"Do you mean his and hers, for the sake of appearances?"

"No, *ours*. He'll be out of the public eye. No one will care if we are living together or separately."

Was she thinking of ex-prime ministers who weren't the objects of fanatical out-of-office attention? I asked, "And your work? How does that fit in?"

"Done and dusted: a boutique on the premises, an eyewear shop with an examination room and all the equipment I need. Getting a Florida license won't be a problem. Donald knows people."

"And people will want to have their eyes examined by the president's partner, I bet."

"We think so. And by the way, my official title will be 'fiancée.' Donald thinks 'partner' sounds gay. I'll have a ring. It doesn't mean we'll have to walk down the aisle. People these days stay engaged for years and no one finds that dodgy."

I asked if she'd talked about these plans with anyone else, such as a reporter.

"I have not."

If I asked the obvious question — you understand that we're on the record? — would it snap her out of her confessional mode, causing her to retract, deny, and threaten me with whatever was in her arsenal?

I *did* ask her. I had to know. "Why tell me this? Weren't you going to write your own memoir?"

"I owe you," she said.

"You owe me?" I repeated. "Because of the accident?"

With her English accent at its most pronounced, she wailed, "Do you know what it's like to hit someone with your car and send her flying, then wonder, as she's lying there in the road, unconscious and bleeding from the head, if you just killed a live person? Until you moved and groaned, it was the longest minute of my life! I hear that *thwump* over and over again. What if I *had* killed you? It's a large car and you're what — eight stone? I have nightmares about that, still! I'm obsessed with the timing of it: Why couldn't I have left my office thirty seconds earlier or thirty seconds later? You wouldn't have been crossing the street at the moment I was driving by! If you'd lost your life, it would be an existential crisis that even being engaged to the president of the United States wouldn't cure!"

After a long, offended pause — how about *my* existential crisis caused by almost being killed? — I said, "But still, I'm the one who called you. It's not as if all of that angst made you pick up the phone."

"I know! I'm sorry. But isn't that what lawyers are for?"

"The money?" I asked. "Can I assume that's a go?"

"You'll get the money. It might bring me peace."

I recited Alex's address, and requested a bank check. I closed with "Good luck, Veronica," followed by what I said automatically in these extraordinary times to friends, strangers and assholes alike: "Stay safe."

39

WHO KNOWS WHEN?

MARY-JO AND MURRAY would be married on Sunday the 7th of June, 2020, at 5 p.m. The invitation came in the mail, obviously printed before the plague, with the synagogue's address crossed out and a Zoom link and meeting ID hand-written in its place.

There was an added note: "Can Alex be there, too? Dying to 'meet' him!"

I called Mary-Jo immediately. "Yes, for sure. And love that it's not postponed until who-knows-when. How are you pulling it all together?"

"Not much to figure out. The rabbi will do it in person, at a distance. We're allowed ten people, total."

"My parents, I assume?"

"Of course! Your father's giving me away. Plus Dougie. Not Mark because of his asthma. My sibs allegedly drew lots for the four remaining spots, but miraculously the winners were the four sisters who'd already bought their bridesmaids' dresses."

"And the bride's dress?"

"Sparkly. A big skirt. Long lace sleeves like Kate Middleton's. 'Gently used.' And it fits!"

I said I couldn't wait to see it. Flowers working out?

"Just a bouquet for me and a boutonnière for Murray. We weren't going to decorate the store, but your mother—"

"Did you say 'store'? Our store? Not at the synagogue?"

"Synagogue's closed. If it's open, they're afraid people will show up for services and get arrested. Your mother's making a chupa from some lace curtains she found on eBay. Very Scarlett O'Hara of her."

And so hands-on Bev, so my mom, so dear, that I choked up.

"Still," Mary-Jo continued, "we invited the whole congregation to attend via Zoom. Dougie figures they won't know how to use it so it won't be a mob."

I managed to say, "I'm sure they'll be thrilled. What else do they have to look forward to?"

There was a pause. "Is that how you feel? Nothing to look forward to?"

I said, No, then yes, then "I worry a lot. I miss Alex."

"Wait. I thought you were isolating together."

"We are. But business has never been better" — a statement that wouldn't have made my voice catch any other time in history.

"What about your job?"

"I go in. I make phone calls. I take notes."

"Do you have to be there full-time?"

"I don't have to be there at all. Kirby's paying me, essentially, to be at the other end of the intercom in case he can't figure out how to flip the image on his phone, or needs his Amazon password."

"Couldn't you help at Alex's store?"

"I've offered."

"But he doesn't want you exposed?"

"He knows where that would lead: to me saying 'I'd get exposed? Then you're exposed. Close the store immediately!'"

"Talk to him," she said. "Tell him you want to help. What about just answering the phone, taking down orders and credit card numbers?"

I said, "Taking orders isn't an entry-level job there. People say 'six bottles of such and such Sauvignon Blanc,' and you have to know if that's in stock. Or 'what do I need for a Negroni?'"

"You're no dummy. You'll pick it up."

I said, "I suppose I could observe for a couple of nights."

"And just like you did at the store, when someone picked some hideous wallpaper. You'd say 'excellent choice. One of my favorites.'"

I smiled at the memory of my retail falsehoods. I said, "I was good at that, wasn't I?"

"You were. And take it from the future Mrs. Feinberg, you find out a lot about a person, working side by side."

I said, "You're forgetting I met Alex at his store. I've seen him in action. And we've been living together for ten weeks."

"And from what I've heard—"

"He's the nicest man in the whole world," I said.

40

LIKE AN EPILOGUE

I DID HELP OUT AT THE STORE. People called. They ordered. I learned to say, "We're low on that particular Pinot Grigio, but how about X, Y or Z?" I'd ask "sweet or dry?" or "liter or pint?" My old gratuitous-compliment habit kicked in, often evoking a laugh from Alex in his personal protective equipment that my mother had sewn from a YouTube tutorial and a shower curtain. Walter and Mr. Dekker seemed happy with less time at the store, on the phone, lugging cartons that Alex kept yelling at them to put down and leave for him.

It did mean that I cut down my hours, way down, at Champion, Inc. I think Kirby was relieved to be free of the make-work projects he'd been so bad at assigning. I pledged that when the scourge was over, I'd return full-time, and we'd write about the landslide defeat that would send Trump and Veronica to Mar-a-Lago for good. Meanwhile, like the de facto assignment editor I'd gradually become, I said, "Keep working on your memoir.

Don't be afraid to speak it, stream-of-consciousness-y, into your recorder. Sandra's so good at finding the most salient points."

The night of Mary-Jo and Murray's wedding, Alex and I dressed up — he in a suit and tie, me in the blue voile dress I'd bought pre-shutdown for the occasion, never picturing us as anything other than in-person wedding guests. I'd chosen a bottle of Prosecco from the store before we left on Saturday night, but Alex said, "No, this calls for Veuve Clicquot."

We watched the ceremony, me alternately weeping and applauding, seeing my mom and dad so handsome in their finery; parental stand-ins; employer-matchmakers.

Best man Dougie deejayed at his laptop, the only guest besides the groom in a tux, generating in me a new fondness for him, especially after a toast that thanked Mary-Jo for bringing his dad, his wonderful dad, some long-overdue and much-deserved happiness.

On cue, we raised our glasses. Then the first notes rang out, Etta James singing "At Last." Murray and Mary-Jo had clearly been practicing, now twirling and dipping. Half-way through, Dougie invited all Zoomers to take to our dance floors.

Alex and I had never danced together. How was that possible? No dips or twirls, but what a good fit, my chin tucked under his. Next song, clearly curated for the baby-boomer newlyweds, was Elvis singing, "Can't Help Falling In Love With You."

My parents joined the showroom dance floor, waving at the camera, blowing kisses — I was sure — directly to remote and sorely missed daughter, me.

"Let's do this, too," said Alex.

"We are," I said.

"I didn't mean dance. I meant this: get married."

How did I answer? Is it too private and personal to describe the teary, noisy, stunned, yelp of a joyful yes and the pitch of the I-love-yous that drowned out Elvis? Suffice it to say, I could see my mother turn toward the camera and mouth, "Everything okay there?"

"Do we tell them?" I ask.

"They know," he said.

Though we'd resumed dancing — well, barely swaying — I stopped again. "Are you saying you asked for my hand, old-school?"

"Not old school. I asked them both. Your father cried. Your mother said, 'Hurry up and pop the question because I don't know how long I can keep this to myself.'"

"And you told your father, too?"

"It's what a guy does when he needs his dad to get his mother's engagement ring out of the safe deposit bank. So, yes. He cried too."

Six weeks later, we live-streamed from Varsity. Present were co-best women Elizabeth and Yasemin, plus Alex's father and his two brothers. I didn't invite Kirby, not from any lack of affection but fear of the faux pas, the gaffe, the potentially loud, embarrassing toast. Family only, I explained, along with the Zoom meeting ID.

I asked, wasn't it odd and wasn't Alex overly blasé about our not virtually meeting with the judge who would marry us? Didn't such officiants get to know the engaged couple, hear how we met and what we did?

"Different times," said Alex.

Soon it made sense. Since Klein Wallpaper & Paint was shuttered, my mother had been sitting down at 11:30 a.m. every day to watch and hear, live from Albany, the good and the bad news about New York. It was, she said, like going to services, her daily devotion, her new rabbi. She never missed a day, so of course she heard of a new executive order allowing weddings to be performed remotely, with the priest or rabbi or judge or imam video-officiating. "Or me!" said the governor, grinning.

So at 5 p.m. on an early August evening, Alex and I were married by Governor Andrew Cuomo, he presiding from his office in Albany, we two at the store, decorated by the multi-talented Walter with party fiesta flags and buckets of hollyhocks. The ceremony was short, just boilerplate vows, plus a Hebrew blessing the governor had learned, as he liked to say, from his Jewish brothers and sisters. He called us pandemic partners, scrupulous observers of CDC guidelines, corona-careful but courageously carrying on. My mother had over-prepped him via some aide to an aide, so that he spoke of the ring — still unsized due to jeweler shutdowns — with which Alex's mother was blessing this union; that he knew something about mothers, and there was one looking down and one watching; oh and another one tuning in — his own mother, the famous Matilda, proud to see him acting like the priest she'd always hoped one of her sons might become.

He couldn't stay for the champagne and the toasts, but before leaving, he said, most solemnly, "One more thing." We waited for the most articulate of officeholders to share with us something patriotically profound. "As governor of the great state of New York, where love wins, where we are tough, we are smart, we are united, we are disciplined, may I recommend that when this is over; when life is back to where you want it to be, when you are free to travel, may I recommend that you honeymoon at Niagara Falls?"

The Zoom audience broke into applause. Elizabeth panned the room where we'd set up dozens of white wooden folding chairs, on the back of each, headshots of the people who would most certainly have been present in the world before.

We didn't hit "leave meeting" till every remote guest had said their goodbyes. Yasemin had made a feast for our wedding dinner, but they refused to stay. "For later, for God's sake. It's your wedding night. We'll take a rain-check. The basket — keep it. Some day surely there will be picnics again."

There was no *Just Married* sign on the Bolt, but Sherman Avenue, relatively speaking, was a busy street, even on a Sunday night. And there we were, unmistakably a bride and a groom, Alex in a tux and bow-tie, me in my blush mail-order dress, bouquet in hand, my mother's veil blowing behind me. We hadn't been looking for a New York moment; hadn't realized we needed one, or that the mere sight of newlyweds could provoke the clapping, the cheering, the banging and honking. We waved back and yelled our thanks. It was, we would say, our receiving line and reception. We stayed longer than modesty would've allowed, drinking it in, two hams prolonging their curtain calls.

People still ask if we're sorry we didn't wait to marry until life returned to normal; sorry that we didn't have a real wedding with friends and relatives in person, a flower girl and ring bearer, a band, a chupa; with handshakes and hugs instead of masked strangers waving from their cars and trucks and balconies?

No, we say every time. Not even close. If only you'd been there, had seen it and heard it. No.

THE END

ACKNOWLEDGMENTS

I am hugely grateful to Scott Pack of Eye & Lightning Books for my British revival and for decisiveness and commitment of the most delightful kind.

My dear friends Mameve Medwed and Stacy Schiff once again provided eagle-eyed and enthusiastic feedback as I finished (or thought I had) every chapter.

I am lucky to know David Ferriero, Archivist of the United States, and grateful for his keen eye and insights about all things D.C.

Great ongoing thanks to agents Suzanne Gluck and Matilda Forbes-Watson of William Morris Endeavor for every single effort on my behalf, especially this one.

For optometric guidance I thank Dr. Doug Hoffman, New England College of Optometry.

And for diagnosis and treatment of Rachel's injuries, I am grateful for the advice of Patrick Tyler, M.D., of my extended family.

My thanks to Atty. Lawrence Siskind, who answers all of my questions related to intellectual property, past, present and future.

I add love and thanks to Jonathan Greenberg, and to Caroline, Ben and Julien Austin, all of whom keep me predisposed to writing happy endings.